"Do you have any computer games, Nick?"

Andrea held her breath until the boy answered.

"Why? You play?"

"Only when I have a worthy opponent, Tony said. "Are you any good?"

"Good enough." Andrea smiled at her nephew's self-confident tone. She released a mental sigh of relief and stood to clear the main course. She refused Tony's offer of help and suggested he stay and talk with Nicky.

In the kitchen, she crossed her fingers briefly, hoping her absence would force her nephew to say more than a few polite words to Tony. When she carried the pie into the dining room, she realized her ploy had worked. The two were discussing the scoring intricacies of some intergalactic game.

Tony looked up when she put a plate in front of him. "Homemade? Nick, do you know how lucky you are?"

The boy picked up his fork and held it tightly in his fist. "Yeah. I'm lucky, all right."

Andrea's stomach twisted with the irony of his comment. Lucky to have lost his parents? Lucky to be living with a single aunt? If only it were simply that he was lucky enough to have someone bake him a homemade pie.

Dear Reader,

I don't suppose there is a fiction writer anywhere who isn't a keen observer of others. In fact, my family jokes about my shameless people-watching and eavesdropping in airports, restaurants or any other place where folks gather. Quite simply, I find the human condition fascinating.

Couple that with a lifelong interest in the legal system, and it was only a matter of time before I set a story in a courtroom. A few years ago, my name was drawn as part of a jury pool. The randomness of the process intrigued me, as did the cross section of citizens represented among the potential jurors. What I found especially gratifying was how sincerely each person on the jury worked to try to arrive at a fair and reasonable verdict. Were we an unusually conscientious group of twelve? Or is that generally how the process works? I pray we were the rule rather than the exception.

In preparation for writing this book, I spent several days as guest in the Court of Common Pleas, Cuyahoga County, Ohio. I came away not only with renewed respect for law enforcement and courts, but with justifiable pride in my gender. Both the bailiff and the judge who assisted me were women—women who performed their jobs with efficiency, fairness and compassion. You know who you are, ladies, and you have earned my utmost respect and gratitude.

You've guessed it. The romance writer in me couldn't resist following the question: "What would happen if a hero and heroine met while they were both serving on the same jury?" I hope you'll enjoy the outcome of this flight of fantasy.

Laura Abbot

P.S. Please check out my new web site at nettrends.com/LauraAbbot or write me at P.O. Box 2105, Eureka Springs, AR, 72632. Your comments are important to me!

TRIAL COURTSHIP
Laura Abbot

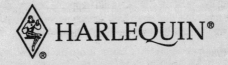

HARLEQUIN®

TORONTO • NEW YORK • LONDON
AMSTERDAM • PARIS • SYDNEY • HAMBURG
STOCKHOLM • ATHENS • TOKYO • MILAN • MADRID
PRAGUE • WARSAW • BUDAPEST • AUCKLAND

ISBN 0-373-70843-2

TRIAL COURTSHIP

Copyright © 1999 by Laura A. Shoffner.

Look us up on-line at: http://www.romance.net

Printed in U.S.A.

For my loving and loyal friend Carol
who asked an important question of me
at just the right time in my life.

With heartfelt gratitude for the hospitality and help so freely
given by relatives and friends, old and new, in the beautiful
city of Cleveland.

CHAPTER ONE

ANDREA EVANS PARKED outside the elementary school to wait for Nicky. The late October sun slanted through the colorful foliage of the massive oaks and maples lining the sidewalk. Across the street in front of a large Tudor-style home, a teenage boy with a rake fought a losing battle against leaves scattered by a stiff wind blowing in from Lake Erie. She buttoned her sweater. Nicky shouldn't be too long. He knew she'd be there.

Shaker Heights, the beautiful wooded suburb of Cleveland, had been a wonderful place to grow up, she reflected, as she watched two girls strolling along the sidewalk, giggling conspiratorially. And the area remained a desirable location for families with children.

Now, unexpectedly, *she* was the one rearing a child, the one waiting for the Science Club meeting to adjourn. The one who, no matter how much love and attention she showered on her nine-year-old nephew, couldn't make up for the tragic loss of his parents.

Despite living with her nearly a year and a half, Nicky still wore that preoccupied, lost look, still appeared some mornings for breakfast with his hair awry, his nails bitten to the quick, his eyes bloodshot. Oh, he loved his Andie well enough—they'd always had a special bond. But she could never replace her older sister Tami as his mother. Nor had she found an acceptable male role model for him, a position her ex-fiancé had refused to consider.

When a boisterous group of students exploded from the school, she searched eagerly for Nicky. He wasn't among them. She checked her watch. He ought to be along any minute. The children split off in pairs and threesomes and scampered away. Maybe she should go inside.

No, there he was. Head down, dragging his book bag by the strap, Nicholas slowly approached the car. She sighed. He looked so lonely. Opening the door, he threw his belongings onto the back seat, pushed his glasses up on his nose, plopped down beside her and, as an afterthought, pulled the door shut.

"Nicky? Are you all right?" She studied the slightly built, raven-haired boy, who sat, hands folded politely in his lap, studying the ink spot on the left knee of his khaki trousers.

He nodded.

She hated to pry, yet the signals he sent off so often concerned her that it was difficult to keep her mouth shut. Every now and then, he would open his shell a crack, permit her in briefly. Then, as suddenly as he'd revealed himself, he'd clam up.

She drove slowly through the residential area toward home. "What was the program at Science Club today?"

"Bats."

"That should've been interesting."

"Yeah."

Nothing about bats hanging by their feet, residing in caves or employing nature's "radar." Just "yeah." Something had happened. She knew it. She tried another tack. "Why didn't you come out with the other kids?"

"I waited."

"Oh?"

As if discovering a curiosity, Nicky rubbed the ink stain with a stubby forefinger.

One more try. "Did something upset you today?" She watched a flush creep up his neck. *"Nicholas?"*

"Jus' Ben again," he mumbled.

"Ben? What now?" She steeled herself for his answer.

"He called me a weenie." He paused before adding, "Said he was gonna beat the crap outta me."

"Did you tell the teacher?"

He shot her an incredulous look. "What good would that do?"

Poor little guy. Caught between a bully and a rap as a snitch. "Would you like me to call Mrs. Elliot?"

He shrugged. "That'll jus' make it worse."

Heartsick, she turned into the drive of the Cape Cod house that had been her sister and brother-in-law's home and was now hers. As soon as the car stopped, Nicky bolted, leaving his book bag behind. She stood, shivering a moment in the cool late-afternoon breeze, then bent and retrieved the bag. He wasn't a thoughtless or bad boy. Just unhappy. And she had no idea how to help him.

Andrea followed him into the house, shrugged out of her cardigan and set water to boil for spaghetti. Then she carried Nicky's bag upstairs to his bedroom, where he already sat engrossed in a computer game. Software and cyberspace—his retreats. She mussed his hair affectionately. "Dinner in forty-five minutes."

He didn't look up. "Okay."

She paused in the entry hall to gather the mail stuffed in the brass door slot. Sorting through the envelopes as she walked back to the kitchen, she flipped past two bills, then stopped short. What on earth did Cuyahoga County want with her? Her heart skipped a beat. Surely nothing involving her custody of Nicky?

Easing onto the chintz-covered breakfast nook bench, she tore open the envelope. "You are summoned to appear in the Court of Common Pleas...Wednesday, November 18...to serve as a juror.''

Jury duty? Could there be a worse time—right before the holiday rush at her store? Perhaps she could get excused. She quickly censored that unworthy reaction. No question about it, fulfilling her duty as a citizen couldn't always be convenient. She bit her lip. Serving would involve making arrangements for Nicholas, securing the cooperation of Phil Norman, her shop manager...

Bemused, she acknowledged a nudge of anticipation. She'd always been curious about what went on behind the closed doors of a jury room. And with uncharacteristic immodesty, she acknowledged her ability to be a fair-minded, impartial juror. Despite the bad timing, she would manage, maybe by adjusting her work schedule and hiring additional part-time help.

The hiss of water splattering on the electric burner brought her to her feet. Grabbing two pot holders, she removed the pan from the stove.

She was eager to show Nicholas the letter. They could talk about the court system at dinner. Maybe he'd think that was interesting. She hoped so.

"WATCH IT, KELL. You're dribbling pickle juice on the contract draft!" Tony Urbanski leaned back in his chair and grinned across the conference table at Kelli Murphy O'Shea, expectant mother and legal whiz.

She waved a dill spear in his general direction. "Just because you're the newest partner in Great Lakes Management Group, Skee, don't think you can order folks around."

He laughed. "Nobody gives you orders. How does Patrick put up with you?"

Rubbing her protruding abdomen, she chuckled wickedly. "Oh, my husband understands there are certain rather delightful compensations."

Tony nodded at the smeared legal document. "That's an interesting shade of green."

She bent her dark head over the page, examining it, then looked up, her blue eyes twinkling. "Ah, laddie, it's the leprechaun touch, doncha know? The luck of the Irish!"

"It damn well better be. I'm going to need all the luck I can get to put DataTech and Cyberace at the same table and hammer out this merger." Already he could feel the ripples of tension in his chest. He had a huge stake in pulling off this deal. Harrison Wainwright, managing partner of his firm, demanded results. As the recently appointed head of the mergers and acquisition department, Tony could ill afford to mishandle his first huge negotiation since making partner.

"Hey, Skee." Kelli reached across the table and patted his hand. "You'll get the job done. I have every confidence in you."

Good old Kell. Always the cheerleader. Ever since they'd joined the Cleveland office at about the same time two years ago, they'd been buddies. Her refreshing nononsense approach to life kept him honest. She had the uncanny ability to see right through him in ways that often made him uncomfortable.

She withdrew her hand and stood, rubbing the small of her back. "And," she continued, "you have every confidence in you. That's what makes you so effective."

"Are you saying I'm cocky?"

She widened her eyes and regarded him archly. "Now would I say a thing like that?"

He scooped up the papers and rose to his feet. "Damn right, you would." He stuffed the contract draft into his bulging briefcase, then checked his watch. "Jeez, Kell, I didn't mean to keep you so late. I hope Patrick won't be worried.''

"I called him earlier. Besides, you saved me. Patrick is putting up our Halloween decorations tonight. He really gets into holidays. You'd think he was still twelve years old. We'll have skeletons hanging from trees, cobwebs draped all over the front porch and enough jack-o'-lanterns to illuminate our entire block.''

"I'm sorry. You're missing all the fun.''

"I'll have plenty of 'fun' getting ready for our party. You're coming, aren't you?''

Tony hesitated. He wasn't much for masquerade parties. "If I'm not too busy.''

"Too busy? Give it a rest. Halloween is on a Saturday night! It'll be a blast. Do you have your costume?''

Costume? A disconcerting childhood memory surfaced of his father telling him boys didn't "play dress-up" and that Halloween was for sissies. As a schoolboy, Tony had been forced to sneak bedsheets in order to transform himself into a perennial ghost. "I'll probably come as Urban Businessman, circa late 20th Century.''

"Wow,'' Kelli said mockingly. "You really let yourself go, don't you?''

Tony grasped for a change of subject. "How about you? What are you wearing?''

Kelli ran a hand over her stomach and smiled ruefully. "It seems to me I have two choices—Buddha or E.T.''

"With your big eyes, E.T.'s a natural.''

"I think so, too.'' Kelli started toward the door.

"I'll get my coat and walk you to your car. It's dark out there.''

"Thanks. I'll meet you at the elevator.'' She paused at the door of her office. "And don't forget to bring a date to the party!''

"Now you've pushed me too far."

She shook her head disparagingly. "Somebody has to help you meet the right woman. Shall I line up one of my single friends?"

He shrugged. "Do I have a choice?" Before disappearing into her office, she shot him one of those looks that clearly said, "Mother knows best." Someday maybe he'd think about marriage, family. But not now. He hadn't worked backbreaking construction jobs to earn his way through Michigan State, driven a cab nights while he finished his MBA and clawed his way up the ranks of Great Lakes Management Group to be sidetracked from his goals. Now that he'd achieved a partnership, he wanted to solidify his reputation as the best negotiator the company had ever had, and that didn't involve distractions of the female variety.

After delivering Kelli to her car, he walked briskly toward the converted warehouse—now a fashionable downtown address—where he had a third-floor flat. The aroma of hot mustard and sauerkraut wafting from the brown paper bag he carried made his stomach grumble. Thank God Kamp's Deli had late take-out service. A guy could do a lot worse than the best pastrami on rye in northern Ohio.

Reaching his door, he clutched his briefcase under one arm and fumbled in his pocket for his key. Although it was already after nine, he still had the latest Cyberace annual report to review. But the prospect of another late night didn't bother him. Deep in his gut, he had the feeling that, despite the obstacles, he could make this merger work.

He pushed open the door to his flat, switched on the lights and set his briefcase and sandwich on the chrome-and-glass table. He was proud of the sleek aesthetic decor—a black leather Eames chair and chrome reading

lamp, a white sofa grouping, matching coffee and end tables, Klee and Picasso prints furnishing the only splashes
of color. A far cry from his father's double-wide trailer,
which Tony had had to call "home." *Take a look, Pops.
Your kid has made it.*

Shucking his suit jacket, he shuddered against the dis-
tasteful image of Stan Urbanski, with the omnipresent ci-
gar stub clenched in his teeth. Stripping off his tie, he then
pulled a bottle of ale from the nearly empty refrigerator.
Slowly pouring the contents into a chilled pilsner glass, he
raised the drink. *Cheers!* An unexpected wave of loneli-
ness swept over him. What good was success when there
was nobody to share it?

Dispelling the maudlin thought, Tony turned his attention to the thick meaty sandwich, idly thumbing through
the day's mail while he ate. A renewal notice for the *Wall
Street Journal,* an invitation to a charity ball at Shaker
Heights Country Club—not bad for a nobody from Detroit—and an envelope with a Cuyahoga County return
address. *What the hell?*

He slit the envelope with his pocket knife and pulled
out the enclosed letter. "You are summoned to appear in
the Court of Common Pleas…to serve as a juror." *November 18?* Shoving his sandwich aside, he stared at the
words. *Not now!* He guzzled the remainder of his ale, then
slammed the empty glass down on the table top. *Joseph
and Mary.* That was only three weeks away. Shortly before
he had to be in New York City to handle the delicate final
merger negotiations.

He started to ball up the offending notice, then thought
better of it. *No need getting in an uproar.* Hell, judges
were savvy individuals. Surely when he explained his role
in a nationally significant business deal, no judge would
insist he serve.

rge jury commission room where, during the orientation,
e'd learned that his only out depended on a trial judge's
ismissing him. He ground his teeth in frustration. If the
ods smiled, maybe he'd get on a jury right away and
uickly fulfill his civic obligation.

Miraculously, he was one of the first to be sent to a
ourtroom. He gave himself a mental high five, gathered
 his belongings and followed a uniformed deputy who
epherded a group of about thirty upstairs to the court-
om. There the deputy directed them to spectators' seats
the large, high-ceilinged chamber, paneled with vertical
ps of wood. A man with the facial features of a tortoise
 the build of a fireplug introduced himself as the bailiff,
 approached Tony and pointed at his laptop computer.
ou, sir. That'll have to go. No electronic devices are
wed in the courtroom.''

Other people brought books and magazines. What's
ifference? I have work to do.'' The woman sitting
to him shied away as if to disassociate herself from

oday your work is this court.'' The bailiff gestured
ently. ''Give it to me.''

w just a darn minute—''

u can pick it up after today's session. You got a
or cell phone?''

u're going to take the phone, too?''

ge's policy. You don't wanna be in contempt. Just
m over, sir.'' There was a definite acidic twist to
''

antly, Tony relinquished his laptop and phone.
s he supposed to do during down times? Count
es?

se,'' the bailiff bellowed. The assembled group
 their feet. ''The Cuyahoga County Court of

Still, it was damned inconvenient. He'd get on the phone
first thing in the morning, speak to someone at the jury
commission. With luck, maybe he'd be permitted to serve
another time.

PALE NOVEMBER SUNLIGHT shone in Tony's eyes as he
faced Harrison Wainwright across the executive's imposing desk. ''How do you plan to handle your work on
DataTech-Cyberace if you can't get excused from jury
duty tomorrow?'' Wainwright leaned forward, his steely
eyes fixed on Tony, his eyebrows meeting in a frown.

Tony met his colleague's gaze. ''I understand the importance of this merger, and I intend to justify your confidence. Once I talk to the judge, there should be no further
problem.''

If only he could be sure. When he'd phoned the jury
commission, Tony had been abruptly cut off. ''You will
have to take it up with the judge on November 18.'' But
he hadn't earned his reputation as a skilled negotiator for
nothing. ''Besides,'' he continued, ''Barry Fuller is really
coming along. I'll be putting in extra time nights and on
the weekends and, with Fuller's help, I don't see a problem, even if it turns out I have to serve.''

''I don't have to remind you that time is critical for Ed
Miller at DataTech,'' Wainwright continued in his deep
baritone. ''The new product launch is the linchpin of this
merger. DataTech has to get the jump on their competition
to secure the projected market share. Their ad agency is
already pressing for some decisions.''

Tony shared Wainwright's sense of urgency. ''I've
spent a lot of time convincing Cyberace's directors that
this is a great deal. And it is. DataTech gets the cash they
need to produce and promote their new product, and Cy-

berace shareholders get a chunk of promising stock in a well-managed company. What's not to like?''

Wainwright started playing with his fountain pen, screwing and unscrewing the lid. "Cyberace is a closely held corporation. Not everyone over there thinks bigger is necessarily better. That concerns me."

Tony seized the initiative. "Understandable, but I feel certain we can address the issues to everyone's satisfaction. Once I'm finished with Cyberace, they'll be begging DataTech for the merger."

Wainwright set down the pen decisively and picked up the phone. "Okay, you're my man, but, Skee, watch your backside with Steelman." He nodded dismissively and began dialing.

Tony stood. "You can rely on me." He left the room, pausing outside the office to focus his thoughts.

Rodney Steelman, the founder of Cyberace. Not exactly your Dale Carnegie honor graduate. Territorial, old-fashioned and blunt. In short, just the kind of challenge Tony liked.

On the way back to his own office, he stopped at the receptionist's station and turned a charming grin on the attractive middle-aged woman. "If anybody's looking for me in the morning, tell them I'm in court."

She raised her eyebrows. "What now, Mr. Urbanski?"

"Nothing. Just jury duty. I'll be back after lunch." He moved away from her desk.

"Don't count on it."

He stopped. "Why not?"

"My sister-in-law was called last year. She had a heck of a time getting excused, even when she explained she was the sole caregiver for her invalid mother."

"They don't call me Henry Clay around here for noth-ing." He backpedaled down the corridor, giving jaunty two-fingered salute.

TONY IMPATIENTLY JABBED the courthouse elevator again. He'd run over from his office and had abou seconds to get to the jury commission on time. N he expected everyone else to be dutifully prompt He couldn't be the only one for whom the summ inconvenient. The whir of machinery announced vator's arrival before the metal panels slid open. H his laptop computer carrier into his other hand to door for departing occupants. That's what he'd a man departing.

As the elevator ascended, he reviewed his p the DataTech-Cyberace merger. He'd holed u weekend, going over the information he had o panies, finding weaknesses in the positions of nesses he intended to exploit with all the sl tech surgeon probing a vital organ. It was re to point out the advantages of a deal, but a needed to know when to apply pressure, v and how to predict the consequences.

His secretary was compiling complete the principals. As he'd explained to Barr associate in his department, tactics we knowledge of personalities and vulner noon he'd scheduled a meeting with for an update on product viability. T game time—December 2, when he'd ting names on the dotted line. Ma even etch a smile on the granite fea wright.

The elevator stopped, and To vacant hallway. He took a dee

Common Pleas is now in session, the Honorable Hilda Blumberg presiding.'' *A female judge?* He'd have to rethink his strategy for getting excused. Wearing a judicial robe, a tall severe-looking woman with straight salt-and-pepper hair pulled back and secured at the nape of her neck, entered, nodded unsmilingly at the potential jurors, then settled into the large leather chair behind the bench. ''Be seated,'' the bailiff barked.

In a dry, matter-of-fact voice, the judge addressed them. ''Ladies and gentlemen, thank you for coming today. Before we begin, let me introduce those in the courtroom.'' She nodded toward the laptop confiscator who studied them through slitted eyes. ''My bailiff, Hershel Schmidt, and Stephanie Reedy, the stenographer. This morning we begin voir dire. The court has several cases awaiting trial. Some of you will be seated on this jury. The others will remain in the pool until you are selected for another trial or are excused after one week.''

One week! Did she expect him to sit for days twiddling his thumbs? He tensed like an anxious prizefighter awaiting the bell.

The judge then began a lengthy explanation of the tradition of English jurisprudence, emphasizing the responsibility of citizens to serve on juries willingly and with open minds. He hadn't been so fidgety since old man Pickins's civics lectures in the eighth grade. He checked the time. *Jeez!* He'd already been in the courtroom thirty minutes. Then something the judge said got his attention.

''...so it should be evident that this court does not take a jury summons lightly. Some of you, no doubt, expect to get excused. There are few, and I emphasize *few,* legitimate reasons persuasive enough for me to excuse you. However, after the bailiff calls the roll, I will declare a short recess during which I will ask those of you who believe you have compelling arguments to come forward. I will listen to a *brief* explanation of your individual circumstance.'' She nodded peremptorily at the bailiff, who began intoning names.

Compelling arguments. Okay, Your Honor, get ready. As the monotone voice continued through the roll, Tony sized up the judge. Definitely a no-nonsense type. He'd lay out the imperatives of his situation and prevail upon her pragmatism. She'd never go for the emotional or personal; she'd require hard-hitting facts.

''Anthony Stanislov Urbanski?''

''Here.'' Nearly at the end of the list. He brushed his pants, tugged on his shirt cuffs, then adjusted his tie. He was ready for her.

After another few names, the judge announced the recess. Tony walked briskly toward the bailiff, who was already surrounded by several impatient potential jurors.

The bailiff checked names and organized them in a line. The judge glanced up from the papers she'd been studying and beckoned them, one by one, to the bench. She sat, a good three feet above them. He recognized the tactic. Intimidation.

As he edged closer, he caught snatches of conversation. ''Do you have help at home, Mr. Smith?''

''...my daughter-in-law, but she works nights...''

''You're excused. Next?''

The young man right in front of him seemed cocky. ''Ain't no way da broad's gonna stop me,'' he mumbled to Tony out of the side of his mouth. ''Yer Honor, ya see, it's like dis. I'm reportin' Friday to Fort Sill. Basic training.''

''Artillery, Mr. Tonaretti?... Good luck to you. Excused.''

Let's make it three for three, lady.

The judge didn't look up. "Mr. Urbanski?"

"Your honor, I represent Great Lakes Management Group in a delicate business negotiation, scheduled to begin shortly—"

"How shortly?"

"December 2."

"That's two weeks away." She still hadn't looked up.

"This is a matter of extreme importance, involving some influential companies. I know you've heard of—"

"Your point, Mr. Urbanski?"

"I'm critical to this negotiation and the timing couldn't be worse for me or for the interests I represent. I'd be more than honored to serve another time," he really meant that, "but right now—"

"I assume others are working with you on this project?"

"Yes, but—"

She finally raised her eyes and stared coldly at him. "No business interests should supersede your duty as an American citizen. Request denied."

Blood drained from Tony's face and his feet remained glued to the floor.

"Move along, sir." The smug-looking bailiff nudged his arm.

Tony stalked out of the courtroom to the pay phone. Hell, he couldn't even use his cellular. He dropped in the change, then slapped a hand against the wall. This was a major complication. "Barry, listen, I've been detained at the courthouse. It might be late afternoon before I can get back to the office. Could you stick around this evening?"

"Be glad to. What's up?"

Tony didn't want to think about what he'd now have to delegate or about how much depended on the unseasoned Fuller. "I need to reassign some work on this DataTech deal."

"Do you need me to notify Wainwright?"

That was the last thing he needed. "No. Leave him to me. I'll call him later." He slammed down the receiver and stood scowling, studying his fellow jurors who, incomprehensibly, chatted animatedly, even with apparent enthusiasm. Surely he wasn't the only one who had other things to do.

Maybe he shouldn't worry. Not even the most incompetent lawyer would want him on a jury in his current mood. The attorneys might still dismiss him. He unclenched his fists and for the first time since entering the courthouse, regained his optimism.

AFTER THE RECESS, Andrea took her assigned seat near the front. So far, she'd found the process interesting and the judge's words about the Constitution and the jury system eloquent. She glanced around at the assembled group, which represented different ages, races and ethnic combinations and, undoubtedly, a wide range of views, biases and experience. She'd visited with several during the break. Most, though not happy to have their daily routines interrupted, viewed the situation as a necessary service.

But she couldn't help noticing the intense man by the phone—the same one who'd been annoyed when the bailiff had taken his laptop. His hawklike eyes were narrowed, his chin thrust forward. Except for the frown on his face, he might have been attractive—close-cropped black hair, ears flat against his head, dark eyes smoldering under thick brows. Broad-shouldered, about five-eleven she judged.

The bailiff's words, "All rise," brought her to her feet. She stood respectfully while the svelte judge made her way to the bench and sat down.

"Ladies and gentlemen, we will proceed with voir dire—that is, the questioning of potential jurors. As the clerk reads off your juror numbers, please take seats in the jury box. The rest will wait and, in numerical sequence, replace any juror excused for cause.''

Andrea clutched the children's books she'd brought from her store to read in the event she wasn't selected right away. During the selection process, she became increasingly apprehensive. What if this was some technical case about money laundering or insurance fraud? Although she was a good businesswoman, she didn't know much about such things; however, she rationalized, neither did most people.

"Juror five."

Her number! Within minutes, the bailiff, who looked like an adorable Chinese pug, had escorted fourteen of them to seats in the jury box. Two men conversed at one of the counsel tables, and a woman seated at the other table made notes on a yellow legal pad. The attorneys, no doubt.

The judge tapped her gavel. "This case involves a juvenile accused of aggravated murder."

Murder? Andrea gulped. The judge continued, "Are any of you acquainted with me or with the two prosecutors Mr. Bedford and Mr. Raines, or with the defense attorney, Ms. Lamb? If so, please rise."

A balding man with a small mustache, who was a member of the judge's temple congregation, was dismissed. When she asked if anyone had ever had a relative or friend who had been the victim of a violent crime, she excused another.

After the judge explained that a juvenile could not be executed for murder in Ohio, she questioned each remaining person about his or her feelings about life imprisonment.

One woman became quite agitated. "I simply couldn't

shut anybody away like that. It's so cruel. Suppose he was innocent? Why, I couldn't live with myself.''

By contrast, a man dressed in overalls and a faded flannel shirt rubbed his hands together. ''We gotta git control of our society. I say lock up all these crim'nals and throw away the key!'' Both were excused.

Andrea's turn came next. Punishment was a serious issue she had long debated, without coming to any conclusion. She chose her words carefully. ''I would be extremely reluctant to sentence a fellow human being to life in prison unless I felt the facts warranted such a sentence, but I also believe that the interests of victims' families must be considered.''

When the scowling man from the pay phone was questioned, he sighed audibly. It was as if he desperately wanted out, but found himself unable to lie. ''Yes, there are circumstances under which I could recommend a life sentence.''

Questioning continued past noon. After exercising several peremptory challenges, the attorneys conferred with the judge, then sat down, seemingly satisfied.

The judge picked up some papers, then addressed those in the courtroom. ''The twelve jurors and two alternates will please remain. The rest of you are excused to report back to the fourth floor. Thank you all.''

Andrea couldn't believe it. She was a juror in a murder case. She felt awed, nervous and slightly sick.

TONY'S STOMACH GROWLED. He checked his watch. Twelve thirty-five. Who was the prisoner here, anyway? Would they ever break for lunch? He couldn't guess what Harrison Wainright would have done in his shoes, but when the time had come for Tony to give his views on life imprisonment, although he could've uttered some outrageous opinion and been excused—at least from this case—he couldn't do it. He'd sworn an oath. And he'd told the truth.

Tony balled his fists. *Hell. A murder trial!* As the eleventh juror selected, he'd come close to escaping. However, he might as well reconcile himself. No use fighting the inevitable. But he wished he could be sure Barry Fuller was ready for the challenge this situation would present. He was a promising addition to the firm, but he had a good deal to learn.

Tony glanced around at his fellow jurors. An interesting crew. A beefy older man in a vintage Cleveland Browns sweatshirt; a short, stylishly dressed black woman; an elderly lady with thick glasses and pursed lips; and the attractive blonde he'd noticed earlier, the one who had attentively listened to every word Her Honor uttered. What the hell was that in her lap? He craned his neck to read the title of the top book in her stack—*Jeremy June Bug's Joke*. He chuckled to himself. She must have the literary tastes of a rug rat.

How long would this case take? Perhaps it would be cut-and-dried. A couple of days max. Maybe his situation wasn't so bad. After all, he could be stuck for an entire week out there with the unchosen. *Spoken like a true compromiser.*

"...and Bailiff Schmidt will suggest nearby restaurants. I admonish you not to discuss any aspects of the case outside the jury room. Please be seated back here at one forty-five for opening arguments." With a bang of the gavel, Judge Blumberg departed.

Like a bunch of schoolkids, they were marched from the courtroom by Bailiff Schmidt. The saving grace for Tony was that, as he left, he found himself behind the blonde, who had a decidedly interesting sway to her walk—the kind that makes any red-blooded man want to reach out and...

"Got a light?" The man in the Browns shirt fell in beside him. "I'm dyin' for a cigarette."

"No." Tony wasn't in the mood for small talk.

"Hope this thing doesn't drag on long. I can't afford to be off work."

"Yeah."

They ambled along in silence. Then Tony's companion poked him with his elbow. "Nice little piece of tail ahead of us."

For some unaccountable reason, the first thought that flashed through Tony's mind was, "She's mine. I saw her first." This guy irritated the hell out of him. "I hadn't noticed."

"Ya dead or something?"

"You might say that." Dead. That's what he'd be if he couldn't pull his negotiating team together, double up on their assignments and hope all hell didn't break loose at the office in the next week!

CHAPTER TWO

NOT ALL OF THE JURORS had seemed enthusiastic, but Andrea had been delighted when someone suggested they eat together and get acquainted. She sat at a long table between a pleasant African-American woman named Shayla Brown and Dottie Dettweiler, a grandmotherly lady with the wrinkled face of a crafts fair apple-head doll.

Dottie, looking to Andrea for reassurance, fingered the menu nervously. "I hope we'll be finished before Thanksgiving. My kids and grandkids are coming, and I've got lots of baking to do."

"We have a week before then, but I have no notion how long a murder trial takes," Andrea said.

Shayla leaned forward. "My brother used to be on the police force. Maybe he'll have an idea."

"It probably depends on the evidence," Andrea suggested.

"But it *is* kinda exciting," Dottie conceded. "Did you ever watch *People's Court*? I was pretty good at figuring out what the judge oughta do."

"No, but I watched the O.J. trial," Shayla commented. "As if that would do us any good. We better avoid discussing that verdict. We might divide this jury into two camps right away."

Andrea laid down her menu. "I hope that doesn't happen. Surely we can all listen to the evidence and come to a just conclusion."

Shayla raised an eyebrow. "Girl, I do believe you're one of those starry-eyed optimists."

"At this point, there's no reason not to be."

"Ma'am, may I take your order?" The waitress stood at Andrea's elbow.

"Oh…maybe the tuna salad plate."

The young man with horn-rimmed glasses sitting directly across the table from her kept glancing around furtively, then taking sips of water. Conversations ranged all around him, but he seemed oblivious. Andrea moved the dried flower arrangement aside, so she could see him better. "I'm Andrea Evans."

He turned bright red, then extended a cold hand. "Hi. Roy Smith."

Andrea grasped his limp fingers briefly. "Have you been on a jury before?"

He shook his head. "Never. I wish I weren't now."

"Really? In some ways, I'm finding it very interesting."

"Not me." He gulped from his water glass again, then leaned forward confidingly. "To tell you the truth, I'm scared."

"Scared?"

"It's too much responsibility. What if we make a mistake?"

"The system should help prevent that. If twelve people conscientiously review the evidence, they should be right most of the time."

Roy ducked his head. "I dunno."

Down the way on the other side of the table, the large man with the Browns sweatshirt drowned out those around him. "It should be pretty damn simple, folks. We listen to the mouthpieces, go in the jury room, take a vote, collect our measly paychecks and go home. Piece of cake."

A frowsy redhead with long carmine nails made a circle

of her thumb and forefinger. "Bingo, Jack. In and out, clean as a whistle."

"You got it right, baby, except for the name." He grinned lasciviously and stuck out his paw. "Chester Swenson. Chet to my friends."

"Well, Chet," she batted her heavily mascaraed eyelashes, "since we're on the same wavelength here, that oughta make us friends, doncha think? I'm Arnelle Kerry."

"But, Mr. Swenson—" Andrea caught the man's eye "—we're talking about a young man's life."

"The kid's prob'ly scum. Shouldn't be too hard."

The waitress set the tuna salad in front of Andrea. *Scum?* The callousness of the remark ruined her appetite. Beside her, she heard Shayla mutter under her breath, "Takes one to know one."

Andrea, feeling color rising to her cheeks, leaned forward so she could look directly at Mr. Swenson. "I have to speak out here. I think that kind of blanket generalization is not only inappropriate, but, frankly, offensive. We haven't heard any of the evidence and—"

Chet, his mouth full, shook a spoon at her. "Hey, lady, it's a free country. I have the right to say any damn thing I please."

"Ordinarily I'd agree, Chet." The man sitting next to him, the one who'd brought his laptop, laid a hand on Swenson's shoulder. "But we have to walk a tight line when we're discussing anything that might relate to the case. I suggest we change the subject."

Chet shrugged. "Maybe. But I don't need no lessons from her." He glared at Andrea.

Smoothly, the man cut through Swenson's diatribe. "We've got a long haul ahead of us. There will be plenty of differences of opinion before this trial is over. It's a little early to start getting on each others' cases, don't you think?''

Chet crumbled a saltine into his chili. "Maybe."

Grateful for the tactful intervention, Andrea heaved a sigh of relief before eating a forkful of salad. Although she hadn't met all the jurors yet, this pointed exchange reinforced her uncomfortable feeling that unanimity would be elusive. Their backgrounds were so diverse. In addition to those she'd met, there was the handsome man who'd just engineered the detente, a sour-faced elderly woman, a fortyish man in a city sanitation department uniform, a young guy wearing a Case-Western Reserve sweatshirt, a weather-beaten man in jeans and a flannel shirt, and a distinguished-looking, silver-haired gentleman. Five women and seven men. Plus the alternates, both women.

To her left, between bites of her chicken sandwich, Dottie was cataloguing all the chores she had to complete in preparation for the holiday. The litany of a true martyr.

Shayla shifted in her chair and whispered in Andrea's ear, "Don't look now, but the hunk who just bested our buddy Chet can't take his eyes off you."

Prickles of discomfort raced down Andrea's arms. Yet curiosity overcame her. She turned her head slightly and, out of the corner of her eye, saw that the black-haired young man was, indeed, studying her. Before she could avert her glance, the corners of his mouth turned up in a lopsided grin, and when he winked at her, her breath caught. When she dared to look back, he was absorbed in winding spaghetti on his fork.

Shayla beamed. "You go, girl."

"Shame on you, Shayla. This is hardly the place for meeting men."

"It's as good as any. So you're not married?"

"No."

"Well, let's see what ol' Shayla can drum up."

artelli. It is he, his widow and children whom you must
old foremost.

"After we present our case, I am confident that the bulk
and nature of the evidence will remove any question of
reasonable doubt and lead you to the only possible verdict—guilty as charged. Thank you." He paused, making
eye contact with several jurors, then returned to his seat.

When the defense attorney rose, Tony watched Andrea
flip to a new page in her notebook, then sit with her pencil
poised.

Dressed in a tailored navy suit, the petite fiftyish bru-
nette, using different words, also thanked the jurors before
launching into her argument. "The prosecutor would have
you believe this trial is a mere formality, that their evidence is so overwhelming you will have little, if anything,
to deliberate. They will try to convince you my client is a
troublemaker with a history of behavioral problems, instead of the bright, responsible young man he is.

"They have told you my client had motive, opportunity
and a weapon. *They*—" she glanced skeptically at the prosecutors "—would have you believe it's all over but the
shouting.

"Now, ladies and gentlemen, if you permit them to plant
such an image in your minds from the very outset of this
trial, you will have done Darvin Ray and the judicial process a grave disservice."

She moved closer to the railing of the jury box. Tony
noted her natural-looking, makeup-free face, the power of
conviction burning in her eyes. He made a mental note. He
wasn't the defendant; the kid, with clasped hands and
bowed head, was.

The defense will prove that Darvin Ray is *not* a criminal, that, in fact, he is himself a victim. We will show
that the defendant was maliciously used by another person
and framed for the unfortunate murder of Angelo Bartelli.

"Really, I'm not—"

Shayla stabbed the air with a fork. "Sure you are. You
just need a little nudge."

After lunch as the jurors filed out of the restaurant into
the bright winter sunlight, Andrea felt someone take her
by the elbow. She looked up. Him.

"Since we're going to be spending time together, we
might as well get acquainted. I'm Tony Urbanski. And you
are—?"

He still had hold of her arm. "Andrea Evans." She was
struck by the breadth of his shoulders and the depth of his
dark brown eyes. His demeanor conveyed confidence, even
a kind of cockiness.

He assisted her over the curb, then let his hand drop.
"Your first time?"

"On a jury?"

He paused a beat, then grinned. "What else?"

She'd led herself right into that one. "Yes. You?"

"First, and I hope last. I don't have time for this."

"You must be a very important man."

"What makes you say that?"

"Because I'm busy, too. We all are. But, as citizens, we
need to make time."

He kicked a bottle cap out of his way. "I agree, but the
timing for me right now couldn't be worse."

She laid a gloved hand on his sleeve. "I'm sorry."

He stopped and looked intently at her. "So am I. But
maybe not as sorry as I was a few minutes ago."

"What do you mean?"

He covered her hand with his. "A few minutes ago I
hadn't met Andrea Evans."

Andrea felt his hand squeeze hers just before they separated and entered the courthouse.

IN THE SECOND ROW, Tony leaned back in the less-than-
comfortable chair, undoubtedly designed to keep bored ju-

rors attentive or at least upright. The judge was explaining trial procedures and rules of evidence. Pretty standard stuff, although several of his fellow jurors frowned in concentration. Fortunately he'd had time at the restaurant to call the office and explain his situation to Wainwright, who, to Tony's relief, had simply said, "I know you'll do what needs to be done about your work."

Since he was stuck in this jury box, maybe he could try to relax and make the best of the experience. And that definitely included a perusal of Andrea Evans, seated to his right in the front row. Light from a ceiling fixture rested on the tendrils of honey-blond hair that curled loosely at her shoulders. She hunched forward, taking notes on a pad the bailiff had provided. He could see only the curve of her cheek, but he had no trouble recalling the perfect peaches-and-cream complexion and the big blue eyes she'd turned on him outside. She came across as both fragile and determined. An interesting contrast. He admired her for taking the bigoted Swenson to task, but damned if he knew why he'd gone out of his way to meet her. *Bull, you know exactly why. You like her.*

The judge's voice droned on, defining the differences among the various degrees of murder and manslaughter. Andrea was really into this jury thing. He'd watched her all morning, nodding in agreement with the judge, now scribbling fast and furiously. She reminded him of one of those red-white-and-blue-sequin-clad chorines strutting across the stage bare-legged belting out "It's a Grand Old Flag."

His amusement faded to acute physical discomfort when he realized what the image of a scantily dressed Andrea Evans had done to him. Clearly he'd been immersed in business too long if one attractive woman could have such a powerful effect.

Beside him, the redhead—what was her name something—drummed her fake fingernails on the She smelled like the bottom of an ashtray, and if up the castanet action, he'd be forced to throttle

Finally, the judge stopped speaking. The attorne their attention on the bailiff who led in a sligh teenager dressed in blue corduroy slacks, a whit size too small and a crimson tie. Huge brown ey nated his pale face as he stared, like a terrifie around the courtroom. *Jeez, he's just a boy.* Tony that sentiment aside. He was just a boy clea groomed to look like a solid citizen and quite ca firing a gun. Dressed in dark clothing with a stoc pulled over his short, sandy hair and holding a n he would look convincingly menacing.

The judge glanced at the lead prosecutor. "Rea your opening arguments, Mr. Bedford?"

"Yes, Your Honor." The portly young man pi his legal pad and stepped to the attorneys' podiu

"Ladies and gentlemen of the jury, on beha state, thank you for being here. We appreciate venience this trial has caused you, but feel certai exercise your obligation conscientiously.

"The state alleges that this defendant, Ray—" he pointed an accusatory finger a "—did, on the night of January 14, with n thought, shoot and fatally wound Angelo prosecution will present evidence of motive nity. In addition, we will furnish testimony accused at the scene of the crime and lin murder weapon.

"Undoubtedly the defense will attemp your sympathies, citing the age and lack o of the accused. However, none of that m

"Look at him—" she gestured with her arm toward the defendant, then waited while the jurors studied the frightened teen. "How in God's name can we incarcerate a young man whose future lies before him for a crime he did not plan and, most assuredly, did not commit?"

She turned back to the jury, her hands folded in front of her. "In good conscience, we cannot. It is my job to convince you that in accusing my client of this crime, a terrible injustice has been done. It is my job to provide the evidence you need to acquit Darvin Ray and give him back his future. A job I take very seriously." She stood for a moment, then uttered a quiet "Thank you."

Tony was used to the rhetoric of persuasion, and this lady was pretty darn good. But she'd have to be able to do more than talk.

The state called its first witness, the homicide detective in charge of the case. He gave details about the police's notification, the securing of the crime scene, the names and positions of other officials who were there and verified the identity of the deceased.

At four-forty, the judge, after listening to Ms. Lamb stipulate some facts regarding the investigation, adjourned the court until nine o'clock the following morning.

Tony leaped to his feet and buttonholed the bailiff, who, after what seemed an inordinately long time, returned his laptop and cellular phone with an admonition to leave them at home from now on.

Hurrying out of the courtroom, Tony dialed the office on his cellular, reaching Barry Fuller after a few moments. He stopped in the corridor, leaned against the wall and reeled off a list of documents he wanted Barry to gather for them to look over tonight. After disconnecting, he lurched upright and strode toward the elevator, passing the pay phone where Andrea was engrossed in a conversation. Just as he stepped into the elevator, he heard "Hold it, please,'' and spotted Andrea running toward him, her arms full of books. He couldn't tear his eyes away from her. She looked as good from the front as she did from the rear.

She turned a dazzling smile on him. ''Thanks.'' The car started its descent. ''Wasn't today fascinating?'' She seemed to have as much energy now as she'd had at lunch.

''I don't know that I'd go that far,'' he murmured dryly.

''I have to pay close attention to catch everything, but the process, I mean—it's interesting.''

''Interesting…and time-consuming.''

''But,'' her lips quirked coyly, ''important.''

''Important,'' he agreed, while in his head he could almost hear the band playing ''Yankee Doodle Dandy.''

BACK AT THE OFFICE, while he looked over the papers in his In box and waited for Fuller, Tony checked his answering machine. Routine stuff, until he heard the whiskey-rough voice of his father. ''Hey, big shot, it's your old man. I need to talk with you. Soon. Spend your nickel.'' Tony frowned in irritation. Rarely did a call from his father signal good news. Better just get the conversation over with. Reluctantly, he dialed the number. The phone rang five times before his father picked up. ''Yeah?''

''It's Tony.''

''’Bout time. I called this morning. Where ya been?''

''Jury duty.''

''That's my kid. Always the model citizen, huh?''

Tony felt the familiar tightening in his chest. Would the world end if the man gave him a compliment?

His father continued. ''What kinda case?''

''Murder.''

''Ooh, nothing but the best for my important son.''

''What do you want, Pops?''

"Can't a father just chat with his son? Enjoy an...exchange of information?"

"Such as?"

"How's that fancy job of yours comin' along?"

"Fine."

"That's it?"

"What else should I say?"

"Aw, the hell with it." He paused and Tony could hear him sipping and swallowing. "Your cousin Denny won the plant bowling tournament."

"Tell him congratulations for me."

"You got Thanksgiving plans?"

Here it comes. The invitation to hole up in that double-wide and watch parades and ball games while dear old Dad gets wasted. As a kid, Tony had dreaded holidays. No family gathered for a loving, bountiful feast. No laughter. No hugs. Just his father's descent into the bottle. Despite the help Tony had offered through the years, some things never changed. "I'm working."

"Big shot can't even take a day off?"

His father knew all about "sick" days. "Let's get to it, Pops. What exactly is the purpose of this call?"

"I need a loan."

No surprise there. "The ponies let you down?"

His father hawked into the phone. "Little streak of bad luck."

"How bad?"

"A grand."

"I'll send you five hundred." Tony had learned the hard way about his father's padded figures. "How soon do you need it?"

"Tomorrow."

"I'll see what I can do." He'd get to the bank during lunch.

After hanging up, Tony stood, drawing deep, punishing

breaths. *So help me God,* he promised himself, *if I ever have kids of my own, I'll bust my ass taking care of them, loving them, so they never feel about me the way I do about my father.* The father who, no matter what, had stubbornly refused his son's many attempts to get him into treatment.

Easing back into his chair, Tony buried his head in his hands and studied the thick Cyberace file on his desk. His secretary's research was thorough. Each bio was three or four pages. On top was Rodney Steelman's. Class of 1950, Penn State. Marine lieutenant with a tour in Korea. MBA, Harvard, 1958. Ten years with IBM. Now he was getting to the good stuff—how an IBM company man bolted, started with little capital but a lot of contacts and built Cyberace into one hell of a software company.

"Ready for me?"

Tony glanced up. Lounging in the doorway and wearing an eager smile was Barry Fuller, Princeton '92; MBA, Stanford. "Sure, c'mon in." Barry was a good man, bright, thorough, ambitious, willing to learn. But—Tony succumbed to a moment of doubt—untried and overconfident. No matter what his flaws were, Tony needed him. And this negotiation was a great opportunity for the kid. Fuller uncoiled himself, entered the office and, carefully pulling at his trouser creases, sat down. "Man, this jury thing is really bad timing for you. How can I help?"

Tony outlined the tasks to be done, suggested some reallocation of personnel and then asked Barry if he felt comfortable spearheading the preparation while Tony was in court.

"Yes, sir, I do. I know things will come up that I can't handle, but I'm not afraid to ask questions. Besides, I'll be in touch with you every day, and I'm planning on being available nights and weekends as long as you need me."

"I'm counting on it." Tony picked up the bio file. "So let's get started."

Fuller scooted his chair forward, placed his legal pad on the edge of the desk and, as Tony outlined their strategy, began taking notes.

ANDREA SPRINTED TO CATCH the outbound Rapid Transit. She struggled down the aisle, juggling her purse and books as the commuter train slid away from the terminal. With relief, she sank into one of the few vacant seats. Though exciting, in many ways the day had been exhausting. Meeting people was nothing new; being in the retail business, she was used to it, but the careful listening was hard work. Especially with so much at stake! Still, she was reassured by the judge's thorough explanations and by the fact most of her fellow jurors seemed to take their responsibilities seriously, except maybe for Chet and Arnelle and...she couldn't tell about Tony Urbanski. At times he'd seemed preoccupied, detached.

But he had a winner of a smile.

And, in unguarded moments, an almost wistful expression. *Listen to yourself. Manufacturing high drama about a virtual stranger.* She allowed herself a slight chuckle. He was a very *attractive* virtual stranger.

She laid her head back on the seat. She hadn't had much opportunity since the deaths of Tami and Rich to think about men. The suddenness of their loss had devastated the family, particularly Nicky. With the upheaval of moving into her sister and brother-in-law's home and the radical adjustment both she and Nicky had had to make— were still making—her personal life had been subsumed. In the past few months, except for the rare date, she had been most decidedly out of the singles' loop. She shook her head. Darn Tony Urbanski's memorable eyes and engaging grin!

She struggled against a sudden, unbidden memory. John and the shock of his departure. She didn't want to recall the pain and betrayal of discovering that the one man she'd thought she loved—her fiancé, for heaven's sake— couldn't handle her changed circumstances after Tami's and Rich's deaths. What kind of relationship couldn't survive the addition of one small, heartbroken boy? Looking back, she wondered how she could ever have thought she knew John, much less loved him!

On the bright side, she was proud of the success she'd made of her store and the concept of combining the sale of children's books with that of toys, clothes and other products related to familiar stories and poems. Yet there was lingering guilt that she'd had to use some of Tami's and Rich's assets as collateral for a bank loan.

The train rattled and bumped along the tracks. Outside, the smoke-begrimed brick of old warehouses and factories passed in a blur, slowly giving way to the fine old buildings and stately trees of the Heights area. When she'd called the shop during the afternoon recess, Phil had assured her the day had gone smoothly. She was lucky to have him, she thought, both as an employee and as a friend.

By the time she reached the Shaker Square station and climbed into her parked car, it was nearly dark. She'd made arrangements for Nicky's grandparents, Claudia and Bert Porter, to pick Nicky up at school and keep him until she could swing by. As usual, they were delighted to spend time with him.

Why, even after all these months, couldn't she shake the fear that one day they'd take Nicky from her? The Porters had not been happy to learn Tami and Rich had named her Nicholas's guardian in their will. They'd stopped short of fighting her in court, but they took no pains to conceal their disappointment about not having custody of their grandson. She walked on eggshells around the two, and their disapproval settled heavily on her. It was as if they were just waiting for her to make a misstep.

It took ten minutes through heavy traffic to reach their imposing home on the southeast edge of Shaker Heights. The gardener was just loading his rakes into a dilapidated pickup when she pulled into the driveway. With the sunset, the air had turned chilly, and she hurried to the back door. Claudia, a denim apron covering her color-coordinated burgundy wool skirt and cashmere sweater, greeted her. "Hello, Andrea." As usual she sniffed out the name. "You're just in time. Dinner will be ready shortly."

Dinner? All Andrea wanted to do was go home, nuke some leftover meat loaf and curl up on the sofa in her sweats, not sit stiffly in the Porters' formal dining room engaging in stilted conversation and listening to Claudia remind Nicky about table manners as if he'd never had any instruction in the social graces. Her jaw ached. "Where's Nicky?"

Claudia turned to the six-burner stove and began stirring the gravy. "Up in Richard's bedroom with his grandfather."

She should have guessed. Bert and Claudia had made a shrine of their only child's room. She shrugged out of her coat and laid it carefully over the back of a kitchen stool. "I think I'll go say hello unless there's something I can help you with."

Claudia's spine straightened. "No, thank you. On your way upstairs, dear, would you please hang your wrap in the guest coat closet?"

Heaven forbid I clutter the spotless kitchen. Andrea escaped down the hall, the ritual offer of help having been refused, as always. What could an unmarried businesswoman who grabbed takeout on the way home from work possibly know about gourmet cooking?

She started up the stairs, caressing the timeworn carved oak bannister. On the fifth step she paused. As it always did, the large illuminated oil portrait of Rich as a college man, which hung on the wall of the landing, overwhelmed her. Dressed in a white sweater, he sat in the stern of a boat, his left hand casually holding the tiller, his curly black hair wind-tossed, his complexion glowing with a sailor's tan. Each time she climbed these stairs, no matter what the angle, his dark, thoughtful eyes seemed to follow her. He had been a striking young man, and her sister Tami had been lost the first time she clapped eyes on him at a frat party her freshman year at Ohio State.

Andrea sighed, then continued toward the second floor. Despite the off-white walls, spacious airy rooms and tasteful, but understated furnishings, the house felt lifeless, as if it would be irreverent to laugh aloud. And this in a home that used to ring with the laughter of Rich and his friends. Ever since the accident, both Bert and Claudia, like the house itself, seemed different—empty, brittle, edgy.

From Rich's old room, she could hear Bert's deep voice. She approached and stood quietly in the doorway. Nicky perched on one of the twin beds, his hands clasped politely in his lap. His grandfather sat beside him holding a trophy between his knees. "…and this one your dad got when his Little League team won the championship. Do you remember what I told you about the double play he made against Creamfresh Dairy?"

Nicky nodded dutifully while Bert extolled Rich's feats on the baseball diamond. Andrea took in the familiar room—done in a blue-and-red nautical theme. Model sailboats lined the long shelf over the beds and on the opposite wall a bookcase was crammed with additional trophies, framed certificates, a leather mitt molded through use to fit a youthful hand and a framed picture of Tami and Rich at a sorority dance. As if his mother had made a concession to youthful idiosyncrasies, on the far wall hung posters of Bruce Springsteen and the Rolling Stones. Not a cobweb or dust bunny anywhere.

"...so what do you think, son? Pretty impressive, huh?"

She could hardly hear Nicky's mumbled, "Yes, Grandpa."

Bert stood, studying the trophy in his hand, then crossed to the bookcase where he carefully replaced it before picking up the stained mitt. He looked at Nicky. "Pretty soon you can use this when you play ball."

Nicky fidgeted, pinching the bedspread with his fingers. "Maybe."

Bert replaced the mitt, then tousled Nicky's hair. "That will be this spring, right?"

Nicky stared at the floor. "I guess."

Determined to rescue her nephew, Andrea entered the room. "Gentlemen, ready for dinner?"

Bert peered at her over the rim of his glasses. "Hello, Andrea. We didn't hear you come in." His tone made her feel like an unwelcome intrusion.

Nicky leaped off the bed and came to stand beside her, his arms around her waist. "Hi, Andie."

She put a hand on his shoulder. "Did you have a good day at school?"

"Okay, I guess."

"Great. Let's go downstairs and you can tell us all about it over dinner."

After they were seated around the antique cherry dining room table, Claudia placed the pork roast, aromatic with garlic and rosemary, on the damask place mat in front of her husband. He dished up the servings, then passed a plate to each of them. Claudia ladled broccoli beside Nicky's meat portion. He bit his lip and looked pleadingly across the table at his aunt.

"Your Mimi wants you to try her special recipe, Nicholas,'' Claudia cajoled. "You and Andrea need to eat more vegetables.''

How would Claudia know? Did she think they consumed nothing but greasy burgers and pizza? Nicky tolerated peas, beans and squash, but he hated broccoli. Andrea watched as he manfully shoveled a teaspoonful of the offensive green into his mouth, his jaws moving mechanically as he attempted to chew and swallow the stuff. She tried to divert Claudia. "The gravy is delicious.''

Claudia smiled smugly. "Thank you, my dear. Richard loved my gravy. Unfortunately your sister never mastered it.''

Bert set down his fork and cleared his throat. "Andrea, Claudia tells me you're on a jury.'' He raised his eyebrows inquisitively while he buttered his roll.

"Yes.'' Why was it such a strain to conduct a conversation with these people? The three of them had loving Nicky in common, didn't they? "It's a murder case.''

Claudia's fork clattered to her plate. "Oh, my.'' She threw a nearly imperceptible nod toward Nicky as if Andrea had just brought up an objectionable topic.

For the first time since she'd arrived, Nicky's face brightened. "Cool. Tell me about it.''

"Must we talk about it now?'' Claudia frowned at Andrea.

"I wanna hear, Andie.''

"Actually, I'm not supposed to discuss the case itself. Mostly this afternoon we listened to the judge and the attorneys' opening—''

"Nicholas, put your napkin back in your lap,'' Claudia hissed, "and finish that broccoli. That's a good boy.''

"How long do you think your jury duty will last?'' Bert asked.

"I'm not sure, several days maybe.''

"I have a wonderful idea,'' Claudia chimed in. "Nicholas can stay with us while you're on jury duty. That way you won't have to worry about him. Don't you think that's best, Bert?''

Andrea's heart sank.

''...pack his things, and I could pick him up from school,'' Bert was saying.

''Excuse me, but much as I appreciate your offer, I think it's important for Nicky to continue with his normal routine.''

Bert turned to Nicholas expectantly. ''What would you like to do, son?''

Nicholas flushed. ''I...I don't care.'' He stared at Andrea beseechingly.

Andrea wiped her mouth with her napkin and tried to pull herself together. She would not be manipulated by these people. ''No. Nicholas will stay with me although I'd appreciate being able to call on you for help. Now, while we finish this delicious dinner, why don't you tell us about school, Nicky?''

Recognizing a reprieve, Nicholas picked up the verbal ball she'd tossed to him and began telling them about some new computer software the fourth grade was using in social studies. Andrea consciously slowed her breathing, unclenched her hands and picked at the pork roast, aware of the frozen expressions on the faces of her hosts.

''WHY DOES MIMI make me eat broccoli?''

Andrea maintained a neutral expression and concentrated on her driving. ''Because it's good for you.''

''Yuck. If I were God and was gonna make somethin' good for kids to eat, it sure wouldn't taste like that.''

''Well, you know how your grandmother is about her cooking.''

He stuffed his hands in the pockets of his parka. ''Yeah. But all she makes is grown-ups' food. I bet she doesn't even know how to make a peanut butter and jelly sandwich.''

''Why don't you ask her sometime?''

He looked doubtfully at her. ''Is peanut butter good for ya?''

She grinned. ''Full of protein.''

''Then maybe I'll ask her.'' He rode along silently for several blocks. Then he spoke again.

''Do I hafta play baseball?''

''Why do you ask?''

''Grandpa wants me to.'' He was kicking the floorboard. ''I don't like baseball.''

Oh, boy. ''Why not?''

Kick, kick. ''I…I'm no good at it.''

''But you've never played.''

She barely made out his mumbled answer over the hum of the heater. ''I wouldn't be any good.''

''Nicky, you don't know that.''

He raised his chin, and his voice was defiant. ''Yes, I do. Everybody knows I can't do sports. And don't try to tell me I can.''

Oh, Lord. A reaction to Ben and the ''weenie'' comment? ''Let's wait and see. Maybe Grandpa and I can practice with you.''

In response, all she heard was the thud of more kicking.

A RAGGED VOICE SCREAMED into the gusting wind. ''Dad! Dad!''

Bert windmilled his arms, struggling through the roiling waves, losing his footing in the sifting sands of the lake floor. ''Hang on, I'm coming!'' He half jogged, half swam toward the sound. Cold breakers, huge and powerful, beat him back, but he thrashed on.

''Bert!'' Something hard—a piece of driftwood?—

aired woman with an olive complexion gasped and
d her mouth with her hand. The widow? Beside her,
ger woman, perhaps her daughter, consoled her.
ehow with that tiny gasp, the dry recitation of evi-
took on painful reality. *That* bullet from *that* gun
bbed a family of their loved one.

rea glanced at the defendant, his white shirt more
ed today, wondering what would possess a teenager,
future lay before him, to kill someone. Well, she
naive. Maybe he was involved in a gang or had
igh on drugs or simply had made a stupid mistake.
ay he sat, his shoulders hunched, his head bowed,
led her of a cowering animal. She'd like to think
is the defense had suggested, he'd been framed.
By whom?

er the defense attorney finished her cross-
nation of the ballistics expert, the judge called a re-
Dottie Dettweiler followed Andrea into the rest room.
't believe it took that man forty-five minutes to tell
ut guns. Why do I need to know about the patterns
vder burns? Why don't they just tell me that gun is
irder weapon and get on with it?''

rea stood at the mirror fluffing her hair. ''Careful,
. We can't discuss the case. Basically, though, the
ution has to prove everything to us.''

olding us captive, more's the like.'' Dottie, in a huff,
eared into a stall.

at would happen when the jurors finally deliberated?
d people like Dottie try to rush a verdict? A few
es ago Chet had groused, ''Fifteen dollars an hour
stin' me ta sit aroun' here listenin' to this garbage.''
rea shuddered and turned away from the mirror. A
f your peers. Among the five scariest words in the
h language.

side in the hall, Andrea wandered to a window over-

knocked against his shoulder. Again the cry. ''Bert! Wake
up!''

He fought onward toward...the red eye of the luminous
dial on the bedside clock-radio, which read two-seventeen.

''Bert, are you all right?''

He pushed onto his elbows, struggling to free his legs
from the tangled sheet. A cold sweat drenched his body.
Shivering, he reached for the blankets at the foot of the
bed. Finally, his respiration slowed. ''Okay. I'm okay,
now.''

Claudia turned on the bedside lamp. ''Was it the dream
again?''

Would he ever be free of it? ''Yes.'' He forced back
the phlegm crowding his throat.

''Bert, it's been eighteen months.''

''Don't you think I know that?''

''Are you sure you don't need to see a profess—''

''No! I don't want to hear any more about it. At least
in the dream, I can see him, hear him....''

''It's not good for you—''

''But I can't reach him. God, I get so close.'' His voice
broke.

Claudia slipped out of bed and put on her robe. ''I'll
bring you some warm milk. It'll help you get back to
sleep.'' She glided from the room.

Sleep! He resisted it, feared it. Because no matter how
hard he tried, how he willed it with every sinew in his
body, he couldn't bring Rich back. He threw an arm over
his eyes and bit back a sob. His son. His only child. Gone.

After a few minutes, he sat up, leaned against the pillows and fixed his eyes on the familiar bedroom furnishings—the massive walnut armoire, Claudia's dressing table, the built-in bookshelves. He concentrated on the
normalcy of his surroundings. Yet the imprint of his son's
anguished face stared back at him everywhere he looked.

God, if it weren't for Nicholas, he didn't know what he'd do. But he couldn't spend time with Nicholas every day the way he'd be able to if his grandson lived here. He couldn't oversee his upbringing. Couldn't fill that empty space Rich used to occupy. It wasn't Andrea's fault, of course. She did her best, but, damn, it wasn't the same as having Nicholas under the same roof.

Claudia eased open the door with her hip and backed into the room, carrying a tray. "Here we go." She turned around and walked toward him, setting the tray on the bedside table. "Hot milk and graham crackers."

"I'm not hungry." Besides, he didn't appreciate being treated like some small boy in a nursery, damn it.

"Now, Bert—" Claudia's voice affected the patronizing tone of a nanny "—it'll make you feel better."

He waved the proffered mug aside. "Why can't you understand, Claudia? *Nothing* is going to make me feel better."

Eyeing him closely, his wife set down the mug and seemed about to say something critical when she apparently changed her mind and merely said, "Well, suit yourself, then. I'm going back to bed. Turn the light out when you're ready."

He couldn't believe it. Within mere seconds, she was sound asleep. They simply didn't understand each other any more. It baffled him that she had been able to go on so smoothly with her life, as if her son's death were just another bump along life's road instead of a cataclysmic upheaval. Most mothers would have disintegrated into grief, their lives forever altered. He couldn't understand Claudia. Maybe denial was her way of coping, but it sure as hell wasn't his.

He leaned over and turned off the lamp. In the darkness, he thought about Nicholas. At least *he* hadn't forgotten Rich. But the lad seemed so sad, so unreachable.

If only he and Claudia had custody…

CHAPTER THREE

AFTER DROPPING NICKY at school the next mo
barely catching the inbound Rapid, Andrea dashe
jury room. The bailiff directed her to the coat
lined up the jurors.

"Girl, you look frazzled." Shayla patted
shoulder as they entered the courtroom. "Tal
breath and calm down."

"I was afraid I'd be late. I had to get my n
to school."

"Mornings are hectic at my house, too. Ro
teenagers outta bed takes an act of Congress."

As the panel settled into their seats, Andrea
at Tony Urbanski, who sat back in his chair, l
studying the ceiling while Arnelle Kerry wh
his ear. He looked distractingly handsome in
button-down shirt, paisley tie and camel blaz
was noticing? When they rose for the judge's
had the feeling his eyes were fixed on her.

The ballistics expert took the stand then.
forced herself to pay attention. The man cle
stuff but, even with charts and photographs,
ficult time making the arcane compreher
about angle of bullet entry and weapon cal
to follow, but she did grasp that the police
identified the weapon that evidence showe
killed Mr. Bartelli. When photos of the en
flashed on the video screen, among the s

looking downtown. A brisk wind roiled the surface of Lake Erie and pedestrians scurried between buildings.

"I brought you a soda." Andrea looked up. Shayla extended a can. "Hope you like Sprite."

"Thanks, I do. What do I owe you?"

"Forget it. You can return the favor this afternoon." Shayla perched on the window ledge. "I also brought news." Her eyes sparkled. "About our fellow juror."

Andrea lifted her lips from the can. "Oh?" Shayla's body language was obvious—she was practically salivating. "Who're you talking about?"

"Don't play dumb with me, girl. Him." She nodded toward the pay phone where Tony Urbanski stood deep in serious conversation.

"Shay-la." Andrea drew out her name chidingly. "I warned you about matchmaking."

"Honey, we gotta do somethin' besides listen to those lawyers. I'm takin' good care of you." She set her soda down and folded her arms. "Now, you wanna hear what Shayla discovered?"

The heck of it is, I really do. "You're going to tell me anyway, right?"

Shayla chuckled. "Listen up, missy. Mr. Tony Urbanski works for Great Lakes Management Group. He has a cushy job and a flat in one of those pricey warehouses over by the river. He grew up in Detroit and got a university education at Michigan State. He's been here two years. And now for the best part—" She picked up her drink and took a maddeningly slow sip.

Andrea pursed her lips and threw Shayla an accusing look. "You're going to make me ask, aren't you?"

"I've gotta have a little fun, too."

"Okay." She enunciated very clearly. "What is the best part?"

"He's single, never been married, and—" She arched her eyebrows suggestively and leaned forward.

Andrea couldn't help herself. "What?"

"He asked me all about you."

Having fair skin was a detriment at times like this. A blush made it impossible to look neutral. But, then, she didn't feel particularly neutral.

When she turned to walk toward the courtroom, Tony, the phone still clamped to his ear, a broad grin creasing his face, followed her with his eyes.

TONY SPRINTED TO THE BANK after lunch to set up the wire transfer of the five hundred dollars. It had always been like this. His father made good money as a forklift operator, but what he didn't gamble away, he drank. Early on, Tony had devised a game plan. If he wanted to get ahead, he couldn't expect help from Pops. He'd have to rely on himself, bust his butt and make it happen. It hadn't been easy, but he took quiet satisfaction in his success.

Crossing the square on his way back to the courthouse, Tony set aside unpleasant reminders of his past and concentrated on Andrea Evans. With all the subtlety of a battering ram, Shayla Brown had invited him to lunch with her and Andrea. Not that he'd minded. Quite the contrary—the perky blonde was easy to look at. Like an inquisitive bird, she had a way of cocking her head when she listened that made him feel as if she really cared, and she exuded...not naiveté exactly...more a zest for life rarely seen in adults. When his eyes strayed, from time to time, to her delicious curves, he felt rather like a ravening wolf creeping up on an unsuspecting lamb.

He'd learned she'd grown up in Shaker Heights, had majored in marketing at Miami University and owned her own toy store. Not bad for such a young woman. A car honked at him, and he stepped back up on the curb. Since moving to Cleveland, he'd had little time for a social life, unless you counted the occasional party like the one Kelli'd had at Halloween. The few women he'd dated had tended to be executive types with an attitude. Andrea's softness was a definite contrast. A welcome one.

He chastised himself. He hadn't gotten where he was by worrying about his personal life. Besides, a workaholic like himself shouldn't be entertaining thoughts about any woman, no matter how temptingly attractive.

That decided, by the time he reached his place in the jury box, he was able to settle back and listen, first to the coroner and then to the fingerprint expert, who established that the print on the murder weapon matched the defendant's. By the time the judge adjourned for the day, he was beat. Did these people have to pass a nerd test to qualify as expert witnesses?

Outside, sunshine faded to dusk and adjacent office buildings disgorged workers into Public Square. Inexplicably, despite his earlier resolve, he found himself rushing to catch up with Andrea and Shayla. "Hey, what's your hurry?"

Andrea spun around, the red of her woolen scarf complementing her rosy cheeks. "Oh, hi, Tony. I'm trying to get to the store before my manager closes." Shayla stood to one side, a knowing look on her face.

"Do you have a minute?" What in the world was he doing? He could almost hear Kelli laughing and saying, "Okay, big boy, what now?" He fumbled for a coherent comment.

Shayla didn't have any trouble finding something to say. "Funny how circumstances have thrust us all together, isn't it? I mean, how else would the two of you have met? And if you'll pardon my interference, I think you should make the most of it." She grinned smugly.

"I beg your pardon?" Tony said.

"Shayla—" Andrea protested.

The older woman ignored them both and hurtled on. "Never a good idea to ignore Lady Luck." With her thumb and forefinger, she picked up Andrea's wrist and held it out for inspection. "Tony, this skinny little gal needs fattening up. Why don't you take her to dinner?"

Andrea shifted uncomfortably, pulling her arm away. "Really, Shayla, I'm sure Tony has plans of his own." She looked pointedly at him. "*Don't* you?"

A conference with Barry, letters to sign…but he'd be through in an hour or so. "Actually, no," he found himself saying. "How about it, Andrea?" Was he out of his mind?

Shayla beamed. "Well, then. That's settled." She glanced up at the Terminal Building clock. "Oops, gotta run or I'll miss my train." And she was gone.

Andrea edged after her. "Wait."

Tony stopped her. "I'm serious."

"Tonight?"

"I'm free. How about you?"

She fingered the strap of her shoulder bag. "I don't know if this is such a good idea."

"Do I need a character reference?"

She smiled. "No, Shayla's checked you out. It's not that—"

"Then what?"

"This jury thing." She wrinkled her nose. "I mean, it would be fraternizing. I don't think we should compromise the process."

She hadn't turned him down…yet. And this was one argument he could handle. "I don't know about you, but I wasn't planning on discussing the case."

"No, of course not. The judge made that very clear."

"So—" he tucked her arm in his and started toward the Rapid station "—I don't see what harm there would be in some off-duty socializing." Harm? Hell, he couldn't wait.

She glanced up at him, her expression wary. "You promise you won't bring up the case?"

He crossed his heart. "I promise. I can pick you up at seven."

"Because of the short notice, the 'you' will have to include Nicky."

"Nicky?" Who the hell was Nicky?

She seemed to be enjoying his bewilderment. "Nicky's my nine-year-old nephew and he'll make a wonderful chaperon."

Oh. "That's great."

"We'll be at Never-Never Land."

"'Scuse me?"

"Never-Never Land."

"Should I fly in?"

She laughed merrily. "That won't be necessary. I forgot. You don't know. That's the name of my store in Shaker Square."

He cracked a wry smile. "What a relief. For a minute there I was afraid you and Peter Pan had flitted off to Honalee along with Puff."

As they neared the ticket booth, she gave him the address. Then she turned and laid a hand on his arm. "You're sure this is okay?"

He covered her hand with his and hoped he wasn't fibbing. "Positive."

"You're on, then." Her eyes twinkled. "Seven o'clock."

As he walked briskly toward his office, Tony had to laugh at himself. After all, he, who made his living as a master of interpersonal communication, had just been adroitly maneuvered by not one, but two women! He plunged his hands into his pants pockets. Nicky, huh?

ANDREA PICKED UP NICKY at the Porters' and made it to the store ten minutes before the six o'clock closing time.

Phil, dressed in his Uncle Wiggly costume, was advising a little girl picking out a birthday present for her best friend. Meanwhile, the child's exasperated mother kept frantically checking her watch. Andrea smiled. Phil was a whiz at the financial end of the business, but his real talent was relating to kids.

Many men would have been uncomfortable wearing a costume, but Phil and her other employees loved the theatrical touch of dressing as storybook characters. Andrea had to admit the idea had been a stroke of marketing genius—that, along with a carefully selected inventory of books and toys, had been a significant factor in attracting and keeping customers. The store had exceeded all her financial projections for this first year, and a strong holiday season would cap things off nicely.

She picked up the cash register receipts and retreated to her office to tally the day's sales. In the corner Nicky lounged in a red beanbag chair reading. Fortunately, he was patient about spending time at the shop and amused himself well. Andrea ran the adding machine, then studied the totals on the tape. Not bad for a weekday. Phil, now in his street clothes, stuck his head in the door. "I've locked up. Okay if I leave now?"

"Sure. I have a few more things to do." After Phil departed, she put the cash into a bank bag and stored it in the small office safe, then glanced at the clock.

"Nicky, may I interrupt?"

With his finger marking the page, he closed his book and looked up.

"I hope you don't mind, but a friend is coming by to take us to dinner. What do you feel like having?"

"*Not* broccoli."

"A cauliflower veggie burger, then?"

He made a gagging noise. "Pizza. Let's have pizza."

"Giorgio's?"

His head was already back in his book. "Uh-huh."

Her friend Daisy Whitcomb, who made all the costumes for the employees, had delivered the new Christmas items Monday, but until now Andrea hadn't had a chance to examine them. She went into the storeroom. Two forest-green elf costumes for their part-time seasonal help; an immaculate uniform—complete with epaulets and gold braid—awaiting only the bearskin headgear to transform Phil into a nutcracker; and her own flowing white gown with attached buckram wings and a glittering halo. Because of her short stature, she was to be The Littlest Angel.

She decided to try on the costume quickly to see if any alterations were necessary. Because of her jury duty, she didn't know when she'd have another chance. She stepped out of her brown tweed skirt and pulled the beige turtleneck over her head before carefully donning the angel robe. Stretching and craning, she finally managed to zip up the back and arrange the wings, which seemed to have a will of their own. Then she gently laid the halo on the crown of her head. Picking up the skirt, she returned to the office to check the effect in the full-length mirror on the back of the door.

Nicky adjusted his glasses with a forefinger, then stared at her.

She pirouetted. "Well, what do you think?"

"It's okay. Don't spill anything on it."

He was right. Anything and everything would show. She'd need to be careful. Not easy to do amid the Christmas rush. Yet it was fun to look in the glass and see an angel reflected. Her gaze went to her feet. The low-heeled brown suede boots spoiled the effect. She'd have to dig out her white hose and shoes. But the length was about right—

"What's that?" Nicky looked alarmed.

"What?"

"That sound."

Then Andrea heard it. Someone knocking on the plate glass at the front of the store. "Oh, dear. That's Tony. I need to let him in." She dashed to the entry, disarmed the alarm and opened the door. "I'm so sorry. The time got away from me."

Tony just stood there, staring. An amused grin spread over his face. Finally he spoke. "First Never-Never Land, and now heaven?"

"No, not the Elysian fields, just a workplace where we wear seasonal costumes—in this case, Christmas." She adjusted the halo, which had tilted during her rush to the door, and stepped aside. "Come on in."

He entered and looked around dazedly. "This is quite a place." He removed his gloves, stuffed them in his coat pockets, then picked up a jack-in-the-box from a floor display. He turned the handle and laughed aloud when a clown jumped out to the tune of "Pop Goes the Weasel."

"Make yourself at home. I need to change."

He set down the toy and reached for her hand. "Not for me you don't. I've never had a date with an angel."

The warmth of his hand enclosing hers sent a shock through her, along with decidedly unangelic thoughts. "Giorgio might not understand."

"Giorgio?"

"The pizza chef." She withdrew her hand.

Tony seemed puzzled. "Pizza?"

"Yes, Nicky and I thought that would be best."

"Sure, whatever you say."

She suspected that, despite what he'd said earlier, the idea of a third party wasn't appealing. Just then Nicky sidled up alongside her. She put an arm around him. "Tony, I'd like you to meet my nephew, Nicholas Porter. Nicky, this is Tony Urbanski."

Nicky averted his eyes as he shook hands with Tony.

She started toward the rear of the store. "If you two will excuse me, I—"

Nicky trailed her. "I thought you said we were going to dinner with a friend," he whined.

Andrea faltered. He was not happy. And Tony had to have overheard. "Tony *is* a friend."

They reached the office. Nicky stood, sullen, his hands deep in his pockets. "But he's a man."

"Does that bother you?"

He shrugged. "I dunno."

She placed her palms on his shoulders. "Tell you what. Why don't you give him a chance? We'll check him out together. What do you say?"

"I guess." He turned away and started stuffing books into his backpack.

In the storeroom as Andrea removed the costume and hung it back on the hanger, she couldn't help thinking about Nicky's possessiveness and the approving glow in Tony's eyes when she'd opened the door. She would most definitely need a guardian angel tonight!

WHEN TONY HAD FIRST seen Andrea—her flaxen hair loose around her shoulders, the diaphanous gown barely concealing her lush body—he couldn't help but think of ravishing that angel right there on the floor. A Never-Never Land fantasy, all right.

He wandered around the store. Train sets, jigsaw puzzles, magician's kits, an entire section of games—he'd had no idea there was this much stuff available for kids. Hell, he'd been lucky to have a secondhand Tonka dump truck and a rusty red wagon. He picked up a pioneer character doll and examined the price tag. The merchandise wasn't cheap either. It must cost a fortune for parents to put on Christmas these days.

He replaced the doll and strolled to the substantial reading corner. He ran a finger along the spines of the books—Babar, Curious George and Horton the Elephant. He supposed most adults had associations with these characters. Not him. He couldn't remember anyone reading to him, except his teachers, after his mother died when he was five. All that came to him was a dim recollection of sitting on her lap playing with the shiny buckles on her overall straps while she told him about a big, bad wolf who "huffed and puffed" and blew down the houses of three little pigs. He'd found the notion of pigs living in houses startling. He and his parents lived in a metal trailer. Could the big, bad wolf blow it down?

He picked up *Goodnight Moon* and thumbed through the pages. He might've been better off to stay at the office, instead of submitting to the very thing that hours earlier he'd vowed to avoid. The possibility of a relationship.

"Ready?"

He hadn't heard Andrea approach. He closed the book and returned it to the shelf. "Whenever you are."

"Nicky, let's go."

While he held Andrea's coat for her, he watched the kid drag his backpack toward the door. "Where to?"

"Giorgio's. It's just down the block. That way you won't have to move your car."

"That's fine with me." He and Nicky waited outside while she set the alarm. "What grade are you in, Nick?"

"Fourth." He glared holes through Tony. "Nobody calls me Nick."

"Mind if I do? Nicholas sounds too formal, and you don't seem like a Nicky to me." He studied the boy—stooped shoulders, longish black hair, goggle glasses, scuffed loafers. "Yeah, definitely more a Nick."

"What's a Nick like?" Tony could tell the kid had debated with himself whether to ask the question.

store near the dairy case, probably thirty feet or so from the register."

"What happened next?"

"I'd just grabbed the milk when I heard voices. Somebody said, 'Please!' in a loud, pitiful voice. When I turned around, there was this man standing by the register with a ball cap pulled low over his face—" here she gestured as if pulling a hat over her eyes.

"Did this man have a gun?"

"He must have. He shot that poor clerk." Her chin trembled with outrage.

"Let me rephrase that. Did you *see* a gun?"

"Well, he had his hand in his jacket pocket, you know, and it kinda looked like this." The woman balled up her fist, extending her index finger.

"Did you hear the man say anything?"

"I sure did. He mumbled something and then, real menacing-like, he said, '...or I'll kill you, old man.'"

"What happened next?"

Mrs. Innes rubbed her hands nervously. "The kid said, 'Hand over the money.' Just then a big display of soda cans that nearly reached the ceiling came tumbling down. Next thing, I heard a shot. My heart was beatin' so fast I like to died right there."

Bedford's dry voice interrupted. "But what *did* you do?"

"I dropped the milk and fell to the floor."

"And then?"

"The alarm went off, and I heard this voice yelling, 'God damn it, what the—'" she glanced up at the judge "—I don't think I'd better say that word, Your Honor."

"I understand. Just substitute 'expletive.'"

Mrs. Innes sighed, apparently in relief. "What the *expletive.*" She leaned against the back of her chair, obviously pleased to have remembered so accurately. "I laid real still until he ran outta the store."

Bedford stood to one side, so the witness had a clear view of the courtroom. "Mrs. Innes, do you see the man you saw that night here today?"

Her mouth set with concentration, she straightened up and studied the teenager at the defense table. "That one looks about the same size, but—"

"Just answer the question."

As if she'd failed a test, Mrs. Innes looked crestfallen. "No, I couldn't be positive."

"No further questions, Your Honor." The prosecutor returned to his table.

Andrea tried to put herself into Mrs. Innes's place. It must be difficult to recall accurately events that had happened so far in the past.

Slowly Ms. Lamb, the defense attorney, rose to her feet. "Good morning, Mrs. Innes. How are you today?"

The witness seemed uncomfortable, as if anticipating a trick. Andrea couldn't help thinking that Mrs. Innes probably wanted the defendant to be found guilty. After all, she'd been scared out of her wits.

"Fine." The woman's chattiness was gone.

"What time of night was this?"

"About eleven-fifteen. My husband and me, we'd finished watching *ER* before he sent me to the corner to get him cigarettes."

Andrea couldn't resist a shudder at Mr. Innes's apparent chauvinism.

"You say you could see what you presumed to be a gun in the pocket of the man at the counter. Is that correct?"

"Yes."

"You also testified you were at the back of the store, a distance of some thirty feet away."

"Yes."

"Could you be absolutely sure the man carried a gun in his pocket and not something else?"

The witness became flustered. "Well, when you put it that way...no."

"In your previous testimony, you referred to the perpetrator as 'kid.'"

"Yes."

"How did you determine he was a youth?"

"He wore those big athletic shoes, the ones with all those colors and flashy things. And he wore, you know, one of those hippie-looking multicolored shirts."

"Could a full-grown adult also wear such shoes?"

"I suppose."

"And such a shirt?"

Mrs. Innes bit her lip. "I...yes."

"So you had no proof that would justify your characterizing this person as 'kid.'"

"I guess that's right."

"That's all I have at this time for this witness, Your Honor."

The judge thanked Mrs. Innes, then glanced at the prosecutor. "Counselor, call your next witness."

Andrea's eyes strayed to the defense table where the defendant was rubbing his hands up and down his thighs. When Ms. Lamb sat down, she touched him gently on the shoulder and his hands stilled.

The next witness, a muscular man of about forty dressed in corduroy trousers and a vividly striped rugby shirt, exuded confidence. From preliminary questions, Andrea learned Ken Mays was the manager of a gym and fitness center in the neighborhood of the store. He sat in the witness box with his feet planted firmly on the floor, knees apart, hands folded casually at his waist.

After the prosecutor asked him to give his version of events, the man responded succinctly. "I had jogged from my apartment to the convenience store, arriving at exactly eleven-thirteen. I know this because I timed my run. I was standing looking at magazines when, over the top of the rack, I saw this guy go up to the cashier. Something about the customer's behavior made me suspicious. I didn't move, not wanting to call attention to myself. I saw him pull a gun, and that's when I moved to the end of the aisle and knocked over a tower of soda cans. I figured maybe I'd scare him away. About the same time, the cashier must've tripped the burglar alarm."

"What happened next, Mr. Mays?"

"I hit the deck and heard the guy yell something like, 'Gimme the money.' Then I remember hearing the shot, and the guy ran like hell. Er, excuse me, Your Honor."

The judge didn't look up from the papers on her desk, but gave a brief nod.

"Did the perpetrator see you?" the prosecutor asked.

"I don't think so."

"Can you describe the man with the gun?"

"He was about five-six or seven. Kinda hard to tell exactly. He wore dark jeans, athletic shoes, a tie-dyed T-shirt, a black goose-down vest and a navy blue ball cap."

"I call your attention to People's exhibit sixteen." Bedford picked up a fuchsia, yellow and purple shirt. "Mr. Mays, is this the shirt the man in the store was wearing?"

"It looks like it to me."

With a flourish of the garment, the prosecutor set it down and continued, "Did you happen to notice if he was wearing gloves?"

"Yeah, I think so."

"Can you positively identify anyone in this courtroom as the man who was in the store that night?"

"No, I can't."

"What happened after the perpetrator fled?"

"I called 9-1-1 and tried to help the victim. But it was too late. He was already dead."

"That'll be all. Thank you."

While the defense attorney sorted her notes, Andrea became aware of the scribblings on Dottie's tablet. A grocery list! Unbelievable. Thanksgiving was still six days away. Surely the woman could pay more attention here. Yet, she had to admit that occasionally her own mind had strayed to what she would cook Tony this evening.

Ms. Lamb began her cross-examination. "You stated that the man at the counter was five-six or seven. However, except for a brief glimpse before you shoved over the cans, your only other view of him was from the floor looking up. Correct?"

"Yes."

"From that latter viewpoint, might he have seemed taller?"

"Because of my work, I'm a pretty fair judge of body types."

"But can you say with certainty, Mr. Mays, how tall the perpetrator was?"

"With certainty? No, ma'am."

"About the shirt you saw. Wasn't the perpetrator also wearing—" she stood at the defense table reviewing her notes "—a vest?"

"Yes."

"Yet, you claim you can positively identify the shirt?"

"Yes. The vest wasn't zipped."

"Indulge me with a little test of your powers of observation." She pulled two similar-looking shirts out of a paper bag and, blocking the witness's view, arranged them along with the one from the exhibit table on the podium. "Mr. Mays, which of these is the shirt you identified for Mr. Bedford?" She stood aside.

He studied them. "The one on my left."

The attorney glanced at the judge and said wearily, "Let the record show that this witness identified People's exhibit sixteen.

"Thank you, Mr. Mays. I have no further questions at this time, Your Honor."

The judge declared a recess during which the jurors milled around the jury room, several noticeably impatient. The trial was now in its third day, and the prosecution had yet to rest its case. "Hell, we'll be here all next week," Chet Swenson complained.

Dottie shook her head sadly. "I don't know how I'm going to get ready for all my company."

"Hey, it's okay with me," the young man who'd worn the Case-Western Reserve T-shirt on Wednesday said with a sly grin. "This beats going to class."

Shayla and Andrea walked to the north window, overlooking the lake, glistening silver in the pale sunlight fingering through the light cloud cover. "So, how's it going with Tony?"

Andrea rued the flush that crept up her neck. "Interesting." She let the word lie between them, unsure whether she wanted to elaborate.

"Hey, girl, you can't stop there. I gotta have something to think about besides crime." She gave an out-with-it gesture. "What do you mean 'interesting'?"

Grinning, Andrea relented. "Thanks to you and your clever manipulation, I had pizza with him last night."

"That's better than 'interesting.' That's progress. So?" Shayla smiled in anticipation.

"He seems very nice. At least he made inroads with my nephew."

"Whoa! Your nephew? Did he go on your date?"

Andrea backpedaled. "It wasn't a date, exactly. Just a casual dinner." She briefly explained about having custody of Nicky. "So, naturally he was along."

"Kinda cramped your style, didn't it?" Shayla waved her hands dismissively. "But, it's a start. And from what I saw this morning, the man's definitely got the hots for you. So what's next?"

Andrea paused, aware that she didn't know anything beyond tonight. Maybe she was kidding herself. Why would there be anything beyond that? Did she even want more? For heaven's sake, she'd only just met Tony. "I've invited him for dinner this evening."

Shayla gave her a high five. "Way to go! I'm proud of you." Then her face fell. "There's only one problem. That means I have to wait until Monday to hear all."

"Maybe there won't be much to tell."

Shayla eyed her up and down, then cackled, "Oh, I imagine there'll be plenty to tell."

To Andrea's relief, the bailiff motioned them to line up again. After court reconvened, Andrea was glad they'd had the break, because the next testimony was highly technical. First, a DNA expert whose tests proved the T-shirt Mays had identified had small bloodstains on it consistent with Mr. Bartelli's blood, followed by an electronics professional, who discussed the surveillance video camera, its angle and range of view. Last, the judge permitted a replay of tape recorded that night. The picture was fuzzy, but was clear enough to show a male entering the store and threatening the owner. Then just as the man pulled a gun, the soda cans fell in such a way that the view of the register was momentarily obscured. Finally the camera picked up a figure running out the front door. It all happened so fast that Andrea had difficulty separating the actions.

The noon recess didn't come a moment too soon to suit her. Walking toward the elevator, she became aware that Tony had fallen in step beside her. "Sorry I can't join you for lunch. I've got to get over to the office. But I'm looking forward to tonight. What time?"

"Seven-thirty okay?"

"Fine." He punched the Down button. "But there's one very important piece of information missing."

The elevator doors opened, and he put a firm hand on the small of her back, merely a courtesy, but heat radiated up and down her spine. She looked into his dancing eyes. "What's that?"

"Where do you live?"

A FEW MINUTES AFTER FIVE, Tony sank into his desk chair to listen to his messages, including a disturbing one from Rodney Steelman, who was obviously getting cold feet again. Something about the insurance and benefits package for his executives. Serving as go-between in a huge merger was like carrying sticks of dynamite across a field of burning coals. No sooner did you avert one disaster than another threatened.

Fortunately the Cyberace offices in Dallas were on Central time. Loosening his tie and unbuttoning his collar with one hand, Tony picked up the receiver and dialed Steelman. He was put straight through. This was one conversation he didn't want Barry Fuller handling. "Steelman, Tony Urbanski. What can I do for you?"

No detail escaped the CEO's steel-trap mind. Tony listened patiently while Steelman recapped his company's current insurance and benefits package and then started in on the inadequacy of DataTech's offer.

When he finally paused, Tony interjected, "So what you're saying is you want your people taken care of handsomely."

"God damn it, of course I do. Urbanski, I have to see some movement from DataTech on this or I'm going to call this whole thing off. Some of the folks on my management team have been with me too long to let DataTech screw 'em at this stage of their careers."

"I understand." Yes, he understood all right. Steelman was going to bleed every last drop of blood from the turnip. "We'll run your conditions past DataTech." Pulling off his tie, Tony hedged his bet. "I can't guarantee they'll go along, but we'll do our best to see if we can't satisfy you and your people."

"Fair enough. I'll be waiting to hear from you."

Tony grabbed the legal pad on which he'd scribbled Steelman's demands, then added a few thoughts on how to approach DataTech. The hell of it was, it was late Friday. He'd try to reach Ed Miller first thing in the morning. He groaned. When would he find time between court sessions to work on the other DataTech people to the point they would make significant concessions? The situation was too delicate to assign Barry or anyone else. Finesse, Urbanski-style, was necessary.

On his desk lay the preliminary merger papers prepared by the DataTech attorneys and reviewed by the Great Lakes Management Group's legal department. Fuller had stuck a memo on top. "This looks doable. Time to break out the champagne." Tony rolled his eyes. Mergers were always precarious, especially one like this, involving millions of dollars. Fuller's confidence struck him as either naive or arrogant, probably the latter. The hell of it was, the kid reminded him so much of himself early in his career it would have been funny if there weren't so much at stake.

A quick glance at his watch brought him to his feet. He still had to go home to shower and change his clothes. There'd be time enough to read the contract tomorrow since he planned to spend most of the day in the office. Besides, he needed to clear his mind of the merger impasse and the damn trial so he could concentrate on the delightful person of Andrea Evans. He shrugged into his topcoat. Oh, yeah. And the more disturbing presence of his buddy Nick.

Yet, later, as he showered, he couldn't shake the image of the afternoon's prosecution witness. Rocco Vincenza's sterling credentials included the fact he was currently serving time for a felony conviction for possession and distribution of drugs. A real sweetheart. Yet he swore on his mother's grave—give me a break, Tony had thought as he'd listened to him—that Darvin Ray had bought the gun from him a few months before the crime. The clincher was the identifying *V* Vincenza had carved into the grip. The defendant held his head in his hands the entire time Rocco was testifying.

Tony turned off the water, stepped out of the shower and began vigorously toweling off. If the damning DNA evidence hadn't done it, the last witness they'd heard today—a policeman—had. He'd testified that the bloody shirt had been retrieved from a locker belonging to the defendant. No doubt in his mind—the Ray kid had shot the old man. Punks. They were all alike.

Punks! Tony grimaced. He knew about punks. Wasn't he one? At least that's what his father had always told him. The words twisted in his gut. "You punk. You're just like the rest of 'em. You'll never amount to a thing."

Tony stepped into his shorts, then ran a brush through his wet hair. *I guess I amounted to enough to help take care of you, Pops.* He grinned sardonically at his reflection. *Who would have thought I'd be having dinner with one of Shaker Heights's finest. Not bad for a punk, huh?*

"OKAY, OKAY, I'LL BE NICE. But I don't see why we hafta have dinner with this guy two nights in a row."

"I thought you liked him," Andrea said.

"Not really."

Nicky's voice had taken on a whining quality that Andrea didn't need at the moment. She carefully spread meringue over the top of a lemon pie. Once she popped it into the oven, she'd have just enough time to straighten up the kitchen before Tony arrived. It was hard to get excited about a man of whom Nicky so obviously disapproved. "Are you finished with the lickings?"

He scraped the side of the pan once more. "I guess." He dropped the spoon noisily into the sink. "Can I go upstairs now?"

Andrea sighed, knowing he would escape into the comfort of a computer game. "All right, but when I call you for dinner, I expect you to come down and be polite."

He slipped off the kitchen stool. "Okay." After he left the room, she heard his footsteps on the stairs, one loud, deliberate clump after the other.

She slipped the pie in the oven, then started washing the mixing bowls and measuring spoons. What was she going to do about Nicky? She could understand his possessiveness of her; after all, except for the Porters, he'd lost everyone else. Even her own parents were dead. But it wasn't healthy to live her life solely for him. And now, just when she'd thought he was finally starting to adjust, he behaved this way.

She wished tonight weren't so important to her. It didn't make any sense. But she couldn't remember the last time a man had made her heart rate double with a mere glance.

She'd just finished rinsing out the sink and putting lotion on her hands when she heard the doorbell. She checked the kitchen clock. You could say one thing for Mr. Urbanski—he was punctual.

To her relief, Nicky managed to answer questions civilly and even comment on the bouquet of flowers Tony had brought, which now graced the center of the dining room table. Yet there was no missing the warning looks Nicky shot her between bites. It was as if the social drama was being conducted on several levels—the pointed nonverbal exchange between Nicky and her, the unmistakable signals coming her way from Tony, and the bland, polite dinner conversation, necessitating, of course, care in choice of topics, since she was determined not to discuss anything remotely connected to the trial. All in all, a Martha Stewart-type challenge.

"Do you always eat like this?" Tony held up a forkful of veal piccata and looked at Nicky. "This is sensational."

Nicky fidgeted with his napkin. "I s'pose."

"Well, then, you're one lucky kid. My old man's specialty was pork and beans out of a can."

"What about your mom?"

"She died when I was a little boy."

Nicky's face flushed. "Oh."

Andrea, trying to bridge the uncomfortable moment for him, filled the awkward pause. "Nicky, it's okay to confess that we eat our share of hot dogs and TV dinners."

"Hot dogs?" Tony grinned. "I'll bet they're gourmet if Andrea fixes them."

"I guess. She sometimes melts cheese on 'em and puts lotsa pickle stuff over the top."

"Maybe I'll have the chance to sample them sometime."

Nicky appeared dubious. "Maybe."

Andrea could tell Nicky was trying hard to forestall any genuine conversation with Tony, but Tony didn't seem to notice. He tried another tack. "Do you have any computer or video games around here?"

"Why? You play?"

"Only when I have a worthy opponent. Are you any good?"

"Good enough."

"Great. After dinner, you're on. But I warn you. I'm very, very skilled."

Nicky shrugged. "We'll see."

passive-aggressive behavior alerted Tony. He needed
d a way to engage Nick in the action before the kid
to believe he was not only inept, but worthless. As
ell knew, no boy should feel that way.

ny retrieved the ball and kicked it toward Nick again
again. Dimly, he heard Andrea say, ''Tony, let's

er his shoulder, he flung his answer. ''No. We're not
ing. Nick's gonna kick this ball, like it or not.'' An-
stalked forward, eyes blazing. Tony held up a hand,
ing her off. ''Trust me, I know what I'm doing,'' he
under his breath before aiming the ball once more at

is time, the boy clenched his fists and, with a brief
lerous look, kicked the ball high in the air halfway
s the yard. ''*There!* Are you satisfied?''

Iey, kid, not bad. Let's try it again.'' Before Nick
I regroup, Tony sailed the ball right back at him. This
, Nick stopped the ball and viciously returned it.
at. Again!''

ny kept up the barrage, not permitting a break. At
half the time, Nick connected with the ball with all
orce of his small body. His face was red and his dark
hung over his forehead. Tony watched him intently.
kid was venting his rage on the black-and-white ball.
could just give Nick a positive outlet for his frustra-

felt someone tugging the sleeve of his jacket. He'd
st forgotten about Andrea. ''Don't you think he's had
gh?''

r eyes held a warning. He had to admit there was a
ine between challenging Nick and pushing him too
st then the ball hit him in the back of the head. When
irled around, ready to explode, he saw a broad grin
k's face. ''Hey, kid, nice shot!'' He scooped up the

Releasing a mental sigh of relief, Andrea stood to clear
the main course. ''Let me help,'' Tony suggested.

''No, you stay here and talk with Nicky.''

In the kitchen she crossed her fingers briefly, hoping that
her absence would create a conversational vacuum Nicky
would be forced to fill.

When she carried the pie into the dining room, she realized her ploy had worked. The two were discussing the
scoring intricacies of some intergalactic game. When she
put his plate in front of him, Tony beamed. ''Don't tell
me it's homemade.''

''Okay, I won't.'' She smiled back at him. His face was
so relaxed that instead of looking hawklike, he looked
downright carefree.

He turned to Nicky. ''The woman is amazing, Nick. Do
you know how lucky you are?''

Nicky picked up his fork and held it tightly in his fist,
then stared at Tony. ''Yeah. I'm lucky all right.''

Andrea's stomach twisted with the irony of his comment. Lucky to have lost his parents? Lucky to be living
with a single aunt? If only it were simply that he was lucky
enough to have someone bake him a homemade pie.

TONY LAUGHED OUT LOUD and held up his hands in sur-
render. ''I gotta hand it to you, fella. You're a master.''

The boy huddled closer to the monitor, his hand caressing the joystick with the instinctive knowledge of a skilled
fighter pilot. Bam! Bam! Two more alien invaders blown
to smithereens. Finally Nick sat back and let his hand fall
into his lap. ''I beat you,'' he said matter-of-factly as he
exited the program.

''Fair and square. Maybe you'll give me a rematch
sometime?'' The kid shrugged indifferently. If winning
Nick over was part of charming Andrea, Tony was in for
a tough sell.

"Whatever."

Through his thick glasses, Nick turned a now-what? look on Tony, who got to his feet, then stretched out his back. "You figure we've stalled long enough to escape dishwashing duty?"

Nick almost grinned, as if realizing he'd been found out. "Prob'ly."

"Then let's go down and see what your aunt's up to."

"Okay." Nick slid from his chair and trailed Tony down the stairs.

In some ways, Tony had hoped the kid would stay in his room, but he was also pleased that Nick seemed minimally more accepting of him now. And why should that matter? Damn. His involvement with Andrea was getting more complicated by the minute.

"Hey, you two, who won?" Andrea sprawled, legs stretched out on the couch, paging through a magazine.

"Not *him!*" Nick said, slumping into an overstuffed armchair. Andrea sent Tony a questioning look.

"I thought I was pretty good," Tony said, sitting on the edge of the raised hearth, hands dangling between his knees. "But Nick's something else!" Tony glanced out of the corner of his eye and noticed the boy straightening up in the chair.

"Now, if I could just get him interested in outdoor games," Andrea said.

"I hate playing sports!" Nick's belligerence exploded into the room.

"No kidding?" Tony regarded him thoughtfully. "Let's see. Wait here. I'll be back." He walked out the front door and returned a few minutes later carrying a scuffed soccer ball.

Nick now sat cross-legged in the big chair, his chin in his hands, his eyes smoldering.

"Last night you said you might like to go to one of my

soccer matches." No answer. "I noticed you on your garage. What do you say we go ou the ball around?"

Nick kept his eyes on the floor. "I won't

"I'm not so great myself," Andrea said, the magazine and jumping to her feet. "But little exercise after that dinner."

"Do I hafta?" He looked pleadingly at he

"Why not? It'll be fun. C'mon."

Nick started reluctantly toward the coat clo I guess I'll try."

Outside the evening was cool but calm. Th illuminated a section of yard and driveway. T the ball from one hand to the other as he waite and Andrea to get in position. Then he dropp and kicked it to Andrea who returned it. Nick s folded across his chest, watching warily. "He Tony called as he kicked the ball toward Nick, an awkward attempt to field it.

"Nicky, honey, it's no big deal. We're just w Kick it back to me," Andrea said encouraging

Reluctantly the kid ambled a few steps, pic ball and threw it in Andrea's general direction. see the disappointment etched in Andrea's fa me." She placed the ball on the ground and ward Tony, who raced forward, captured it feet, executed a dribbling side step, then ki on the ground to Nick. "Kick it!"

"I hate this," Tony heard Nick mutter desultory kick that sent the ball a few feet on the grass.

Tony strolled over, grabbed the ball, th Nick's side. "Here, let me show you." through Tony's brief explanation, before and making a halfhearted effort. Some ball and sauntered toward him. Gently laying a hand on his shoulder, he leaned over and said, "Not bad for your first time. How's about we make a deal? You teach me computer game strategy and I'll help you with sports. What do you say?"

"I'll think about it." Then, for the second time in a matter of minutes, Nick smiled.

Tony tousled his hair. "That's a start." Over the top of Nick's head he watched Andrea's hunched shoulders relax. She was probably mad at him, but somebody needed to toughen the kid up.

Andrea beckoned to them both. "Let's go inside. It's time for your shower and bed, Nicky." She started toward the back door, assuming he and Nick would follow. Tony couldn't help wondering what she'd have to say to him after Nick went to sleep.

ANDREA WAS STILL STEAMING as she tucked Nicky under the covers, kissed him, then dimmed the lights. What had gotten into Tony? He knew Nicky wasn't good at sports. What had he been trying to accomplish? Whatever it was, he'd been way out of line. Nicky was *her* responsibility, not his.

She walked downstairs slowly, considering what she could say to Tony to ensure he would not interfere with her nephew again. Tony sat on the sofa, feet casually resting on the coffee table, watching her as she entered the living room. Deliberately skirting him, she settled in the small upholstered rocker and tried to collect herself.

Tony gazed around. "Attractive place you have here."

She took in the furnishings as if she'd never seen them before. "We like it."

"You've got nice stuff." He gestured toward the mantel and adjacent shelves, which sported Rich's collection of model ships. "Are you into boats?"

"Not really. Those belonged to my brother-in-law." She gripped the arms of the rocker, hoping to avoid an explanation of her family history. She didn't want him getting that close to her, not after what had happened in the backyard. She changed the subject. "Tell me about your job."

He gave her a brief overview of his duties and mentioned the big merger he was currently working on. When he finished, he abruptly put his feet down and eyed her speculatively. "You're angry with me, aren't you?"

"Is this part of your negotiating strategy? Taking the offensive?"

He smiled lazily. "I've been known to go for the frontal attack, yes." The smile faded. "I imagine you think I was too hard on Nick."

She folded her hands tightly in her lap. "Yes, I do."

"You think I overstepped my bounds, don't you?"

"No 'think' about it. You did. Nicky isn't used to such rough treatment."

"Did it ever occur to you he might need to get used to it? After all, he's a boy, and much as I hate to resort to stereotyping, boys need to know how to hold their own."

She bit the inside of her cheek. "Is that what you thought you were teaching him—how to hold his own?"

"In part, yes. Did you notice how angry he was?"

The last thing she needed was Tony Urbanski explaining the obvious. "Certainly, I did. And he has every right to be angry."

"With me?"

"With you, me, the world in general."

Tony moved to sit on the raised hearth beside her chair. He turned the rocker so that she faced him. "And why is that?"

Before she could stem them, the words burst forth in a flood of emotion. "Put yourself in his place. An only child with two parents who adored him. When he was seven, they went sailing on Lake Erie and got caught in a freak storm and never came back. As best as we can tell, Tami, my sister, was hit by the boom when a sudden wind caught it. She fell overboard. Rich knew he couldn't stop the boat, so he did the only thing any loving husband would do. He took the life ring and jumped in after her.'' Andrea, faintly aware that Tony was gripping her hands, felt her breath coming in gasps. ''Neither one of them was wearing a life jacket. The Coast Guard found their bodies later that same day.''

''Andrea, I'm so sorry. Tragedy doesn't begin to describe something like that.'' He closed his eyes briefly, then shook his head. ''The poor kid.''

His words brought Andrea back to the immediate situation. She jerked her hands away and forced a steely tone. ''Now do you see why I'm not crazy about the rough treatment you dished out tonight?''

''I understand where you're coming from, and I know you think you're doing what's best for Nick. But let me ask you a question. Did you *see* how angrily he kicked the ball? Maybe, just maybe, sports would give him an outlet for all the grief and rage he has bottled up inside of him.''

Something painful in his voice made her look at him closely. ''But he doesn't like sports.''

''Of course he doesn't. He's not any good at them. That doesn't mean he couldn't be, though. He just needs someone to teach him.''

Her heart thudded. ''Who? You?''

''Why not me? I know all about anger. If I hadn't had sports, I'd probably have ended up in jail for assault and battery.''

''Why? What happened?''

His eyes narrowed and his jaw tensed. He stood up and turned away, leaning against the mantel. After a long hesitation, he faced her. ''I lost my mom when I was five.

She had breast cancer. The night she died, my father wasn't there. He'd gone to the tavern to 'hoist a few,' as he put it. Needed to 'calm his nerves.' I've never forgiven him. He didn't even care enough to stick around. And he certainly never cared enough to be much of a father. So anger? The kind a little kid can have? I know all about it. Believe me, Nick needs a target. Why the hell not a ball?''

Andrea could hear the edge in his voice, see the effort it took him to reveal so personal a confidence. She rose to her feet and laid her hands on his shoulders. "I'm sorry. I didn't know," she said softly. He ran his palms over her hands, then captured them in his own. The way he was looking at her—openly, vulnerably—stirred her deeply. "I guess I never thought about sports as therapy.''

"Isn't it worth a shot?'' He squeezed her fingers.

She hesitated. "I don't want to obligate you. After all, we hardly know each other.''

He released her hands, put his arms around her and pulled her gently toward him. "But we're about to do something about that, aren't we?'' His eyes held hers as deliberately and ever so slowly he lowered his mouth to hers. Then, before she had time to consider the consequences, she surrendered to a need she was powerless to resist.

CHAPTER FIVE

ANDREA SMOOTHED DOWN the frilly organdy apron of her Alice in Wonderland costume and reached across the window display to retrieve a Cinderella pop-up book. "Is this what you wanted?" She smiled at the small girl clutching her grandmother's hand.

"Grammy, lookie. She got it. That's the one!"

The grandmother nodded indulgently. "Good. A book is always a treat, isn't it, Jordan?" The child bobbed her head up and down and pulled her grandmother toward the cash register.

After Andrea had rung up the sale and waved goodbye, she sat down on the counter stool, realizing this was the first time all day she'd been off her feet. But then Saturdays were usually like this—busy. And busy was good. Over by the puzzles and games she spied Phil, decked out in his Mad Hatter costume, explaining the intricacies of a board game to an elderly gentleman. He'd done a great job of running the store the past three days, and Andrea had been impressed with the applicants for part-time work that he'd lined up for the interviews she'd conducted earlier. Even though Phil had things well in hand, Andrea knew if the trial went on much longer, she'd begin to worry. As if in stark reminder, a huge sign across the square blazoned, Only 28 shopping days till Christmas!

Startled out of repose by a voice chanting from the rear of the store "I'm late, I'm late, for a very important date," she twirled around to face her costumer, Daisy Whitcomb, who'd obviously come in through the employees' entrance. Andrea couldn't help smiling. Irrepressible, unconventional Daisy wore green suede boots, purple leggings, an orange tunic top and a jeweled belt anchored over her hipbones. Her freckles paled only in comparison with her short mop of carrot-colored curls.

Andrea slipped off the stool and embraced her friend. "What are you doing here? Isn't this your day off?"

Daisy linked her arm through Andrea's. "It is. And what I'm doing is dragging you away for a steaming latte. Even Alice in Wonderland needs coffee now and then. That tea party must get pretty old. C'mon."

Andrea stopped Daisy in her movement toward the front door. "Daisy, thanks, but I really can't. Phil's being a trouper while I'm on jury duty. I just can't cut out on him today."

"We won't be gone long." Daisy waved her hand frantically at the Mad Hatter. "Okay, if I take Alice for a little break?"

Phil grinned and gave a thumbs-up. Again, Daisy propelled Andrea to the door. "I give up, Daisy. You're the most stubborn woman I know."

But Andrea had to admit as she sat across the table from Daisy sipping latte, it was relaxing to leave the store for a few moments and think about something else. She listened as Daisy prattled on about some sexy jazz musician she was seeing. "…and he has the most fantastic pair of hands," Daisy concluded before sitting back with a cat-that-ate-the-canary grin.

"Alice doesn't know quite what to make of that remark," Andrea said, batting her eyes innocently.

Daisy chuckled smugly. "Make as much as you want to, girlfriend. When I say 'fantastic,' I mean *fantastic!*" She leaned forward. "But enough about me. What about you?"

Andrea began telling her about jury duty, but Daisy interrupted. "I don't care about that. I want to know about the man."

"What man?"

"You may look like a dewy-eyed innocent in that outfit, but don't try to fool me. Our pal Giorgio put a little bug in my ear."

"Oh." Andrea felt her stomach cave in. Was nothing secret around here? Besides, what could she say?

"I'm waiting."

Daisy was too good a friend to ignore. "Okay, you win. Believe it or not, I met Tony on jury duty. We've had dinner a couple of times, that's all."

Daisy studied Andrea's face. "You know those two little spots of rouge Alice always wears on her cheeks? Well, honey, right now, yours are natural. Don't give me the 'that's all' line. I don't believe it. Not for a minute. Now tell me about Tony."

Andrea fought a desire to confide in her friend, to tell her how confused she was by this assertive, laughing, brooding, vulnerable contradiction of a man. She settled on a half truth. "He's very attractive. I enjoy his company and he's interested in Nicky. But I don't see any future in it. He's really involved in his business."

"Well, for God's sake, divert him."

Remembering last night and the kisses they'd shared until she'd become shaky and breathless, Andrea didn't answer right away. Instead she stirred her latte and took another swallow. Finally, she looked straight into her friend's merry eyes. "You know, Daisy, I believe I'll try." Suddenly she giggled. "Somehow, I don't think Tony Urbanski's ever considered being seduced by Alice in Wonderland!"

THE SOUND OF A HACKY SACK ricocheting off the wall echoed loudly through the deserted office area. Tony had grabbed the first available object and hurled it mindlessly when he'd gotten off the phone with Ed Miller, CEO of DataTech. Damn, what had Barry Fuller been thinking? Fortunately for Tony the Hacky Sack that he often toyed with when he was contemplating strategy had been closer than the heavy pewter paperweight. So much for a calm, peaceful, productive Saturday at work.

His day had started with Harrison Wainwright awakening him with a terse message. "Call Miller ASAP. Here are his numbers at home, at the office, and for his cellular.... You got 'em?... He's mad as a hornet. Don't blow this, Skee." How the hell could Barry have screwed up so monumentally? Times like this he wondered if he really wanted to spend the rest of his life mother-henning trainees and maneuvering so-called adults into civilized accord.

It had taken a couple of hours to reach Fuller and discover what the hell was going on. Apparently in his zeal, the kid had assumed the deal was done and had indicated as much in a conversation with Ed Miller yesterday afternoon. Miller had called Wainwright later to exult. When Wainwright had indicated there were further points to be ironed out, the DataTech CEO had gone ballistic. Lord, if only Tony had been able to reach Miller after court yesterday, this whole problem could probably have been downplayed. Didn't Barry know you never tipped your hand or counted your chickens or... Damn, Fuller's actions had reduced him to using mindless clichés. Tony ground his teeth in frustration before taking a deep breath. Barry was young. He was bound to make mistakes.

Although Miller had calmed down some by the time Tony reached him, he still wasn't happy. Tony salvaged what he could from the tense conversation, but demands that might have once eased past DataTech were now deal breakers. It had hardly been the time to go into the particulars of the concessions Cyberace wanted from DataTech. He'd told Miller he'd follow up with him Monday.

Tony shoved his chair back and retrieved the Hacky Sack. He stood in the middle of his office, bouncing the small leather ball off his foot and thinking. When he was satisfied he'd come up with a viable strategy, he kicked the Hacky Sack into his hand and decided he'd had enough of work for one day. He grabbed the phone book, made a couple of calls and then left the office on a mission.

A foolish mission, maybe, he thought as he drove toward the large discount store. How had that kid gotten to him so quickly? He was a skinny little computer nerd with a sullen attitude. Spoiled, too. Yet the absorbed look on his face, the intensity of his coiled body, the uncontrolled fury of his kicks had hit Tony in the gut. This was one angry little guy. It took one to know one, all right. Except for the fact that he had been a natural athlete, he might have been watching himself at the same age.

Nor could he discount the effect Andrea was having on him. A warm rush flooded him as he remembered how perfectly her body—her wonderfully curvy, ripe body—had molded to his, how heartstoppingly responsive she'd been. He'd kissed women and he'd kissed women, but damn it, she was something else again. *Watch yourself. Can you afford to be diverted from your work right now, even though it might be pleasant?*

Caution was prudent. But he had to admit that all day long Andrea's sweet, open face had hovered in the forefront of his awareness.

Smiling to himself, he nearly missed the turn into the shopping center.

"WHAT DID YOU DO TODAY?" Andrea asked Nicky when she picked him up from his Saturday with his grandparents.

"The usual stuff." Nicky sat in the front seat fiddling with the GameBoy he held in his hands.

"Like?" Andrea concentrated on her driving, wondering why it was often so difficult to get anything out of him.

"This morning Grandpa and I played checkers. Big whup. Then we ate lunch."

"What did you have?"

"This gross stuff with spinach. Mimi said it was kish."

"Quiche?"

"Whatever."

"How about dessert?" She knew Nicky had a sweet tooth and Claudia often redeemed herself there.

"It was this mooshed-together glop. With whipped cream and these little cookies called ladyfingers." He made "ladyfingers" sound like a noxious vegetable.

"Trifle, I'll bet."

"Yeah. Mimi said it was a special treat."

Head down, he concentrated on his game, clearly signaling disinterest in further conversation.

It was like pulling teeth to get information out of him. "What about this afternoon?"

"Grandpa took me to the science museum. That was kinda cool. But I've been there lotsa times."

Rounding the corner of their street, Andrea reflected that it couldn't be much fun for Nicky to go to his grandparents' every Saturday. They meant well, but they didn't seem to know what to do with him. Maybe if they'd invite one of Nicky's friends occasionally... What friends? Even she was at a loss to name one.

"Who's that at our house?" Nicky was looking out the window.

Andrea spotted a black Jeep Cherokee in their driveway. Her accelerated heartbeat betrayed her attempt at calm. "I think it's Tony."

"I didn't know he was gonna be here."

From his neutral tone, she couldn't interpret his reaction. "Neither did I."

Pulling in behind his vehicle, Andrea realized what Tony was doing. He'd hauled the rickety old ladder out of her detached garage and was balanced precariously at the top, struggling to secure a basketball backboard.

As she and Nicky got out of their car, Tony shouted over his shoulder. "Nick, can you give me a hand here? I need those screws on the hood of my car."

Nicky ran forward, picked up the screws, then stood watching Tony position the backboard. "What's *that* for?"

"Well, sport, I thought you and I might play some hoops."

"Hoops?" Nicky hadn't moved.

"Yeah, your new basketball's in the front seat. Go on. Get it."

Andrea approached slowly, unable to curb her wondering smile. "Tony?"

He backed down the ladder, then stood, hands on his hips, surveying his work. "Cool, huh?"

She walked closer. "It's great, but—"

"I know. I shouldn't have done it." He grinned mischievously, then winked at her. "If you're a good girl, Nick and I may let you play, too."

For reasons she didn't want to think about, Andrea's heart was light.

Nicky returned, holding the ball as if it were made of Waterford crystal. "I'm not—" he scuffed the toe of his shoe on the driveway "—I'm not very good."

"Here, toss me the ball." Tony held out his hands and caught Nick's inept pass. "The great thing about not being very good is you can always get better."

Andrea watched Tony patiently begin instructing her nephew about dribbling.

Before she went into the house, she came to a decision. "Tony, would you like to stay for dinner?"

He gave her a look over Nicky's head. A look that echoed the words he spoke. "I thought you'd never ask."

Three nights in a row. What in the world was she thinking?

"A FELLA COULD GET USED TO your cooking," Tony said patting his stomach and smiling at Andrea. "That was great chili."

"Didja like the corn bread, too?" Nicky seemed very interested in the answer.

"Best I ever had."

"You guys. You'll turn my head."

After seeing how much his remark pleased her, Tony felt expansive.

"If you're both finished," she continued, "why don't you play one of your computer games while I clean up. Then we'll have our ice cream."

Nicky scraped back his chair. "C'mon, Tony."

Tony wiped his mouth with his napkin and followed the boy toward the stairs. "I'm ready for you, Nick. Tonight's my night to win."

"Yeah, sure!" Nick challenged, as he took the steps two at a time.

Following him, Tony admitted to himself he'd much rather have stayed in the kitchen helping Andrea with the dishes, watching her hair curl around her face and thinking prurient thoughts. But Nick's sneering tone had whetted his appetite for competition. "Yup, tonight's the night," he repeated, rubbing his hands together as he sat down at Nick's desk.

Later, while Andrea tucked Nick in, Tony sat on the flowered living room sofa idly watching the flames in the gas fireplace flicker and flare. Homey. He guessed that's

"True confession. You want to know the worst thing I
[e]ver did?"

"Your secret will be safe with me."

She straightened up, as if relishing the telling. "When
[I] was sixteen, Mom and Dad went to an out-of-town
[chu]rch conference. I invited five of my friends over to the
[ho]use for the express purpose of seeing how much beer
[I] had to drink to qualify as drunk."

"What happened?"

"A neighbor stopped by to return some books to Dad.
[H]e caught us red-handed." He loved watching her. Right
[no]w, she was as pleased with herself as if she were an
[Ol]ympic torchbearer. "The good news is that not only was
[he] not a member of the church, but he took care of us and
[ne]ver said a word to my parents."

Tony laughed. "Now there's a true saint."

"But now," she faltered, "Nicky's my only family."

"How's that?"

She swallowed. "Mom died several years ago. Dad,
[sh]ortly before Tami and Rich drowned. Facing that loss
[wo]uld have been horrible for my parents. But I miss
[the]m...all."

Her wistfulness was tearing him apart. "It must be hard
[for] you living here with all these reminders." He nodded
[tow]ard the sailing ships.

"Oh, Tony, that's just the start. This house belonged to
[Tam]i and Rich. Most of the furniture, the paintings, well,
[just] about everything was theirs. When they died, as
[Nick]y's guardian, I inherited the house, and Nicky and I
[were] the beneficiaries of their will."

"You've been through a tough time, involving lots of
[adjus]tments, I'll bet." Not many women could experience
[what] she had and come out on the other side as positive
[and o]ptimistic as Andrea was. Not many women? Hell,
[f]ew people!

how a decorator would describe the room with its antique
walnut tables, overstuffed chairs, milk-glass lamps. Even
a brass bed warmer leaning against the hearth. Not exactly
his style, but nice. Very Andrea-ish.

"I guess I owe you an apology," Andrea said as she
came into the room after settling Nick.

Tony turned and patted the place next to him. "How's
that?"

Almost too carefully, she sat down, leaving a space between them. She drew up one leg and faced him. "I think
you're quite possibly right about athletics. Maybe I
should've been doing something all along. His grandfather
talks about sports with him, and I suppose I thought that
was enough."

"Talking and playing are two vastly different things."

"Apparently. But what I want to say is thank you. Nicky
really seems to like you."

"I like him, too." And he realized it was the truth. The
kid was fun and tougher than he looked. He'd hung in
there with him out on the driveway, practicing dribbling
over and over. "I just wish he weren't so darn good with
computers."

She arched her eyebrows. "He beat you again?"

"Sure did. And, believe me, I was trying to win. None
of this pretending so that the kid can gain confidence. Not
me."

"He told me you asked him to go to your soccer game
tomorrow."

"If it's okay with you. I could pick him up around
three." Had he invited Nick to the game because he
wanted to spend time with the boy or because he couldn't
wait until Monday to see Andrea again?

"If you're sure it won't cramp your style..." Her voice
faded away.

"I'll tell you what's cramping my style." He put an

arm around her shoulders and drew her closer. "There, that's better." She nestled her head against his arm and he could smell a wonderful fragrance like...like those purple bushes that bloom in late spring. Lilacs. Yeah, that was it. He could remember helping his mother plant a lilac bush outside their double-wide not too long before she died. It was huge now and always reminded him of her and of her gentleness and sweetness.

"Do you think we should talk about what happened last night?" she finally asked.

"Why spoil something so special with words?"

She looked up at him, a darker blue rimming the edges of her pupils. "I'm not usually so...so—"

"Cuddly?"

"Responsive. At least not when I hardly know a man." She ducked her head and settled back against him.

A sensation, like shock, ran through him. He reached down and turned her face toward his. "I don't know, I have the sense you know me fairly well." He grinned abashedly. "Maybe too well."

She opened her mouth to speak, then hesitated, and all he could do was watch the unintentionally erotic way she moistened her upper lip with the tip of her tongue. "It doesn't seem possible we only met Wednesday." Then she smiled up at him and he could no longer control himself. He pulled her close and kissed her in a way that would leave no doubt as to how she affected him. She moved in his arms, and he seized the moment to let his hand stray down her side until he cradled one hip, urging her even closer. Lord, she felt good!

Finally, she drew away. "Tony?" He could tell from her flushed face and the quaver in her voice that she, too, was aroused. "Do you think we could just...talk?"

"Too soon, eh?" She nodded. Well, he could be a gentleman. If only he could convey that message to his body.

"All right. Let's talk. But would you plea[se] here?"

"Yes. I like snuggling with you."

He settled her more comfortably against hi[m] fingers play through her silky soft hair. Sn[uggling] good. "Now then. I'm ready. What do you [want to talk] about?"

"Tell me where you grew up. What you l[iked.] That kind of stuff."

Great. The illustrious family history. Well, sh[e hadn't] heard the worst of it. He launched into the laun[dered ver]sion—his childhood in Detroit, his love of sport[s, the] group of high school buddies he'd run with, hi[s determi]nation to excel. He finished with his university [years.] "Okay. Fair is fair. You?"

"I had an almost idyllic childhood, right here i[n Arbor] Heights. My father was a minister, much belove[d by his] congregation. Sometimes, when I was little, I us[ed to re]sent that he couldn't spend more time with me, [especially] on Sunday. But he always made very sure I k[new I was] loved." She absently rubbed his thigh. He su[pposed she] had no idea how that slight movement excited [him.]

"My mother was a perfect minister's wife[—home]maker, confidante, organizer deluxe."

"Did you ever feel you had to behave just [better] than other kids?"

"Oh, absolutely." She affected a maternal [tone. "']Andrea, remember, everything you do reflec[ts on your fa]ther.'" She chuckled. "That didn't mean [I al]ways obeyed, of course."

"The proverbial preacher's kids?"

"We weren't *that* bad. Tami was actu[ally a good] girl. You know the type. Miss High Scho[ol . . .]

"So you were the renegade?" Someh[ow, picturing] her in that angel costume, he couldn't q[uite . . .]

"Sure, I've had to make some changes. Give up my apartment, adjust to living with a child. But I don't mind. I'd do anything for Nicky. I love him so much, but I know that will never be enough for him."

"It's a lot more than many kids have." *I ought to know.*

"But still..." she bit her lip before continuing "...it's not the same."

"We can't change the past," he said, realizing belatedly he sounded more bitter than he'd intended.

"No," she said simply. Then, brightening, she looked at him and said, "Maybe Never-Never Land is the silver lining."

"You love your work, don't you?"

"I really do. It's exciting to be around kids all the time and to have employees who get a kick out of giving in to their imaginations."

"I wonder what that would be like...."

She eyed him thoughtfully. "I assumed you liked your job."

He considered her remark. "I do. Don't get me wrong. I guess I'm good at it, too. But I don't think I'm as enthusiastic as you sounded a moment ago."

"That's because I'm a gushing female."

There was more to it than that. Buried in this conversation was something important he needed to think about. "Shame on you, Ms. Evans. That was a sexist remark, if I ever heard one."

She giggled, then laid her head against his chest, her palm resting over his heart. "You know, you're right."

He sat quietly, caressing her shoulder. Instinctively he sensed calm was what she needed tonight. He closed his eyes and relaxed his muscles, aware only of their quiet breathing. Several minutes passed. Slowly he raised his arm and checked his watch. Nearly eleven. She stirred and sat up. "I know it's not that late, but, lady, you nearly went to sleep there."

"I know," she murmured, running her fingers through her hair.

"So, I think I'll be on my way." He stood up and stretched to unkink his back.

She walked to the coat closet, retrieved his jacket and held it out to him. "It's been lovely, Tony. Thank you for the basketball hoop."

He shrugged into the jacket. "I'm the one who should be thanking *you*. After all, you've fed me two nights in a row. Maybe one evening next week, we could hire a sitter and you and I could have a *real* date."

She stopped his breath with her smile. "I'd like that."

"Good." He pulled her into his arms. "Do you realize we've accomplished two things this evening?"

"We have?" Her skin was luminous in the half light of the hallway.

"Yes. We made up after our first argument and—"

"Argument?"

"Yes, about Nick and sports. And, second, with very little effort, we succeeded in avoiding any discussion of the trial."

"The trial? You know, I haven't given it a single thought."

As he lowered his lips to hers, he whispered, "Neither have I, neither have I." And for the next few seconds, he couldn't have given rational thought to much of anything, most certainly not the trial!

BERT PORTER STIFLED a yawn as he and Claudia exited the small auditorium. Chamber music. Not his idea of the best way to spend a Sunday afternoon, especially when the Steelers were playing on TV.

Claudia, chic as always in a plum-colored wool suit, laid

a birdlike hand on his arm. "Wasn't that wonderful? I especially liked the Vivaldi."

There were times in a marriage when small deceits were called for. "Yes, dear, it was quite well executed, maybe a little heavy on the cellos." He was no music lover, but years of being dragged to symphonies and intimate concerts like this one had given him the ability to dissemble.

"Oh, did you think so?" Claudia sounded dismayed. "Maybe it was the acoustics. I thought the program was nearly flawless." And she was off and running, maintaining a constant critique of each and every number, which left his mind free to roam as they walked toward their Lincoln Town Car.

The chill in the air was invigorating after the stuffy concert hall. The way the setting sun shone through the nearly leafless trees, streaking the lawn with fingers of shadow, reminded him of so many days when he and Rich had returned home late in the afternoon after attending a football game at the old Browns' stadium, now razed to make way for the new one. Why was it that simple things like one sunset could trigger such vivid memories, memories excruciating in the recalling but which were, nevertheless, comforting? The void in his life, even after nearly two years, was still painful, made all the more acute by moments like these.

If it weren't for Nicholas and, on some level, Claudia, he couldn't have made it through these recent empty months. But Nicholas, precious boy, was his hope, his future. Claudia had mourned Rich, but then had seemed to resume her life almost as if nothing had happened. Oh, she had her occasional moments of grief, but they were growing more and more infrequent. He couldn't understand how she could skim over the surface of the days so unheedingly while he continued to be haunted by his memories. She had grown increasingly impatient with his nightmares. He stifled a sigh. What had become of their closeness?

Claudia was still dissecting the concert as they drove into Shaker Heights, although she periodically interrupted her soliloquy to remind him to slow down or watch for a car at an upcoming intersection. The best way to preserve peace was simply to tune her out.

"Bert, let's go to the club for dinner. That would be a pleasant way to end our day. Here, I'll call and make a reservation." Without waiting for his answer, she dialed the mobile phone, then hung up in mid-call. "Wait. I've got a better idea. Why don't we pop by Richard's house and see if Andrea and Nicholas will join us?"

For the first time during the long afternoon, Bert brightened. "Good thinking." He made a right at the next intersection and followed the gracefully winding road through the neighborhood of stately, well-kept homes.

"Nicholas didn't seem to enjoy the quiche we had for lunch yesterday." Disappointment and irritation were obvious in her voice.

"Then we'd better let the lad order a big juicy hamburger tonight." He might even do that very thing himself. He'd never admit it to Claudia but he was growing weary of curry, arugula and shitake mushrooms. Yes, a thick hamburger, oozing with juice. Maybe even an order of cottage fries and—

He felt a sharp slap on his right arm. "Bert! Bert! Who in the world is that person in Richard's yard?" Except for decorum, Claudia would have pressed her nose against the side window of the car. As it was, she did a very unladylike thing—she pointed.

He glanced up from the road. In the driveway was a black sports utility vehicle with a swarthy-looking individual leaning against it, tossing a soccer ball from one hand to the other. Bert eased the heavy car to a stop beside the curb. Something was different about Rich's house. It bothered him. What was it?

Claudia didn't even wait for him to come around and open the door for her. She was striding across the lawn, a woman with a mission. Before she could accost the man, the front door opened and Nicholas ran down the porch steps and across the grass before stopping in his tracks. "Mimi? Grandpa? What are you doing here?"

"We've come to see if you and Andrea are free for dinner with us tonight at the club," Bert said.

"I dunno," Nicholas said, looking tentatively at the stranger with the soccer ball.

"Nicholas," Claudia approached him, her mouth pursed, "you'll have to change those awful shoes before we go." She pointed at his feet, shod in huge, gaudy athletic shoes.

Nicholas looked crestfallen and turned in appeal to Bert. "Grandpa, what do you think? These are so cool!"

Bert cleared his throat. "Well, yes, they undoubtedly serve a purpose. But I agree with your grandmother. They're not suitable for the club."

Nicholas, hanging his head, walked over to the man, who had been watching the entire exchange. "Nick, I think I'd better be going. First, though, how about introducing me to your grandparents?"

"Oh, yeah, I forgot."

Nicholas had just completed his fumbling introductions when Andrea joined them. She looked from one adult to the other. "Claudia, Bert. Have you met Tony Urbanski?"

Bert spoke up. "Er, yes. Nicholas did the honors."

Claudia approached Andrea. "Dear, we've come to take you and Nicholas to the club for dinner."

Andrea seemed uncomfortable. On one level, Bert didn't blame her. Claudia had made it very clear Mr. Urbanski was not included in her invitation.

"Claudia, I don't see how we—"

Urbanski turned to Andrea. "I have to go. That way you and Nick can have a nice dinner and I can get some work done." Then nodding to Claudia and him, Urbanski laid a hand on Nicholas's shoulder. "Enjoyed having you along today, Nick."

"Thanks for the rad shoes, Tony."

"No problem."

"Rad" shoes? Who was this fellow? Why was he buying his grandson shoes? Urbanski waved to the group before he climbed into his vehicle and drove away.

No sooner had he cleared the driveway, than Claudia hissed, "Who is that man?"

Andrea's eyes seemed unnaturally bright and a flush suffused her face. "Tony? I met him on jury duty. He's been very nice to Nicky."

"Didn't Nicholas say his name was Urbanski? Just who are his people?"

"His father lives in Detroit."

Nicholas looked at his grandmother. "He took me to his soccer game today. I got to go to this cool restaurant place afterward with the team."

Claudia all but cringed. "You don't mean a tavern, do you? Were those men drinking?"

Nicholas hung his head as if belatedly realizing he'd revealed too much. "Only beer."

Claudia made a clicking noise with her tongue, then sidled closer to Andrea. "Is this something serious, Andrea?"

"Oh, for pity's sake, I just met the man last week. As I said before, I'm grateful to him. He's showing Nicky how to play soccer and basketball."

Bert didn't always read people's expressions accurately, but from the way Andrea had straightened up and was holding her head high, he guessed that this Urbanski chap was interested in her, as well. And that maybe that feeling was mutual. Judging from the disapproval stamped all over Claudia's face, he was overdue to intervene. "Well, how about dinner, ladies?"

"Thank you, Bert. But not tonight." Andrea drew Nicholas into the shelter of her arms. "Nicky's had a big day, and I already have a roast in the oven. Thanks, anyway."

On cue, the boy mumbled, "Yeah, thanks."

"Some other time then," Bert said as he took Claudia by the arm and propelled her to the car.

"Bye, Mimi, Grandpa."

"Goodbye, Nicholas. Andrea," Claudia replied frostily. She climbed in the passenger seat, where she sat staring straight ahead. Bert took his time rounding the car, puzzled. Then it came to him. He knew what was different. A basketball hoop that hadn't been there before. Urbanski?

No sooner had he reached the first intersection, than Claudia started. "What in the world is Andrea thinking exposing Nicholas to such a person? Why, the very impertinence of the man calling our grandson 'Nick.' It's so…so common."

Bert fumbled in his coat pocket for his antacid tablets. There went his hamburger. No way his stomach would tolerate all that grease tonight. Claudia's condescension bothered him.

But, then again, so did the longing on Andrea's face when she looked at that Urbanski fellow.

CHAPTER SIX

TONY SQUIRMED in his chair Monday as the testimony droned on. He checked his watch. Nearly one. Would the judge ever declare a lunch recess? He had to get to the office to call Ed Miller, who was probably wondering why the hell he hadn't heard anything further from Tony. When he'd called the office before today's court session, he had made it abundantly clear that Barry wasn't to do anything else. He would handle the situation—but not from this damn jury box!

The prosecutor's next words pulled him back to the scene before him. ''Your honor, the state rests.'' Tony was on his feet almost before the judge finished announcing the recess. He grabbed his coat from the jury room and sprinted toward the elevator. At least Judge Blumberg had allotted an hour and a half—plenty of time provided he could reach Miller. If he couldn't...? He didn't even want to think about it.

Pigeons fluttering in Public Square scattered as he cut across the open space, then dashed down the block to his office where he took the stairs two at a time.

The receptionist glanced up as he cleared the door. ''Mr. Urbanski? A Mr. Miller has been trying to reach you all morning.''

Great. ''Thanks, Karen, I'll take care of it.''

She fluffed her perm. ''How's the jury thing going?''

He turned and strode down the hall, calling over his

shoulder. "Don't ask." Hell, the defense hadn't even started its case.

He hung up his coat, then flopped in his chair and, while he caught his breath, reviewed the notes he'd made Saturday. His approach just might work—satisfying Steelman, yet permitting Miller to save face, an element vital to any successful compromise. He spread out the papers on the desk, took a deep breath, then dialed. Luckily, Ed Miller was available.

"Urbanski, I'm glad you called." The "at last" reverberated in his undertone. "I hope you have some solutions to the problems we discussed. I'm still rather distressed since, as you know, your man Fuller led me to believe we had this deal all sewed up." Tony cringed. *Your man Fuller.*

"I'm sorry he gave you that impression, Ed. His work on the project was basically finished, but I regret the implication that there would be no fine-tuning." Then Tony adopted his best man-of-the-world delivery. "You know how these things are. Nothing's settled until the ink is dry."

"At this rate it may never be dry." Miller's impatience was evident. "We're not interested in a one-way proposition with Cyberace calling all the shots. I want to know what the bottom line is and whether we can still play ball."

"I can appreciate how you'd be upset, Ed. Now let me make sure I understand your concerns, then suggest alternatives."

Tony pushed back the chair and got to his feet. He thought better when he could move. He paced between the desk and the window, gesturing with his free hand, using every ploy at his disposal to sway the dangerously skittish CEO. Tony's stomach roiled, but he couldn't permit himself the luxury of anger.

Finally, his tone softening, he introduced what he hoped

would be a persuasive analogy. "You've got daughters, haven't you, Ed? Any of them married yet?" From his research, Tony knew damn well Miller had three married daughters. "Well, you know how it is, then. Consider this a little case of prenuptial jitters on Steelman's part. He needs reassurance. You can't blame him. You care about your employees, he cares about his. In his position, wouldn't you do the same for your people?" This was the crucial part—bringing the principals closer together by giving them a common bond. "Why don't you think about my suggestions for changes in the benefits package? Consider the overriding advantages?"

And now for the final point. "So you've got a jittery bride. Is that any reason to scrap the wedding? Or the potential for a long, happy, mutually satisfying marriage?"

When Miller hesitantly agreed to reconsider, Tony slumped into his chair and concluded the conversation. After hanging up, he briefly rested his head on the desk. For the moment, he'd dodged the bullet. Now he had to be patient, wait for the ideas to percolate and keep Rodney Steelman calm. He grabbed the phone again. Twenty minutes to reach Steelman, stall him and get back to the courthouse.

After ten minutes of placating Steelman, Tony dashed past the receptionist on his way out. "Tony, wait up." Stopping and glancing over his shoulder, he saw Kelli hurrying toward him. "You on your way to the courthouse?"

He smiled wryly. "Where else?"

"I'm headed that way, too." She linked an arm through his. "Care to be a good Boy Scout and assist a helpless woman great with child cross the streets?"

"Helpless?" He laughed. "That's the last word I'd use to describe you, pregnant or not." He steered her into the elevator. "But if you don't mind long strides, I'll be happy to escort you."

"I take it you're in a hurry?"

"Neither the bailiff nor the judge reacts kindly to truants." He frowned. "I feel like I'm back in high school, afraid I'll end up in detention."

"This trial's made it hard for you to get your work done, hasn't it?"

When they reached the first floor, he stepped into the doorway of the elevator to allow her to exit first. "That's an understatement." As they hurried through the lobby and out onto the sidewalk, he felt her studying him.

"Where's the old Urbanski confidence?"

"It's wondering why the hell I think all of this wheeling and dealing is so important. I mean, it's not like I'm finding the cure for cancer or orchestrating a Mid-East peace agreement."

She squeezed his arm. "Did anybody ever tell you you take yourself too seriously?"

"No, but why do I think you're about to?"

"Because I am. You're a bright, talented man and if anybody can work under pressure, it's you. What's the worst thing that can happen? The deal falls through?" She eyed him, allowing no room for evasion.

"It falls through, and Wainwright thinks I'm chopped liver."

She scoffed. "I doubt that very much. You're his fair-haired boy, and he's been around. He knows deals don't always come together. No, I think there's a lot more than Wainwright's good opinion at stake."

They paused at the pedestrian crossing and he waited, fearing where this conversation would lead them. "I think it's your stubborn Urbanski pride."

"Gee, Kell, don't hold back or anything."

She poked him with her elbow. "Well?"

"Okay. Have it your way. I don't like failure." The light changed and he propelled her across the street.

"Now you've said it. And while we're at it, my ambitious friend, did it ever occur to you that you have all your eggs in one basket?"

Women! What was she getting at? "What the hell are you talking about?"

"A life, for heaven's sake. Something besides Great Lakes Management and work, work, work!" Her coattail flapping, her short hair ruffled by the wind, she waved her free arm in frustration. "Something novel, like maybe a woman? Marriage? A family?"

"Impending motherhood has turned you into a crusader. Why am I the target?" Thank God, they were nearly to the courthouse.

She stopped and shoved him emphatically in the chest. "Because you're too decent a guy to think success in business is all there is." She grinned, then took his hand and started walking again. "Besides, some lucky lady just might make something of you yet."

He avoided looking at her, not wanting her to see the effort it was taking not to grin. He kind of liked the idea of somebody, Andrea, making something of him.

"So tell me. Who is she?"

Who is she? What had he missed here? "What're you talking about?"

"The woman."

"What woman?"

"Don't play dumb with me. I'm your best bud, remember? I couldn't reach you at home either Thursday, Friday or Saturday night, and you sure as heck weren't at the office. Then, of course, there's that lovesick expression on your face. This is all new behavior since the trial began, so it has to be somebody you met at the courthouse."

"Good God, are you psychic?"

She punched him on the shoulder. "I knew it!" she exulted. They'd reached the courthouse lobby, and she was studying him, as if he were an interesting piece of sculpture. "Love looks good on you, buddy. Enjoy it!" She waved her fingers airily and darted toward a crowded elevator, stepping inside just as the doors closed, leaving him standing there wondering what in hell all that had been about. Love? Kelli was out of her mind!

He made it to the jury room just as the bailiff summoned the jurors. Andrea gave him a quizzical glance before falling in line. He supposed he needed to think about where their relationship was going. If he ever had time! The trial wasn't enough of a distraction from business, no. Now in less than a week, Andrea had become important to him. The kid, too. How had that happened? Where was his renowned self-control?

While he stewed, he stared at the back of Andrea's head, then at her profile, imagining the honeycomb depths of her mouth and the soft, welcoming curves of her body pressed tightly against his. He was in deep. Too deep?

ANDREA OBSERVED THE TEEN at the defense table. His eyes darted nervously back and forth from the judge to the attorneys huddled beside the bench. Almost unconsciously he rolled a pencil back and forth on the table surface with the palm of his hand. What would it be like to be seventeen years old and facing a lifetime in prison? He had to be terrified.

But if he committed the crime…? The state had made a persuasive case, yet there were some areas that bothered her. The eyewitnesses for example. They'd seemed almost too eager to testify. In the interests of fairness to the victim, she let her eyes fall on the ravaged face of Mrs. Bartelli and imagined her waiting, unaware, for her husband to return home from work as he had every other night. Who had knocked on her door instead? Who had delivered the wrenching news? The poor woman. In what unimaginable ways had her life changed, just as Andrea's had when she had heard about Tami and Rich?

She pulled herself up short. It wasn't time yet to weigh the evidence, not when they hadn't heard from the defense. And she certainly wouldn't permit emotion to rule logic in something this important.

As the sidebar continued, Andrea felt prickles at the base of her neck. Slowly she turned around and caught Tony watching her. He looked speculative, then seeming to catch himself, he smiled and nodded. Quickly she swiveled her head back to the front. Even though the two of them scrupulously avoided discussing the case, it wouldn't do for others to draw the conclusion they might be. Besides, the judge had been forceful in her caution to the jurors about inappropriate communication. Maybe it hadn't been such a good idea to agree to see Tony socially, at least not until after the trial.

And yet…she'd enjoyed the past few days more than any in a long while. She hardly dared admit to herself how good it felt to have a man around the house, helping with Nicky, making her laugh, listening to her and—she felt a quickening of her pulse—caressing and kissing her in ways that made the proverbial sparks seem an understatement.

"Call your first witness, please, Ms. Lamb." At the sound of the judge's voice, Andrea focused on the courtroom. For just an instant, the defendant stopped rolling his pencil and, instead, gripped it tightly. As the attorney gathered her files and walked to the podium, the boy's eyes followed her, a mute appeal on his face.

"Your Honor, the defense calls Margaret Grant." A motherly-looking woman of about fifty, dressed in a plain blue suit and a white blouse took the stand. After she was sworn in, she stated she was a social worker employed by a community teen center.

"How long have you known the defendant?"

"Five years."

"In what capacity?"

"Darvin's mother brought him to our facility when he was in seventh grade. She had a full-time job and was terrified that if he wasn't involved in an after-school program, he'd be approached by gangs. He started coming, reluctantly at first, but soon became involved in our computer classes—" she smiled at the young man "—to the point that for the past two years he has taught the course."

"During your tenure at the center, has the defendant ever been involved in any trouble?"

"Only once."

"Tell us about that." Ms. Lamb leaned her elbows on the podium, as if encouraging the woman.

"About a year ago, there was a very belligerent young man hanging around. He did his best to undermine our work at the center. Things like questioning the manhood of our participants, even painting personally-directed graffiti in the rest rooms. When Darvin, er, the defendant, was accosted by this individual, he drew a knife."

Andrea watched keenly as the woman glanced at the jury as if assessing how much damage her statement had inflicted.

Ms. Lamb continued, "What happened then?"

"One of our staff intervened and separated the young men."

"Do you think the defendant intended bodily harm?"

"Objection. Calls for a conclusion."

The judge made a note. "Sustained," she said without looking up.

"What did the defendant say to you concerning his motives?"

"That he had intended to march the assailant to the office and seek adult help."

"Did you believe him?"

Mrs. Grant folded her hands over her stomach, nervously twiddling her thumbs. "I had no reason not to. In my dealings with him, he was always truthful."

"And did you have reason to believe Darvin was ever involved in a gang?"

"No."

"To your knowledge, has Darvin ever had prior trouble with the law?"

"Not to my knowledge."

Andrea noticed that the defense attorney had begun calling the defendant by his name. To humanize him perhaps? Make him seem more vulnerable?

"Two significant events related to this charge occurred before Mr. Bartelli's murder. Tell the court about them."

The witness shifted uncomfortably in her seat. "First of all, Darvin's mother was killed in a drive-by shooting." Next to her, Andrea heard Dottie Dettweiler gasp. "Then—"

"Let me stop you right there, Mrs. Grant. From your point of view, how did his mother's death affect Darvin?"

"He was devastated. And, as you might expect, angry. His first instinct, quite naturally, was revenge. But he's a bright boy, and we were able to help him understand that taking the law into his own hands would only ruin his life."

"So, though justifiably outraged, he was not violent?"

"No, he was not."

"What was the second event?"

The woman nodded her head in Darvin's direction. "That young man, the defendant," she added anticipating the judge's instruction, "won a city-wide computer competition and was offered a college scholarship."

"How do you believe these two events are related?"

Mrs. Grant smiled broadly. "Darvin loved his mother,

and she was very proud of him. I don't think he would do anything to jeopardize his future.''

Ms. Lamb tamped down her folders loudly. "Thank you, Mrs. Grant. No further questions.''

Judge Blumberg looked acerbically through her half glasses, eyeing the prosecution side. "Counselor?''

Andrea watched Mrs. Grant's chin jut forward slightly as Mr. Raines, an assistant district attorney, approached the witness box. After preliminary greetings which fooled no one about his intentions, he went right to the point.

"You've told the court the defendant came to your center for five years. How often per week would that be?''

"Well, it varied. He'd come more in the winter than in the summer, and there was some inconsistency. But, on average, I'd say four times.''

"Four times.'' The way the attorney chewed the words, made four sound downright infrequently. "For how long at a time?''

"Usually from three-thirty until about nine o'clock.''

"Can you testify with certainty what the defendant did after he left the center?''

"No.'' Nervously, Mrs. Grant smoothed her skirt.

"Can you say positively that Darvin is not and never has been a member of a gang?''

"I have no reason to think he—'' She turned, in confusion, toward the judge.

"Answer the question as it was put to you, Mrs. Grant.''

The woman closed her eyes briefly, then opened them and gazed at her lap. "No,'' she said softly.

"We can't hear you, ma'am,'' the attorney stated, gesturing toward the court stenographer.

Mrs. Grant raised her head. "No.''

"Are you telling this court that in five years the defendant had an unblemished record except for one incident when he just happened to pull a knife on another human being?'' The attorney's expression suggested he knew a lie when he heard one.

The witness's face reddened, and Andrea felt defensive on her behalf. ''That's exactly what I'm saying.''

''But you testified earlier,'' he made a show of flipping through his legal pad, ''that after his mother's death, he wanted revenge. That he was very angry.''

Mrs. Grant lost *her* cool. ''You'd be angry, too—''

The prosecutor stepped neatly between the witness and the jury, letting the word ''angry'' hang in the silence. ''That'll be all for this witness, Your Honor.''

The judge turned to Mrs. Grant, who was still stewing. ''You may step down. This court will take a short recess.''

So rapidly had the judge concluded the session that the sharp rap of the gavel took Andrea by surprise. ''All rise.'' Judge Blumberg had swished out of the room even before Andrea had gotten her legs under her.

Back in the jury area, Tony approached her. ''Sorry I've been so preoccupied today, but things are nuts at work. In fact,'' he consulted his watch, ''I need to make a phone call right now, but how would Wednesday night suit you for dinner?'' He hesitated. ''Unless you're traveling somewhere for Thanksgiving. Or cooking. Or something,'' he finished lamely.

Andrea felt a smile she was helpless to control spread over her face. She'd wondered if he'd forgotten their ''real'' date. She certainly hadn't. ''I'll try to get a sitter and let you know tomorrow.''

He took hold of her elbow and gave it a squeeze. ''Good luck. See you later.''

She gazed out the window. What she wouldn't give for some fresh air. The vertical lines of the courtroom paneling were hypnotic, and as the day wore on, it was increasingly difficult to concentrate. Especially when she'd lain awake half the night fuming about Claudia.

Andrea tried to be fair, charitable even, and to empathize with the Porters. But nothing gave the woman the right to snub Tony as obviously as she had yesterday. It was as if Claudia was determined to purge Andrea's life of any male who might threaten the Porters' hold over Nicky. And, regardless of how she felt about Tony, she resented Claudia's assumption that he was unworthy. *Who are his people?* Andrea had taken grim satisfaction from imagining a meeting between Claudia and Tony's father.

"Where are you, Andrea?" Shayla laid a hand on her shoulder. "A million miles away?"

Andrea collected her thoughts and faced her friend. "Yes, I guess I was."

"Wouldn't have anything to do with Juror Number Eleven, would it?"

Guilt must have been written all over her face, because Shayla laughed. "Honey, if a man looked at me the way he looks at you, I'd melt into a big pool of molasses. What's going on?"

"I'm not sure. I like him." She gazed into Shayla's warm, twinkling brown eyes. She lowered her voice. "A lot. But—"

"But what? You worried about meeting him like this?" She glanced over her shoulder toward the jury room.

"Not how we met." She hesitated, forcing herself to consider her answer. "More how the judge might view the propriety of our relationship if it's as obvious as you say it is."

Shayla laughed again. "It's obvious, but only to those who're looking. Which is mainly me. Anyway, I imagine you two have lots of things to talk about that don't include this trial. Am I right?" Sheepish, Andrea nodded. "Well, then, enjoy it while you can get it. That's my advice."

The bailiff motioned to them. Court was resuming. *Enjoy it while you can get it?* What did Shayla mean exactly?

Then an image Andrea thought she'd confined to the dark of the night came to the surface and she felt her face flood with embarrassment. Surely Shayla didn't think they were… Oh, mercy!

THAT EVENING TONY balanced a pizza carton carefully as he unlocked the door to his flat. He was starving! The testimony had continued late in the day—first that social worker type obviously trying to paint the kid as deserving of sympathy, then a couple of other character witnesses, including one of the defendant's high school teachers.

Tony threw his coat down on the couch, grabbed a bottle of beer and attacked the pizza. His entire lunch hour had been spent on the DataTech problem. Without the candy bar he'd bought during the recess, he'd have been even hungrier. One week from Wednesday he was due in New York City, supposedly with the merger finalized and ready for signatures. Surely there couldn't be much more than one additional day of testimony, then, at the most, one day of jury deliberations. They should be easily finished by Thanksgiving on Thursday.

Whether Ray was a model citizen or delinquent, there couldn't be much doubt—the evidence pointed to his guilt. The kid had really messed up. Tony couldn't help thinking, though, that he could've ended up just like Darvin. His tenth grade year, he'd been headed for big trouble until several teachers and coaches had cared enough to straighten him out. He was living proof it *was* possible to rise above your circumstances. So why did kids like Darvin insist on squandering their lives?

After eating what he wanted, Tony put the leftover pizza in the refrigerator and stretched out in his chair with the morning paper, which he hadn't yet read. This was the first time he'd had to relax since the trial began. Of course, part of that was his own fault. He hadn't been able to stay away from Andrea Evans, which was new for him. Usually it was the other way around. He'd have a couple of dates with a woman, then before he could move on, she'd hound him. But Andrea was different.

Letting the paper fall to his lap, he gazed absently at the stark white wall opposite, unrelieved except for the vivid Picasso print. As he looked around his apartment, he realized that it seemed barren, cold. It didn't have any of those decorator touches that Andrea's house did. He'd always thought utilitarian, modern was his style. But, he had to admit, it wasn't comfortable, not like her cozy living room.

Disgusted with himself, he brought the sports page back into focus. When he finished the paper, he'd call Andrea and make arrangements for Wednesday night. Something out of the ordinary, something…romantic.

"SURELY NICHOLAS ISN'T wearing those ungainly clod-hoppers to school!" Andrea slumped against the kitchen counter Tuesday morning clutching the phone and wondering why she'd invited Claudia to attend the fourth-grade assembly that afternoon. Was the woman really blind to fashion trends or was this something else?

She struggled to sound reasonable. "Nicky is so proud of them, Claudia. If you watch today, you'll see all of the boys are wearing them."

Claudia made no effort to conceal her disdain. "Nicholas isn't 'all boys.'"

"No, but it's important for him to fit in. If he feels better about himself, then I think that's the most important consideration."

Never graceful in defeat, Claudia went down with one final volley. "Well, after all, you are his guardian. We're only his grandparents."

Andrea hung up and stood quietly, trying to calm herself. Claudia had never been an easy person. Even so, Tami had been genuinely fond of her. As her sister had often said, "She's done something right. Look at Rich." As for Bert, he'd thought the world of Tami. But, Andrea wondered, how long could she go on making excuses for Claudia? Even grief didn't give her the right to be rude or insensitive.

The thump-thump in the driveway broke into her thoughts. She looked out the window. Nicky was shooting baskets. Only about one in three or four attempts came near the rim, but Nicky looked happy. She continued watching until he scored, then grabbed her purse and hurried into the chilly morning.

"C'mon, kiddo. Time for school."

"Just one more, please, Andie?"

Andrea relented. "Just one. Otherwise, we'll be late."

When Nicky climbed in the car beside her, his cheeks were flushed and he looked relaxed. "I made twelve buckets," he said proudly.

Andrea grinned. She knew "buckets" was an expression he'd learned from Tony. "Great. Keep up the good work and, before you know it, you'll get really good."

"I wanna get good enough so Ben'll leave me alone."

Andrea gripped the wheel tightly. "Is he still bothering you?"

"He calls me a wimp. He thinks he's such a hotshot, bein' good at sports and stuff."

"How does that make you feel?"

Nicky hitched his glasses higher on his nose. "Mad."

Even though she knew it wasn't very helpful, she launched into a monologue about how there would always be Bens in the world, about how there were things more important than sports, about the fact another person couldn't make you feel bad without your permission, yadda, yadda. She didn't blame him for sitting there staring at the book bag in his lap. She sounded like yet one more adult who couldn't remember how it felt to endure the scorn of your peers. She finished lamely with, "I was watching you out the window. You were doing great."

She pulled into the curved driveway in front of the school. As Nicky opened his door, he caught her off guard with his next question. "Do I hafta spend Wednesday night with Grandpa and Mimi?"

How could she admit that she couldn't find a sitter and that she didn't want to miss her date with Tony? "It'll be a lot more convenient, honey, since we're going over there anyway for Thanksgiving dinner."

"But why can't I go with you and Tony?"

Before she could answer, the driver in the car behind her honked. "I have to move, Nicky. Run on in. Enjoy your program. Sorry I can't be there to watch."

Without a backward glance, he melted into the crowd of children moving toward the entrance, few of whom walked alone as he did. Slowly she eased up in the car-pool line waiting to exit onto the city street. What could she have said about Wednesday night? How could she help him fit in with the other children? The answers eluded her. The best thing that had happened to him in a long time was Tony.

And, though she didn't dare hope, he was also the best thing that had happened to her.

CHET SWENSON slammed his fist on the jury table Tuesday morning. "How much longer is this gonna take?" The force of his voice interrupted several peripheral conversations. He reminded Andrea of a cartoon character with smoke coming out of his ears.

"Nip it, Swenson." Arnelle Kerry, in the process of applying hot pink fingernail polish, was clearly in no mood for Chet's complaints. "You're not the only one who's getting sick of this."

The elderly graying man whose name, Andrea had learned, was Willard Feldman, held up his hands. "People, it won't do us any good to get impatient. The whole thing is out of our control." He ignored those who shot him menacing looks.

Shayla, who had been sitting at the far end of the table reading the *Plain Dealer,* looked up. "If it will make anyone happier, I'll ask the bailiff how much longer he thinks the trial will take."

"Go for it," Arnelle said, screwing the lid on the polish bottle.

Just then, Tony dashed into the room, nearly knocking into Shayla. "Sorry." He glanced around like a truant showing up late for class. "Have they called us yet?"

"No, we're havin' a jolly old time sittin' on our butts," Chet responded sarcastically.

Tony threw down a newspaper. "Slow start, I guess."

"Damn attorneys. They're so fulla hot air, it ain't even funny."

Andrea watched as Tony adroitly shifted the topic. "How'd the Patriots and Dolphins look last night?"

Thankfully, Chet had plenty of thoughts on that subject. While he talked, Andrea studied Tony. He had a deft way of deflecting conflict but he also gave the impression he could more than handle any confrontation. That he almost welcomed it. Against that picture was the contrasting image of a gentle, patient man instructing Nicky about dribbling, almost as if Tony longed for a human connection every bit as much as Nicky did. She had to acknowledge that Tony aroused in her two very powerful and incongruous feelings—an almost maternal desire to soothe the hurt she sensed he'd experienced as a child coupled with a fierce longing, hot and sensual, which she hardly dared think about.

Fortunately, before Andrea was forced to examine these feelings, Shayla appeared, clapping her hands preparatory to an announcement. "They're getting ready to call us in, folks. But the bailiff said there were several more defense witnesses. Then, of course, the closing arguments and the instructions to the jury. I'm thinkin' we're looking at the end of the week."

The chorus of groans subsided when the bailiff appeared immediately and lined them up for court. Andrea fell in behind Dottie, who was wringing her hands. "I'll never get all the pies made, now."

"Couldn't you order from a bakery?" Andrea suggested.

Dottie had just enough time to send her an appalled look before they were back in their accustomed seats in the jury box. The bulk of the morning was spent listening to the defense's expert witness concerning the angle of the video camera and its distortions of distances. The defense was making the case that, since none of the witnesses could positively identify Darvin, neither could the surveillance tape give any proof of the murderer's exact height or identity. Something again about the angle of the camera. Andrea furrowed her brow in concentration to follow the testimony. So far as she could tell, the defense had succeeded in planting doubt about that. Still remaining, though, were the disturbing matters of the T-shirt and the fingerprint on the gun.

The noon recess came none too soon. Andrea and Shayla, avoiding Chet, Arnelle, and other testy jurors, opted for a quick bite at the snack bar in the courthouse lobby. Shayla regaled Andrea with the story of her unconventional courtship, carried out under the watchful eye of her grandmother. "I'll tell you somethin', though, that

Walter of mine, he just kept comin' around. Wasn't anything gonna keep him away. My mama said he was the 'most persistentest' fellow she ever saw.''

"I'd call that real love. You're a lucky woman."

"I sure am. And listen here, honey, don't you settle for anything less." She grinned wickedly. "I think there may still be a few of 'em growin' in the cotton patch." She nodded toward the east entrance.

Andrea raised her eyes. Tony strode across the huge atrium lobby, hell-bent for the elevator bank.

"Are you playin' your cards right?" Shayla sported that out-with-it smile.

Andrea wadded up her chip bag before rising to her feet. "I'll know more after tomorrow night."

Shayla arched her brows. "Big date?"

"We'll see," Andrea said as she threw her trash away and sauntered beside Shayla toward the elevator.

Any jurors suffering from after-lunch drowsiness were immediately roused when the defense attorney called her next witness, Darvin Ray. Andrea studied the young man, who shuffled across the floor and, with a nervous duck of the head, sat down in the witness box. Through the preliminary questioning, he kept darting glances around Ms. Lamb's shoulder in the direction of the prosecutors. Deftly, she would move, blocking his view of the other attorneys who, with sharpened pencils, bent over legal pads, as if waiting to pounce.

"Darvin," Ms. Lamb moved closer to the witness box, but on the bench side so the defendant was in full view of the jury, "were you in Bartelli's Kwik Shop on the night of January 14?"

"No, ma'am."

"Would you tell the court where you were between eleven and midnight on the night Mr. Bartelli was shot?"

"I was home."

"Can anyone verify that?"

"No, I 'spose not." He visibly squirmed.

"Why is that?"

"The landlady, she doesn't ever come outta her apartment after dark. So she couldn't 'uv seen me. And nobody's at home any more. Not since…" his Adam's apple bobbed "not since Ma died."

Ms. Lamb bled the emotional moment by taking her time getting back to the podium.

"Now, Darvin, I want you to look at the gun." She turned to the stenographer, "Prosecution, Exhibit Four." She went to the exhibits table, picked up the revolver and held it out to Darvin. "Have you ever seen this weapon before?"

"I—" he cleared his throat "—it looks like one I had."

The attorney glanced at the judge. "The defense will stipulate, based on the identifying *V* on the butt, that this weapon is the one Darvin Ray acquired from Mr. Vincenza." Then she turned back to her witness. "Can you explain how your gun was found in the vicinity of Mr. Bartelli's store on the night in question?"

"No."

"You didn't loan it to anybody?"

"No."

"When was the last time you saw it?"

"Maybe around Christmas time."

"Why did you own a gun?"

"After Ma got shot, my uncle thought I oughtta have protection. He gave me money to buy the gun from Rocco. I kept it in the closet. I'd clean it sometimes, but I never shot anybody."

"Can you explain how your gun got to the store?"

Darvin Ray gripped the edge of the witness box. "I can't say for sure. Only sometimes some other dudes, they'd come to my house."

"Did you ever show them the gun?"

"Yeah." A small spark of hope gleamed in his eyes as he glanced furtively at the jury.

"Is it possible the gun was stolen from you?"

"Objection." Mr. Bedford was on his feet. "Calls for conjecture."

"Sustained."

"Let me rephrase. The whereabouts of the gun were known to other people?"

"Yeah."

Ms. Lamb backed up and took another tack. "Is there anyone who would want to get you in trouble, Darvin?"

The boy took a deep breath and rubbed his knees. Then a look, almost like an animal pleading to be released from a trap, passed from him to his attorney. "Yes." His voice cracked.

"Who?"

"Cue Ball."

"I beg your pardon?"

"Cue Ball. He's the dude that messed with me at the center."

"Can you give the court his legal name?"

Again the youth hesitated. "Maylon White."

Ms. Lamb approached the box. "You seem frightened."

"Cue Ball, he's one mean man. He told me, 'You mess with me, son, I'll fix you good.'"

"In other words, Mr. White threatened you."

"Yes, ma'am."

"Would Mr. White have any way of knowing where you kept your gun?"

"His brother, he used to hang out at my house."

"Do you own a shirt like this?" She picked up the T-shirt from the exhibit table.

"Yes."

"Where do you keep it?"

"In my locker at the center. It's my lucky basketball shirt."

"Could anyone else have access to your locker?"

"Sure. I never locked it. Too much trouble."

"I see." Ms. Lamb paused, one hand on the rail of the witness box. "Is there anyone else who might have reason to cause you trouble?"

Darvin's eyes darted back and forth. "Maybe," he said softly.

"You don't need to be afraid. Tell the court, Darvin."

"A week or so before Ma got shot," he took a deep breath, "I saw these two guys down the street."

"What were they doing?"

"I couldn't see good enough to tell for sure, but it looked like they were makin' a deal."

"A deal?"

"Yeah, a drug deal."

"Did they see you?"

"I dunno, but then when Ma got killed, I wondered…you know, if they were really after me." He stared into his lap.

Ms. Lamb waited until he looked up. "Darvin, how tall are you?"

"Five foot five."

"How do you know?"

"The cops measured me when they booked me."

"Now, Darvin, I'm going to ask you a very important question. Remember, you are under oath." She stepped back a pace. "Did you on the night of January 14th kill Angelo Bartelli?"

Darvin squared his jaw and looked unflinchingly at her. "Never. I'd never do anything like that."

Slowly Ms. Lamb gathered up her notes and made her way to the defense table. "That's all I have for this witness, Your Honor."

Andrea cringed waiting for what she knew would be a grueling cross-examination. She desperately wanted to believe in the boy's innocence. Based on how she'd sized up his character, she'd have no trouble. But it was the evidence alone the jury had to consider.

The lead prosecutor, Mr. Bedford, took his time getting to the podium and laying out his notes. Darvin's eyes locked on Ms. Lamb.

"Darvin, do you really expect this court to believe you weren't in that store that night?"

The defense attorney turned red in the face. "*Objection,* Your Honor!"

"Sustained." The judge gave a withering look to the prosecutor. "Really, Mr. Bedford. You know the rules."

He nodded curtly before going on. "Do you know Mrs. Grant, who works at the community center?"

"Yes."

"Has she been helpful to you in the past?"

"Yes."

"Can you explain, then, why you didn't just tell her that Maylon White was harassing you?"

Darvin studied the fists balled in his lap. "I don't need any woman fighting my battles."

"So it's a manhood issue, then?"

"I guess."

"So if manhood is an issue with you, wouldn't you want to do something to make your mother proud?"

Darvin looked wary. "Y…yes."

"Going to college would've made her proud, right?"

"Yes, sir."

"Mr. Ray, did you have enough money, even with the scholarship, to go to college?"

Looking down, he finally mumbled, "No."

"So you might have found robbery an easy way to augment your funds?"

"I didn't rob anybody!"

"And when the robbery didn't go as you expected, you panicked and shot that man, didn't you, Darvin?"

The youth, halfway out of his chair, raised his voice. "No! I didn't do anything. Can't you people believe that?"

"Please be seated, Mr. Ray." The judge paused before nodding consent to resume questioning.

"Do you have trouble with your temper, Darvin?"

"Objection!"

"Sustained."

Andrea was on the edge of her seat. The questions continued, badgering away at Darvin about his state of mind, establishing again that he had no alibi for the night in question, indirectly reinforcing to the jury that the defendant had motive, opportunity and weapon. As the interrogation continued, Darvin seemed to shrivel before her eyes. Finally, Bedford gathered up his files and returned to the prosecutors' table, but not before shooting the jury a what-more-do-you-want? look.

The courtroom was stifling and a bad taste welled up in Andrea's mouth. This was gut-wrenching. Through her discomfort, she only half heard the judge's words. "This court will be in recess for thirty minutes."

"All rise!" The bailiff led the jury from the courtroom. Andrea realized that there was no way she was going to be able to eat dinner. She felt sick. There would be no postponing the serious duty that lay before her and eleven others.

IN THE BACKGROUND a public television program, serious and pretentious as far as Bert was concerned, rolled on the TV screen. He tried to watch, but his mind kept returning to the question that had bothered him all day. For the life of him, he couldn't recall. Was it '87 or '88 when Rich had won the yacht club Labor Day regatta? He did remember how pleased the members were that somebody had finally defeated Carleton Slade, the longtime champion. And, of course, who could forget the maneuver Rich had made around that final buoy to put himself in perfect position for the homeward tacking duel.

He winced. Sailing. If he'd never taught Rich to sail… If he'd never given him the down payment for that state-of-the-art racing sloop… He leaned his head back in the leather chair, then closed his eyes. Never again. He couldn't change a damn thing. It was too late.

"Bert?"

He sat up, muted the television and looked over to where Claudia was sitting, leafing through back issues of *Bon Appétit* and *Gourmet* magazines. She took off her reading glasses and rubbed the bridge of her nose. "What is Andrea thinking of?"

"In relation to what?" The woman expected him to be a mind reader.

"Well, for one thing, that man. For another, those shoes." She shook her head wearily. "Nicholas actually wore them today for his school program."

"They're just shoes, Claudia."

"Ugly shoes. Nothing like what Richard would've worn."

Bert stifled the sigh that rose within him. "You know very well Rich wore whatever the other young men were wearing. You always made certain he was in style." Before she could interrupt him with a correction, he hurried on, "And that's all Nicholas is doing. Wearing what's in style." He turned the knife slightly. "That doesn't mean you have to like it."

"Rest assured, I don't." She put her glasses back on and began snipping out a recipe, probably for some terrifically complicated, spicy way to prepare turkey. What was wrong with plain old oven roasting, he'd like to know. When he reached for the remote control, eager to escape this line of questioning, she spoke again. "I'm not half as worried about the shoes as I am about that man."

"That man has a name, dear. Tony Urbanski."

"Foreign sounding."

"You've lived in Cleveland most of your life. Ethnic names, ethnic cultures are part of the diversity of this city." He knew he sounded pompous, but Claudia had become increasingly close-minded since Rich's death. As if she could stave off disaster by insulating herself from all but the very familiar.

"But what do we know about him?" She laid down the scissors and looked straight at him.

"He's a friend of Nicholas and Andrea's. And he cared enough to install a basketball hoop for Nicholas. That's all."

"You men. That's just the beginning. I think she's seeing him."

"'Seeing him'?"

"Yes, we're keeping Nicholas Wednesday night because she has an engagement. Bert Porter, I'll bet you anything it's with that man."

Bert felt a pinching sensation at the base of his skull. "Is that so bad? Or really any of our business?" Yet even as he asked the question, the sense of dread he'd felt Sunday evening mushroomed like an ominous storm cloud. If Andrea married… He could hardly bear to complete the thought, but he couldn't help himself. Would Nicholas forget his own father? Forget Rich?

"Any of our business? When she may be staying out until all hours with him? Why else would she want Nicholas to spend the night with us?"

"Because she couldn't find a sitter, what with the holiday and all?"

She shot him a disbelieving look before picking up her scissors and commencing to snip. "Why are you always so willing to believe the best?"

As he picked up the TV remote, then activated the sound, he muttered, "Because you never do."

Damn, why had Claudia had to voice his worst fear? It made the possibility seem ever so much more real. And yet it was obvious. Andrea was attractive. Some man, Urbanski or somebody else, was going to find her interesting. Interesting and attractive enough to marry. So, like it or not, there it was.

And what would become of Nicholas then?

For that matter, what would become of Claudia and him?

CHAPTER SEVEN

WEDNESDAY, BECAUSE the courtroom was warm and stuffy and because testimony from the defense's fingerprint expert was difficult to follow, Andrea found her mind wandering. Nicky had sulked all the way to school, unhappy because he was spending the night with his grandparents. Andrea couldn't help wondering, though, if his snit wasn't, in part, calculated to make her feel guilty for going out with Tony—alone. The Porters had been both disapproving of her date and eager to have their grandson.

The anticipation of being alone with Tony fueled the heat rising beneath her collar. Always before, she and Tony had had Nicky for a buffer, at least until he went to bed. Tonight? Anything was possible, and she had a case of nerves to prove it.

"So is it your conclusion the fingerprint is in the wrong position to prove the defendant fired this gun?" The defense attorney's pointed question grabbed Andrea. She focused on the slight, balding man in the witness box.

"Yes. The only print we were able to lift, the thumbprint, indicates the defendant was holding the gun grip out, as one would do if one was cleaning the gun or replacing it in a case."

"But not as if he were firing the gun, correct?"

"Correct."

When Ms. Lamb finished with the witness, the prosecutor moved in and asked only one question. "However, if the perpetrator wore gloves in the commission of the crime, we could not rule out the defendant as a possible suspect, is that right?''

''Correct.''

After the witness stepped down, Andrea was relieved to hear Ms. Lamb say, ''The defense rests, Your Honor.''

The judge shuffled through some papers, then addressed the three attorneys. ''I will expect closing arguments to begin promptly at 9 a.m. Friday. Is that understood?''

After they nodded their assent, the judge turned to the jury. ''Because of Thanksgiving tomorrow, we will recess early today. However, when you come in Friday morning, be prepared, if necessary, to continue your deliberations into Saturday. Enjoy your holiday.''

Saturday? Andrea groaned inwardly. Surely it wouldn't take that long. Given the amount of circumstantial evidence, reasonable doubt seemed a likely possibility. After all, no witnesses could identify the killer, and the frame-up theory was definitely plausible. The prosecutor had shown—and the defense had admitted—that the gun was Darvin's but couldn't prove he'd pulled the trigger. Besides, Darvin Ray just didn't have the look of a killer. Whatever that was, she acknowledged. And what about the others—Chet, Dottie and Arnelle, for example? There was no way to know what they were thinking except that they wanted the whole ordeal behind them. And Tony? She had no idea where he stood.

EVEN THOUGH TONY ALREADY knew Andrea was lovely and that by merely looking at him a certain way she could reduce him to putty, he was unprepared for just what a knockout she was in the V-necked, form-fitting black dress or for what two-inch pumps did for her legs. All night long, he'd barely been able to take his eyes off her. In fact, she rendered him disconcertingly speechless.

Le Bistro had been an inspired choice—great food, four-star service and an intimate, candlelit decor. Best of all, the band knew exactly when to throw in a dreamy number—about the time he could no longer stand not to hold Andrea tightly against him.

He nuzzled her forehead and nestled her even closer as they swayed in place to an old James Taylor tune. When she released a soft, contented sigh, he realized that despite all the pressures of his job, tonight he was truly happy. And it felt good.

At the end of the song, he dipped her and held her there momentarily, the two of them suspended in that fraction of a second between the cessation of music and the resumption of conversation. Reluctantly, he pulled her upright, hugged her, then raised an eyebrow. "Another dance?"

She tipped her face and smiled languidly. "It's tempting. Very tempting."

He put an arm around her waist. "Why do I hear a 'but'?"

"I guess because you do." She picked up his wrist and checked his watch. "It's after midnight and it's a long way home."

"Afraid your coach will turn into a pumpkin?"

"Maybe just that I'll lose one of my glass slippers."

He gently steered her through the couples on the dance floor to their table, then pulled out his billfold. "I'll settle up and we'll be on our way." Part of him wanted one more dance, but the more insistent part wanted to get to a comfortable, private place where he could show her just exactly what she did to him.

He retrieved their coats from the hatcheck stand and made sure she was bundled up before linking an arm through hers and escorting her out the door. Unexpectedly they found themselves in the midst of a swirling snowstorm, barely able to see the lights of the parking lot down the hill. Already, the street was packed with several inches of snow and the storm showed no signs of abating.

"Damn! The weatherman blew this one big time." He turned up his coat collar. "Let me take you back inside to wait while I get the car."

"This is one time I don't mind being a woman," she said, her words nearly lost in the howl of a northwesterly wind.

He left her in the lobby, then started down the street. Snow seeped into his shoes, and his face was numb with cold. Under the snow, the sidewalk was pure ice. Literally sliding down the inclined entrance to the parking lot, he began to question whether, even with four-wheel drive, he could get out of the lot, much less up the steep hill leading from the Flats into the downtown area.

Surveying the situation, he finally acknowledged that even if he safely escaped the parking space, he'd probably never navigate the slope up to the street. He'd have to call a cab.

The deserted street was ominously quiet except for the wind. He retreated to the club, where he found Andrea huddled on a love seat. She looked up hopefully, then registering his expression, said, "No luck, huh?"

"Not tonight. Cleveland is having one of its famous lake-effect storms." He stamped his feet, leaving a trail of snow on the entry carpet. "I'm going to call a cab. They'll have chains."

The hatcheck girl leaned forward. "Sir, several other customers have called taxis, but I'm afraid the cab companies are reporting a three to four hour delay. Of course, you're welcome to wait here."

Wonderful. A classic lesson in how to impress your date!

Andrea looked worried. "How bad is it?" she asked the hatcheck girl.

"Bad. They're predicting eighteen inches or more."

Tony cursed under his breath. Of course, there was an alternative. If they could make it. He brightened. It was a very attractive alternative. He took hold of her hand and led her to the door, directing her attention to the small window. "See that building up there at the top of the hill?" She nodded. "That's my apartment. We'd be a lot more comfortable there." He did his damnedest not to sound too eager.

She didn't bat an eye. "I can't argue that."

"But—" he eyed her evening shoes "—I'm not sure you're very well equipped for the walk."

"Excuse me," the hatcheck girl interjected. "I couldn't help overhearing. If you're trying to walk in the snow, please take these." She handed Andrea a pair of plastic overshoes. "A customer left these here last winter. They were never claimed."

Andrea slipped them on. "They're perfect." She smiled at Tony. "Now I'm better prepared than you are." She squinted out the window. "It doesn't look too far."

Struggling up the hill a few moments later, he acknowledged there was some truth in her analysis. Though she was shivering in the curve of his arm, she seemed better able to get traction than he did. Leather soles were great for dancing, lousy for Arctic expeditions.

Halfway there, Tony decided this had been a foolish decision. They were covered with snow, and shards of ice, blown off the lake, pricked their heads and faces. "Are you okay?" he managed. "Maybe we should turn around."

She grabbed his hand and tugged him forward. "Going up has to be easier than sliding back down."

Their breath coming in short gasps, they finally reached level ground. Snow whispered around them; otherwise they were enshrouded in an eerie silence—the normally bustling city was a ghost town. "We're almost there," he said encouragingly, pointing to the dimly lighted lobby entrance.

"Lead on. I love snow, but I'm f-freezing," she said, mushing forward.

The welcome warmth of the lobby was almost a shock to his stinging hands and frozen feet. Tony knew Andrea didn't need to walk much farther, so instead of taking the stairs, as was his custom, he pushed the elevator button. "I'm not sure this was such a good idea. Are you all right?"

"I'll l-let you know when I thaw out." Then she managed a half smile. "It's okay, T-Tony, really. I'll b-be fine."

Inside, he went immediately to the linen closet and pulled out a goose-down sleeping bag and a bath towel. Next he retrieved a pair of wool socks from his underwear drawer. She sat huddled on the sofa, shaking. "Here." He handed her the towel, hunkered in front of her, removed her overshoes and pumps, then massaged her frigid feet briefly before pulling the heavy socks over her nylons, trying not to think about the intimacy of the gesture. Then he bundled her in the sleeping bag, tucking it carefully around her. When he stood up, he said, "I'll have the brandy ready in a minute."

But instead of moving, he stood there stupidly, staring at her. Flakes of snow still clung to her hair. Her face was flushed from the cold and her eyes sparkled with relief. She was beautiful. He continued watching, mesmerized, as she began drying her hair.

"What about you?"

He started. She'd said something. "Huh?"

"You. What about you? Change your shoes and socks, get into some dry clothes." She shooed him toward the bedroom. "I'm much better. I may even be warm again in this lifetime."

He stumbled over himself hurrying to change his clothes. He couldn't wait to get back to warm her up—the old-fashioned way!

Shortly, dressed in wool socks, jeans and a turtleneck sweater, he poured two snifters of brandy and handed one to her. "Cheers." He sat beside her, then after a healthy sip, he put down the brandy, fumbled under the sleeping bag, pulled her feet into his lap and began rubbing her toes and instep. She held the snifter in both hands, as if the glass would somehow warm her fingers. "Getting warm?"

"Slowly." She closed her eyes briefly. The contentment on her face stirred his groin. "Mmm. That feels so good." Then her eyes fluttered open and she glanced from the Eames chair to the black-and-white European-style kitchen, then to the Picasso print. "Funny," she said. "I wouldn't have taken you for a modern kinda guy."

If anybody else had said that, he'd have felt insulted. But from her it sounded strangely like a compliment. "It's the latest in bachelor-executive decor." God, he was making a joke out of the huge chunk of change he'd spent on this place. At the same time he felt the heel of her foot come into contact with his erection. He reached out and took a gulp of brandy. How could scratchy wool socks be so incredibly erotic?

When he looked at her again, she had stopped shivering, and her hair was drier, but what if she caught pneumonia or something? Maybe they should've stayed at Le Bistro. "Look," he patted her feet with finality, "I hope you won't misinterpret this, but wouldn't you feel better if you could take a hot shower, dry your hair, then get under the covers? I have a big robe you could put on along with—" he nodded at her feet "—those stylish socks."

She pulled her feet back under her. "Not only will I not take that wrong, I think it's exactly what I need to do, if you don't mind."

Mind? Hell, it would drive him crazy imagining her standing in his glassed-in shower letting hot water spray over her naked body. He'd need every ounce of self-control. But she was a lady. And a wrong move would ring the death knell to their relationship. Making the right moves was very, very important to him.

NEVER HAD A SHOWER been so welcome. Andrea luxuriated in the invigorating hot spray, the cloud of steam, the blessed warmth finally permeating even her feet. She picked up a bottle from the shelf and lathered her hair with a wonderful woodsy-smelling shampoo. As rivulets of water dripped off her breasts and ran down her legs, the nerve endings of her body tingled, and she could no longer conceal from herself what she was thinking and feeling. Tony Urbanski set her on fire.

First the romantic dinner. Then the heaven of dancing, their bodies locked together. And only a few moments ago, that yearning look, his dark, sensuous eyes warming her better than the finest brandy.

She shut off the water, then toweled herself, the friction of the terry cloth against her skin succeeding in arousing her further. Quickly she donned an oversized pair of pajamas he'd located, pulled on the wool socks and tied his flannel robe around her waist. Then she dried her hair, using his brush and hair dryer. The intimacy of these acts was not lost on her.

Then she knew. Knew precisely what was going to happen. And knew, without a doubt that she wasn't going to fight it even if giving in to the powerful attraction might change the nature of their relationship in ways she couldn't predict. Quite simply, she wanted to make love.

When she emerged from the bathroom, some new age instrumental was pulsing through the sound system and

Tony had refilled her snifter. He drew her down beside him on the sofa. "Better?" he asked.

"Infinitely. Thank you."

He ran a finger along her jawline. "I'm glad." He kept looking at her as if he'd never seen her before. She swallowed with difficulty, unable to lower her eyes, seeing in his the reflection of her own feelings. Something clenched inside her belly. If he didn't touch her soon...

The moment stretched unbearably until they moved toward each other, his lips meeting hers, her arms twining around his neck, his hands pressing firmly against her back. She lost herself in the vortex of his kiss, in the welcome release of pent-up emotions. His mouth was warm and firm on hers and she couldn't get enough of him. She wanted those lips everywhere all at once—on her neck, her breasts, her abdomen. Dimly, she felt his hands move to cup her face, then, ever so slowly, he pulled his mouth away and just looked at her.

Finally he spoke. "Wow!" His voice was low, husky. When she smiled tentatively, he ran a forefinger over her bottom lip. She traced the sharp planes of his cheek and jaw, never breaking his gaze. "Andrea, I—"

She pressed her palm against his mouth. "Shh. You don't have to say anything." She snuggled closer. "Just hold me. You feel so good."

"Tell me about it," he growled, pulling her across his lap, snugging her head into his shoulder, running his hand up and down her arm. Beneath the cotton pajama top, she could feel her breasts swelling and peaking in anticipation. She wanted his hands there. Now. She blushed against the wool of his sweater. She was shameless. But it had been so long since...since she'd thought of herself first, of what she wanted, of what felt good. In their refuge from the storm, with snow blotting out the rest of the world, leaving them in the warm cocoon of their entwined arms, far from their daily concerns, she knew what mattered most at this moment. With a fierceness she would not have thought possible, she wanted Tony.

They sat for what seemed like several minutes. Occasionally his lips would trace a warm trail of kisses across her forehead. Other than that, he was unnaturally still, as if holding himself in check.

Finally he shifted. "What about that brandy?"

She looked at the snifter, then back at him. "You're a better warmer-upper than any brandy."

His face contorted briefly, as if he were fighting for control. "My pleasure." He swung her legs around and slowly stood up. "But now I'm going to tuck you into bed." He took her hand and drew her to her feet. "I don't want you catching cold." He led her to the bedroom where he had already turned down the comforter. Awkwardly he undid the knot at her waist and helped her out of the robe.

He was going to leave. She didn't want him to. Her body throbbed with desire. He gently pushed her down on the bed, picked up her legs and swung them under the covers, before tucking the comforter around her shoulders.

"What about you?" she managed.

"I'll be fine on the couch. That sleeping bag is mighty warm." He kissed her forehead, turned off the bedside lamp, stuffed an extra pillow under his arm, and then paused, studying her in the dim glow cast by the night-light. He cleared his throat. "Well, pleasant dreams."

Dreams? She knew what would fill hers—images of Tony's smoldering eyes, taut body, exciting hands, broad chest. Like distant thunder, her heart pounded.

He walked to the doorway, where, hesitating, he turned around. "Good night, Andrea."

"Tony?" Her voice, muffled by the comforter, came out as a croak.

He stilled, like an animal scenting something different in its surroundings. "Yes?"

She felt her tongue thicken. "Don't go."

He stepped toward her. "What did you say?"

"You heard me." She flipped back the covers and held out her arms. "Stay. Here. With me."

Before she'd finished speaking, he'd tossed his pillow to the floor and lay stretched out beside her on the bed, his face buried in her neck, his arms clutching her against him. "Lady, you're driving me wild." His lips, hot on her bare skin, followed his fingers as, one by one, he worked his way down, unbuttoning each pajama button until he eased her arms out of the top and, with an impatient gesture, threw off his sweater, and held her, his warm skin kindling hers. "Is this the preacher's daughter's idea of rebellion?" he whispered.

Involuntarily, she writhed against him. "Oh, no." She could scarcely breathe, so intense was her wanting. "This is pure self-indulgence," she murmured, glorying in the rush of heat produced deep within her as his tongue teased one taut nipple. "But, Tony, what about—?"

"Shh." He raised up, dropped a fleeting kiss on her lips and reached for the bedside table. "I'll take care of it."

In some distant part of her brain she registered the impossibility that only a brief time ago, she had been freezing. Now she was melting in a tropical ocean of sensations, driven wild by a man who was every bit as intense a lover as he was a person.

And then, propelled by a spasm of desire, she didn't concern herself further with thinking. Only with Tony. And her own frantically responsive body. And how very good they were together.

"NICHOLAS, WILL YOU *please* turn down that television? Mimi can't think." From his leather armchair in the family room, Bert looked over his shoulder into the kitchen where Claudia stood, her cheeks flushed with heat from the range, stirring some concoction for their Thanksgiving dinner. He felt a tic of irritation. She'd refused to let Nicholas go outside to play in the snow. Whether because she was afraid he'd catch cold or because he'd track it in, Bert couldn't say. You'd think, at the very least, for Nicholas's sake, she could tolerate the Macy's Thanksgiving Day parade. He glanced at his grandson, sitting upright on the couch, his feet dangling, the remote tucked in his hand. He'd already muted the sound.

"Thank you," Claudia intoned with asperity. Bert wished the sounds coming from the kitchen were half as appealing as the smells—pumpkin pie, roast turkey, hot mulled cider. He closed his eyes, remembering one particular Thanksgiving when Rich had brought several fraternity brothers home from college. The house had been filled with laughter and noise. Wonderful noise.

"Grandpa?" He snapped open his eyes and looked at Nicholas. The boy was swinging one leg back and forth against the sofa. "Do you think I could call Andie? I'm worried she may not be able to get here. You know, with the snow and all." His anxious expression touched Bert. He didn't like to see Nicholas upset. Much as he appreciated the boy's affection for Rich's sister-in-law, he hoped his grandson was equally attached to him.

"Of course." He picked up the portable phone from his chairside table and handed it to Nicholas. "Help yourself." While the boy dialed, Bert glanced out the window where snow still fell, though now in large flakes sifting slowly through the bare tree limbs.

"Grandpa?" Nicholas's voice sounded strained. Bert looked at him. The boy's brows were contracted with worry. "There's nobody home. Where is she?" The question came out shrilly. Ever since losing his parents, he'd been quick to overreact. He clambered off the sofa and came to stand at Bert's elbow. "Do you think she's all right?"

Exercising her uncanny ability to hear what she wanted to hear, Claudia moved quickly into the family room. "What are you talking about, Nicholas?" She stood, one hand on her hip, the other holding a potato masher.

Bert took hold of Nicholas's hand and pulled him down to sit on the ottoman. "Now, Claudia, it's nothing." With his voice, he'd tried to convey a warning. She didn't need to upset the lad further. "He can't reach Andrea. She probably slept in and is in the shower."

"Do you think so?" Nicholas's expression was heart-breakingly hopeful.

"I'm sure of it, son." Bert patted the boy's knee.

Claudia approached the ottoman and laid a hand on Nicholas's shoulder. "I imagine that's it, honey," Claudia said. Before returning to the kitchen, she paused, threw Bert a skeptical look and muttered, "Remember where she was going last night and with whom!"

Bert bobbed his head meaningfully in the boy's direction. "Claudia," he mouthed, "that's enough." Then he said for his grandson's benefit, "There's a perfectly reasonable explanation why Nicholas can't reach her just now." He turned solicitously to his grandson. "Don't you worry. I'm sure Andrea is fine." He stood and walked to the window, staring out at the drifts. "However, she may have trouble getting over here today because of the storm." He swiveled to face his grandson. "And we wouldn't want her to try if it isn't safe, would we?"

Nicholas hung his head. "No. I guess not." Then, picking at an upholstery button on the ottoman, he looked up. "Grandpa, what did Mimi mean—about last night?"

Bert felt his chest constrict. Little pitchers and their big ears! "You know how Mimi is," he offered conspiratorially. "She's always imagining things."

Nicholas appeared to consider the words. Then with a shrug, he moved back to the sofa and glued his eyes to the television set, seemingly oblivious to the nuances of Claudia's ill-considered words.

But when Bert picked up his magazine, he was unable to concentrate. Damn it all, anyway. Claudia had a point. What if Andrea had spent the night with…with that Urbanski fellow? Tiredly, he set down the magazine and rubbed his eyes. Surely not.

And what would Claudia say when he had to confess he no longer had much appetite for the Thanksgiving feast? Guiltily, he glanced into the kitchen. Now what was the woman doing? She had the phone book open and was apparently looking up somebody's number. Oh, well. Probably checking with one of her friends about how long to boil the sauce or heat the rolls. Some damn woman thing.

TONY OPENED ONE EYE, then closed it against the icy glare from the window. Still snowing. Behind him, he felt warm skin against his bare back. Andrea. Then it hit him—the unbelievable night, followed by a truly memorable daybreak. Slowly, so as not to disturb her, he rolled over and gathered her against his chest. Tendrils of blond hair trailed across his shoulder and her cheeks, flushed with sleep, reminded him of ripe peaches. He felt the erection stirring and knew he was totally powerless to resist this woman. He held his breath with longing even as, in some part of his brain, he acknowledged this shift in their relationship might cause problems for a guy who wasn't looking for commitment. Women were funny that way. The hell of it was, if he *were* looking for a wife, Andrea would be at the top of the list.

"Tony?" She moved her hand, capturing his and tucking their entwined fingers beneath her chin.

"Uh-huh?" He kissed the pulse point in her neck.

"You feel so good." As she drew out the "so," she moved against him.

She was driving him wild. If she wanted more, he was her man. But before he could act on his impulse, she scooted to the edge of the bed and sat up. "Tony, it's already ten-thirty." She leaped to her feet. "I've got to call Nicky. He must be worried sick."

Disappointed, Tony flopped on his back, cradling his head in his locked hands. "Isn't he okay? He's at his grandparents', isn't he?"

She was hurriedly knotting the robe. "Yes, but I told him I'd call this morning and tell him when I'd be joining the Porters."

"Have you taken a gander out the window? You may not be going anywhere for a while. What time is their dinner?"

"Two."

"I wouldn't count on it, then. The streets are probably treacherous."

"Oh, dear. I better let them know not to count on me." She looked around, then spotted the phone concealed under a stack of newspapers. "Mind?"

"Of course not." He slipped out of bed and circled the foot, putting his arms around her from behind, pulling her tight against his chest as he tenderly cupped her breasts. "It's just I was hoping we'd have a more leisurely morning. But I understand." With one hand, he lifted her hair and nuzzled the nape of her neck. Then he patted her gently on her nicely rounded ass. "Call him. I'll be in the shower. That'll give you some privacy."

When he came out ten minutes later, a towel wrapped around his waist, he smelled coffee. Going into the kitchen, he found her sitting on a stool, nursing a cup. She looked contemplative, even distant. Oh, God, had he blown it? He settled on the stool next to her, then captured her fingers in his. "You okay?"

She turned troubled blue eyes to his. "Nicky was worried. He tried to call me at home." Her shoulders slumped. "I wasn't there, of course."

"He'll be fine. You can't be expected to live every hour of your life for Nicky."

"Think about it, Tony. He's already lost his parents. He gets frantic when I'm not where I'm supposed to be."

"That's gotta be tough on you, though."

She pulled her hands free and traced a finger back and forth over the handle of the mug. "I have to put him first right now. Anyway, it's what people in families do—take care of each other."

Right. Like his old man had done? "Even at the risk of your own happiness?"

She looked directly into his eyes. "Even then."

He stood up, rounded the counter and poured himself a cup of coffee. Caffeine would be damn little comfort for the ache inside. "You're too good, Andrea." As soon as the words were out, he regretted them. Too good for her own well-being? Or too good for him? A flicker of uncertainty jolted through him. He was used to doing what he needed to in order to get what he wanted. But her singleminded, selfless devotion? He didn't know quite what to make of it.

She shrugged. "It's not a matter of 'good.' It's a matter of necessity and devotion and…love." She paused, sipping delicately from the mug. Then she looked at him in silent appeal. "You have to understand one thing, Tony. I love Nicky as if he were my own."

The unstated part of any understanding between them rang loud and clear. As he'd known all along, any future with Andrea involved Nick. He leaned both elbows on the countertop. "Of course you do. No problem."

The hint of a smile played over her face. "Unless you consider *this* a problem."

He stood up. "What?"

"You apparently didn't hear the phone ring when you were in the shower. The answering machine picked up. It was Claudia Porter. Basically, I've been busted. She oh-so-sweetly invited both of us to join them for a belated Thanksgiving dinner on Saturday, necessitated, of course, by our ill-considered rendezvous."

Tony felt the implied insult deep in his gut. "Never mind the snowstorm."

Andrea smiled resignedly. "I think it's my punishment for being caught spending the night with a man. You know, 'living well'—or in this case graciously—is Claudia's best revenge." She hesitated. "You don't have to come, Tony. I'll understand."

One look at her—tousled hair, creamy skin, the tops of her breasts showing where the robe gaped open—and the anger drained right out of him, replaced by confidence. He had never met an opponent he couldn't charm. He grinned and raised his mug in a toast. "Bring it on, woman!"

When he held out his arms, she set down her coffee and moved into his embrace. In the distance he heard the siren signaling the raising of the bridge over the Cuyahoga River. Some ship battered about by the storm was entering the safety of port. He knew the feeling.

ANDREA STOOD IN Tony's kitchen studying her outfit and listening to the weather report. Before he left to dig his car out of the lot once the snow had finally quit mid-afternoon, he'd loaned her an old pair of sweats and a turtleneck. Though the pants drooped around her ankles, by cinching up the drawstring, tucking in the shirt and pushing up the sleeves, she looked reasonably presentable. In a self-important baritone, the newscaster was reporting twenty inches. Because of the ice and snow, traffic on the interstates was snarled, hundreds of holiday travelers were stranded and city street crews were making slow progress. All unnecessary travel was being discouraged.

She glanced around. Tony's kitchen was as bare as the apartment itself. None of it was unattractive exactly. It just looked sterile and made her feel...lonely.

She curled up in his Eames chair and thumbed through a copy of *Sports Illustrated.* But her mind kept straying from the images of the athlete's bodies to her memory of the live warm body she'd enjoyed last night. Tony's love-making had been tender, imaginative, passionate, provocative. Encased in his cozy, soft clothes smelling faintly musky, she felt tingly all over again.

No doubt about it. She'd been loved. And it had felt very good!

She leaned her head back. How long had it been since she'd last made love? She pursed her lips. It had to have been with John, long before...Nicky came to live with her.

The incredible part was that she'd met Tony exactly one week ago, yet she'd known from the very beginning that he was special. Despite his confident, take-charge demeanor, he had a gentler side that, for whatever reasons, he didn't seem comfortable revealing. Yet he had, both with Nicky and with her. When she got to know him better, maybe she'd discover why he kept a part of himself hidden.

She must've dozed off in the chair, because the next thing she knew, she heard Tony stomping his feet inside the door of the apartment. She opened her eyes and watched him rub his hands together, then hang up his parka. She stretched her arms over her head and yawned. "Any luck?"

"With the help of some other guys, I managed to get out of the lot. I had to go around the long way to get back here. The city crews have cleared the main streets, so I think I can get you home if we take it easy, especially if you're willing to hike into the side streets if necessary." He walked across the room, leaned over and pinned her with his arms. "Sure you don't want to stay another night?" He arched his eyebrows leeringly.

She laughed. "And do what? Go to court dressed like this?"

He stood back up. "Oh, hell. You know how to ruin a guy's fantasy. I'd forgotten all about the trial."

"Do you think they'll postpone it because of the weather?"

He shook his head. "Not if there's any other way. Nobody, least of all the judge and attorneys, wants to carry the thing through the weekend. All the way around, it'd be great to have it over and done with."

She frowned. "Do you really think we can hear closing arguments and jury instructions and arrive at a unanimous verdict all in one day?"

"Piece of cake." Did he have his mind made up already, she wondered. She knew which way she was leaning, but surely it would take twelve people quite a while to deliberate and agree. He went on talking. "The sooner the better, as far as I'm concerned. Wednesday I have to be in New York, ready to go on that merger."

Something about his stance shifted. He looked more…controlled. Like a big cat, ready to pounce.

She stood up. "Could we leave soon? While it's still light?"

He rubbed his hands over her shoulders and down her arms. "Sure you won't reconsider my offer?"

She stood on tiptoe and kissed him lightly. "I'm sure. Let me get my things."

They were putting on their coats when the phone rang. "Never mind," Tony said. "The machine'll get it."

A voice grated out into the apartment. "Tony, ya punk. Where the hell are ya?" Tony stood stock-still. Andrea noticed his fingers curl into loose fists. "Thought you'd at least call me on Thanksgiving." There followed a garbled sound like glass against metal. "Too big for your britches, huh? Look here, kid, I needa talk with ya. *Today*." Then the tone sounded. The end of the message.

Tony, his face a rigid mask, grabbed her by the arm and hurried her out of the apartment. As they waited for the elevator, he avoided looking at her.

Tentatively she laid a hand on his shoulder. "Tony? You seem upset. Who was that?"

Finally he looked at her, his eyes hooded in the same way an untrusting stray animal's are. "That?" He shrugged. "Nobody. Just my old man."

Like a sliver of ice, the cold in his voice pierced her heart.

TONY SAT THE NEXT MORNING, drumming his fingers on the hard wood surface of the jury room table. Most of the jurors had arrived, but they were still waiting for three, Andrea among them. He hoped to hell she hadn't had any difficulty.

He'd tossed and turned most of the night, alternately longing for her—his bed seemed so empty—and resentful of the way his father had succeeded in spoiling the mood yesterday. When Tony had reached him after taking Andrea home, it was more of the same. Pops needed money. He was never satisfied. As soon as the DataTech merger talks concluded, Tony decided, he'd have to fly up to Detroit and try to talk some sense into his father. He raked his fingers through his short hair. Fat chance. Why would this time be any different from the others?

He looked up just as Andrea arrived, cheeks rosy with cold. The two others came in right behind her. They barely had time to deposit their coats before the bailiff appeared, scowling even more than usual. "Mr. Urbanski?" He scanned the room, then locating Tony, he pointed an index finger at him. "You and—" again his eyes made a circuit of the room and landed on Andrea "—Ms. Evans, come with me. Now."

Andrea glanced at Tony questioningly. He shook his head. He had no idea what the hell was going on. Once the bailiff had the two of them in the corridor, with a tone Tony could only interpret as satisfaction, he said stonily, "Judge Blumberg has requested to see you in chambers."

"What's this all about?" Tony asked.

The bailiff ignored him. "Follow me. Both of you." And he bustled officiously down the hall.

Andrea looked at Tony, worry in her eyes. He wished he could put an arm around her, comfort her. But, of course, he couldn't.

CHAPTER EIGHT

HILDA BLUMBERG GLANCED up briefly from a stack of papers on her desk, waved a hand toward the two padded armchairs and said absently, "Be with you in a minute." Andrea's hands trembled. Full of apprehension, she sat down, then fixed her eyes on the floor-to-ceiling shelves lined with official-looking reference books. She didn't dare glance at Tony.

After several minutes, the judge set down her pen, whipped off her glasses and looked from Tony to her. "We have a potential problem here. A serious one." She leaned back in her chair and linked her fingers at her waist. "It was reported to an officer of this court that the two of you were seen in what was described as affectionate circumstances at a nightclub Wednesday evening. What exactly is the nature of your relationship?"

Andrea knew she and Tony hadn't compromised the trial, but that knowledge did nothing to alleviate the tinny taste in her mouth.

"Your Honor, Andrea and I are friends." Tony's voice didn't waver.

"Where did you meet?"

"Here."

"I see." The words were clipped. "And you—" she stared at Andrea "—how would you characterize your relationship?"

Andrea's pulse throbbed. "The same, Your Honor. We've become good friends."

"Have you been seeing each other socially?"

Tony jumped in. "Yes, Your Honor, but I can assure you nothing about our relationship is cause for concern."

To Andrea, his words sounded forced. She couldn't bear the thought of being seen as less than honest.

"I will remind you that you have been selected for a vital and sacred duty of citizenship. I expect a truthful answer to my next question." Judge Blumberg leaned forward, clasping her hands on the desktop. "Have you discussed this case with one another?"

Andrea sat up straighter. "Absolutely not, Your Honor."

Tony jerked his head in Andrea's direction. "Andrea made that an emphatic condition of our relationship." He grinned his knock-'em-dead grin. "And as you might expect, we had many other topics of conversation."

His charm was lost on the stern-faced woman. "I have a decision to make. As you know, the case goes to the jury today. The question is whether you should continue to serve as jurors or whether I should dismiss you and seat the two alternates. This court and the defendant can ill afford a mistrial."

Tony hesitated for a fraction of a second, and Andrea wondered if he was considering how an extra business day would benefit his all-important merger preparations. "We have not discussed this trial, Your Honor, and nothing in our behavior would, in any way, compromise our ability to deliberate fairly and impartially."

"Ms. Evans?"

"That is exactly how I feel, Your Honor."

"Would I be correct that taking this lady dancing is not against the law?" Tony asked.

"You would. But, Mr. Urbanski, perception is important." She picked up her glasses, tapped the earpiece against her desk and appeared to be considering her options. Finally, she spoke. "One last time." Her eyes bored right through Andrea's skull. "You are absolutely certain of your ability to proceed impartially with this case?"

"Yes, Your Honor."

The judge repeated the question to Tony. Apparently satisfied with their responses, she stood and slipped her arms into her judicial robe. "Do not give me any reason to question my judgment on this matter." She reached under her desk, pressed a buzzer and, shortly, the bailiff appeared. "Mr. Schmidt, please escort these jurors to the jury room."

Andrea was grateful they were immediately summoned into court; otherwise she'd have had an awkward time handling the quizzical looks of her fellow jurors. But as she filed into the courtroom, she couldn't help questioning her *own* judgment—as well as wondering who had seen them.

TONY SAT IN THE JURY BOX, his mind churning. On the one hand, there was nothing to be upset about. The judge had simply done her duty. But who the hell had reported them? Andrea's stricken look said it all. He doubted she was accustomed to having her integrity questioned and, the heck of it was, he felt responsible for putting her in that position. He was the one who'd talked her into dinner that first night. Looking at the situation objectively, he could see how it might appear to others. But anyone who knew Andrea would realize she was incapable of collusion or deceit. And she certainly didn't deserve this embarrassment.

After prolonged conversations between the judge and the attorneys, the judge asked the prosecutor to present his closing argument. With difficulty, Tony banished thoughts of Andrea and leaned forward, determined to concentrate while Bedford laid out his case.

"Ladies and gentlemen of the jury, according to Mrs.

Grant's testimony, we have before us a bright young man severely traumatized by personal tragedy, who, uncharacteristically we are told, is subject to outbursts of anger.'' He went on to tick off the facts as he saw them. The defendant owned the gun. His fingerprint was on the weapon. A T-shirt, unique in design and stained with blood consistent with that of the victim, belonged to the defendant and was found in his locker. The physical description of the assailant matched that of Darvin Ray. The defendant needed money. Finally, his emotional profile suggested volatility.

''The defense has tried to convince you that the defendant was framed for this crime. But have they produced a single witness who can corroborate their hypothesis? The answer is no, ladies and gentlemen. Have they given you any plausible reason to exonerate this defendant? No. Are you willing to take responsibility for turning this defendant out on the streets, knowing that the next time his anger erupts someone else may be a victim?'' He lowered his head and shook it sadly, then pausing a beat, looked into their eyes, one by one. ''Again, I'm confident your answer is 'No!'''

Tony leaned back in his seat. The prosecutor had emphasized the very points Tony found compelling. Although the evidence was circumstantial, it was convincing. He was curious to see what the defense attorney would do with her closing. She was a damn good orator, but you could drive a semi through the holes in her case.

ANDREA HAD HAD NO IDEA listening to the closing arguments would fill her with such tension. She willed her muscles to relax, but when she next looked down, her hands were clamped together. How could anyone be an attorney and undertake the responsibility for another hu-

man being's fate? Her stomach lurched. Oh, God. Soon it
would be her responsibility, along with eleven others.

During the prosecutor's remarks, she studied the faces
of Mrs. Bartelli and her daughter—grief, anger and hopefulness all were present. An open-and-shut case would
have made her decision automatic, but Mr. Bedford had
not convinced her that the police had charged the right
man.

She sat up expectantly and watched Ms. Lamb approach
the jury box. "Ladies and gentlemen, the prosecution
would have you believe that we have concocted some elaborate fiction in an attempt to exonerate my client, Darvin
Ray. But, if you will consider the evidence, you will see
that it is Mr. Bedford who is using smoke and mirrors here.
He has piled one half-truth on top of another in the hopes
that if the pile gets high enough, you'll decide it must
represent capital "T" Truth. But, I submit, a pile of manure, no matter how tall, is still merely a pile of manure."

She proceeded to recap Darvin's record at school and in
the community and to raise the question why he would
jeopardize his promising future by committing, at the very
least, armed robbery. An act that would hardly garner him
sufficient sums for college expenses. Furthermore, she suggested, bright as he was, in the unlikely event he had un-
dertaken such a venture, he would surely have planned and
executed it more intelligently.

As she talked, Andrea concentrated on listening for a
misstep, something that would cause her to change her
mind. But the arguments were flawless. The defense attorney concluded with the exact thoughts running through
Andrea's mind. "The prosecutors want a conviction, ladies
and gentleman. They cannot have the public think that law
enforcement is less than efficient or that there is still a
murderer roaming the city." She turned, directing their
attention to the wide-eyed teenager. "So, in their mis-

placed zeal, they have produced Darvin, a young man with no criminal record, as a convenient scapegoat.''

She approached the railing, fire blazing in her eyes. ''Since when are we as a society content to permit a young man with such potential to be sacrificed on the altar of expediency? Not, ladies and gentlemen, while I have breath to defend him and not while you, in your wisdom, agree that we are well beyond 'reasonable doubt' here. On the contrary, there is no case whatsoever. I ask you to make the only possible humane decision and acquit Darvin Ray. Thank you.''

Andrea sighed with relief. Thank goodness. The lady had done her job. In a few short hours, this ordeal would be over—for the jury and for that innocent young man.

DURING THE NOON RECESS, following which the judge would issue the jury instructions, Tony slogged to his office through snowdrifts and along sidewalks soggy with salt and melting ice. He wanted to be sure everything was nailed down, with no possibility of a repeat of Barry Fuller's blunder. Fortunately, Harrison Wainwright hadn't left yet for lunch and Tony was able to see him in his office.

After Tony gave a summary of the presentation he intended to make to the principals Wednesday in New York, Wainwright sat without speaking for several moments, hands folded, thumbs rotating. His silence put Tony on edge. Wainwright ought to be satisfied. Finally he spoke. ''You've invested a lot of time in this, Skee. I appreciate the work you've done. Will you be ready for the closing?''

Tony affected nonchalance. ''Why wouldn't I be?''

''You've been sidetracked with this trial. Had your mind elsewhere. We can't afford less than your best.''

''And that's what you'll get, Harrison. The case goes to the jury this afternoon. I have every reason to believe we'll reach a verdict soon. That'll give me the weekend and all day Monday and Tuesday to focus on Cyberace and DataTech.''

Wainwright looked thoughtful. "This afternoon, huh?" Tony nodded. "That should give you enough time." He rose to his feet and, by way of dismissing Tony, said, "I hope all goes smoothly in court."

Since he'd missed lunch, Tony grabbed a bag of chips and a soda from the lobby vendor, then beat it back to the courthouse, his nerves on edge every step of the way. Had he screwed up by not getting out of jury duty somehow? He couldn't let anything—even Andrea—distract him from the most important negotiation of his career.

He reached the jury room just as the bailiff was checking roll. He barely had time to say hello to Andrea. It might have been better if he hadn't, because she whispered to him, "What do you think we should do about the dinner with Nicky's grandparents?"

Hell! In his preoccupation with the trial and business, he'd forgotten all about that little date with destiny. A lobotomy might be preferable to the ordeal he imagined the Porters had in mind for him. Worse yet, there went an entire evening of work.

"Why don't we wait to see if we get a verdict today before we decide?"

She nodded, looking relieved. Obviously their little session with the judge had shaken her. Appearances mattered.

ANDREA TRIED HER BEST to follow the judge's instructions concerning the statutes regarding aggravated murder and the duty of jurors to set aside their own intuitions and biases in the interests of weighing only the evidence presented. Yet, despite her best intentions, she found her mind periodically wandering to the hurried phone conversation she'd had with Phil at lunch. He'd said the store was inundated with customers, so much so that he was ringing up sales as he talked. That was good news. But she still had qualms about leaving him shorthanded on one of the busiest shopping days of the year.

The judge's voice cut into her thoughts. Well, nothing could be done about Never-Never Land while she had this critical afternoon ahead of her. Nor about the strange look on Tony's face when she'd mentioned dinner at the Porters'.

"Your first duty is to select a foreman. Should you need to review any of the testimony or exhibits, ring for the bailiff. Any communication with the bailiff or with me must be in written form signed and dated by the foreman. When you reach a verdict, please notify the bailiff." The judge drew herself up in her chair and paused to look at them. "Ladies and gentlemen of the jury, the case of the State of Ohio versus Darvin Ray is in your hands."

After she stood in response to the bailiff's "All rise," Andrea swayed for a moment. The enormity of their task fell on her shoulders like a sledgehammer. Before she followed Dottie out of the courtroom, she took one last look at Darvin's ashen face and, for a brief moment, feared she might vomit. Blindly she followed the others into the jury room and swallowed two or three times when the bailiff closed the door behind him with a finality that shook her.

As if they didn't know quite what to do with themselves, the jurors milled around, some getting drinks of water, others using the rest rooms. Finally, however, when they were all seated around the table, an unnatural silence fell over them. They'd been together for a week, yet now no one seemed interested in speaking. Some bowed their heads, unwilling even to meet the eyes of the others. Count on Chet. He couldn't stand it. "What the hell's the mattah with you guys? Ya want outta here, doncha? Let's get this show on the road!"

Arnelle Kerry, who sat to Tony's right near the other

end of the table, picked up the tablet in front of her place and tamped it. "Second the motion."

Beside Andrea, Dottie cleared her throat. "I guess we need a foreman."

"Or forewoman," Shayla cracked.

"Any volunteers?" Charlie Franklin, the young Case-Western Reserve student asked.

Silence followed. By breathing deeply, Andrea tamed the butterflies in her stomach. Who would want the job of steering this group through the complicated deliberation process?

Tony nodded toward the silver-headed gentleman at the far end of the table. "I nominate Mr. Feldman."

Although he didn't seem eager to accept what by now was a vote of acclamation, Willard Feldman agreed to serve. Again the room fell quiet and all eyes rested on their "volunteer." They expected him to take action. He spoke quietly. "Perhaps we should begin by asking if there are any questions about the instructions."

"Sounds reasonable," Tony agreed.

"The instructions seemed clear," Charlie said. "We review the evidence, take a vote, and we keep doing that until we get a unanimous verdict."

"Whadda we need to review the evidence for?" Chet asked. "We were all there, listenin' to the same buncha bull. Let's just vote so we can get outta here."

Andrea found herself speaking without making the conscious decision to do so. "Darvin's whole life is involved here. The least we can do is take the necessary time to review the evidence so we have a basis for discussion."

"Discussion? Why do we need one if we all agree anyway?" Dottie asked.

"Very well," the foreman said. "Let's take a straw vote to determine how close we might be to a verdict."

When all had voted, the foreman collected the ballots,

then carefully counted them out in two piles. "Seven guilty, five not guilty."

A groan went up from Chet, Arnelle and several others.

"Now what?" Shayla asked.

The foreman looked around the table. "Any suggestions?"

This was insane, Andrea thought. How many people serving on juries had ever had any practice at it? What were they supposed to be doing?

Tony shoved his pad to the center of the table. "Why don't we go around the room and each lay out the reasons we feel as we do? Might give us food for thought."

"Good idea," Willard responded.

Tony continued. "Could we agree not to interrupt so that each person gets a fair shot at expressing their ideas? In other words, no arguing."

A hum of general agreement followed. Andrea appreciated the skillful way Tony focused the group on the matter at hand and at the same time attempted to circumvent dissension. After four others had commented, it was Andrea's turn. To that point, only the college man, Charlie, had argued for acquittal, because he felt the framing theory was a plausible explanation and therefore raised doubt in his mind.

Andrea chose her words carefully. "I am troubled that neither of the eyewitnesses could positively identify the defendant as the perpetrator. Also, he is a young man with no history of trouble who had a bright future, so I think it's highly unlikely that even an upsetting event like his mother's murder would cause him to jeopardize it."

Relieved to pass to the next person, she sat quietly, studying her hands, primly folded on the table like those of a model pupil. From across the way, though, she could feel someone staring at her. Slowly she lifted her eyes.

Tony gazed at her with a look she couldn't interpret. Puzzlement, maybe? Or disappointment?

When his turn came, with a sinking heart, she learned what the look had signaled. He spoke forcefully, decisively. "Darvin Ray is guilty. His T-shirt had Bartelli's blood on it, he has no alibi, he had a motive, and, like it or not, his gun shot the bullets that killed Angelo Bartelli."

Once again, bile rose in Andrea's throat. Oh, God. In Tony's voice she'd heard not one shred of pity.

Then a second thought overwhelmed her. Did she really even know the man?

BY FOUR O'CLOCK, the jurors were getting testy. Tony was familiar with this phase of group dynamics. The facade of civility had worn off, and personal agendas were moving to the forefront. Even two hours of being closeted was starting to affect those who suffered in any degree from claustrophobia, and as it became increasingly obvious that they were a long way from unanimity, tempers began to fray.

"People, let's try to reason with one another here," Tony suggested. "Getting overly emotional doesn't help anybody."

He might as well have saved his breath because Chet had already started in on Charlie. "Damn it all, kid, how can you buy that cock-and-bull story about a frame job? Can't ya see? Darvin's trying to save his sorry ass."

The foreman cleared his throat and shot Chet an admonishing look. "Sir, could you moderate your language?"

"Moderate? Hell, it's gonna take a little tough talk to move this group off dead center."

Tony spoke in a mild tone. "Chet, I think you'll find we'll get further with logical arguments than with loud talk."

Arnelle, who'd been combing her flamboyant mass of red hair, spoke up. "Whatever. Face it, we've been talkin' till we're blue in the face. But the five of you won't give it up. What's it gonna take?"

Roy Smith pulled a handkerchief out of his pocket and blew his nose. Tony wondered if it was an avoidance technique. The man was afraid of his own shadow, and now that he was on the unpopular side of the issue, he was decidedly uncomfortable, darting continual glances at Andrea that seemed to say, "Help me."

Ferris Klein, the city sanitation worker, rubbed his face, bearded with a five o'clock shadow. "Tell me again why you don't think the murderer could have been someone else?"

Before Chet could start in, Tony carefully and thoroughly reviewed the evidence. Motive, opportunity, weapon, DNA testimony. When he'd finished, Dottie turned to face the holdout. "There. Like the man said, it's perfectly logical. And if I were you, " she raised one eyebrow knowingly, "I wouldn't assume the defendant always looks as clean-cut as he did in court." She leaned forward as if conveying ultimate truth. "You know these lawyers take prisoners to the barber and fix them up with fancy clothes so we'll think they're model citizens."

"Gimme a minute," the man said, closing his eyes and slumping back in his chair.

Tony waited, hoping for the defection, suspecting that if one broke, the rest would soon follow. He pulled back his cuff and looked at his watch. Jeez! Pushing four-thirty. It would be a hell of an inconvenience if this thing dragged over into Monday. Already Saturday was looking all too probable.

"Okay." Heads swiveled toward Klein, who'd straightened up and opened his eyes. "You got a point. I kept thinkin' Darvin looked too...nice. But, I see what you mean.'' He drummed his fingers on the table, then looked at the foreman. ''All right. Change my vote.''

''So we're eight to four, correct?'' Willard glanced over the rims of his glasses.

''I—I'll—make that nine to three,'' Smith croaked, deliberately ignoring Andrea's incredulous look.

Tony stuck his hands in his pockets and sat jiggling his change. Two down, three to go—Willard, Charlie and Andrea. The men might ultimately be persuaded. But Andrea? How were they going to get her to come around? He'd heard the conviction, even passion, in her voice. He could appreciate where she was coming from with her assessment of Ray's character, and it was her nature to see the best in every situation. It would require powerful reasoning for her to send a kid with—what had she said earlier?—a bright future off to prison for the rest of his life.

When Shayla asked, ''Anybody else hungry?'' the question was greeted by near unanimity.

''I'll ask the bailiff for some snacks,'' the foreman suggested.

Others took that as license to get up and move around. Tony noticed that no one approached Andrea. Looking pensive, she helped herself to a glass of water. Her face was pale and she'd chewed off most of her lipstick. He wanted to go to her, hold her. But, at the same time, he was irritated with her. She was the key. In any negotiation it usually came down to this. You make some progress, then one determined person with a different agenda creates a logjam.

He brought himself up short. He was being unfair. She wasn't the only holdout, and she did seem to be listening intently to each person's viewpoint. He watched Shayla walk over and touch her arm. Andrea smiled wanly, then just shook her head. If Shayla couldn't reach her…

"Sorry, folks," the foreman announced loudly. "No food allowed during deliberations."

Arnelle threw back her head, flailing her arms dramatically. "Gawd, even prisoners get bread with their water!"

A chorus of grumbles went up. Tony noticed Andrea's hand shake as she set down her water glass.

"Let's get started," Willard said.

Chet glared at Andrea. "Okay, we've heard from the kid here and from old Willard again. Whaddaya got to say for yourself, little lady?" The contempt in his voice set Tony's teeth on edge.

Andrea, her back stiff, faced her inquisitor. "I fully understand that Darvin's gun killed Mr. Bartelli, just as I concede that it was his shirt with Mr. Bartelli's blood on it. And that Darvin's thumbprint was on the revolver. But don't you see?" She looked imploringly around the table. "The fingerprint is inconclusive, and no one, certainly not the two eyewitnesses, can prove to me that it was Darvin in the store that night."

"Oh, jeez," Chet knocked his forehead against the table. "Whaddya want—a picture?"

"As a matter of fact, yes. And speaking of pictures, that figure on the videotape could have been any number of young men."

"Only those five-foot-six or seven," the prune-faced elderly woman said.

"And Darvin's only five-foot-five," Andrea snapped. "Even the experts couldn't establish with precision the height of the perpetrator."

"Crap," Arnelle muttered. "Does this mean you're not changing your mind?"

Andrea's face was flaming. "That's exactly what it means. I have reasonable doubts about Darvin's guilt. And I am not—repeat *not*—going to be railroaded into a decision I might regret the rest of my life."

The table was rimmed by faces with raised eyebrows. Tony was torn by admiration for her spirit and frustration with her reasoning. God, she was such a softie. Somebody needed to keep the pressure on her, though, and nobody else was leaping into the fray.

"Andrea," he began quietly, "nobody's trying to railroad you. All of us feel terrible for the Bartelli family, and nobody wants to make a mistake here. But the judge instructed us to use the facts—not emotions, suppositions or previous experiences—to arrive at a verdict. How much of your decision is based on your feelings about the case and how much on the facts themselves?"

She looked as if he'd slapped her, then recovering, stared at him defiantly. "Are you suggesting I'm an overwrought, emotional female?"

He held up his hands, palms out. "Whoa, I didn't mean to offend you, but, gender distinctions aside, yes, I'm wondering if you aren't basing your decision more on intuition, emotions, call it what you will, than on logic."

She stood and faced him across the table. "Logic? What's logical about a young man with all kinds of opportunity ahead of him throwing his future away in some senseless convenience store robbery? Darvin isn't that big a fool."

He couldn't stop himself. "And how would you know? All you know is what that bleeding-heart social worker told you."

"'Bleeding heart'? Are you sure you're not the one making value judgments based on gender? Why wouldn't that woman be telling the truth? She surely doesn't want a murderer teaching computer courses at her community center!"

Tony had had enough. He stood up, nearly knocking the chair over, and began pacing. "How can you be so damn trusting?"

The air was charged. Tears of…what? rage? disappointment? stood in her eyes. "How can you be so cynical?"

"Where I come from, it goes with the territory. Not all of us have had your advantages."

"Don't patronize me. This is about Darvin Ray. His *life,* for God's sake. Not about me, nor you either, for that matter."

No one spoke.

Tony stopped dead. He couldn't believe it! He'd lost control. She'd egged him over the edge. Something a good negotiator never lets happen. Something *he'd* never let happen. Only his father had ever gotten to him that way. How could this have happened with Andrea?

But, damn it, she was wrong. Wrong and pigheaded! With despair, he saw hours and hours of this impasse stretching before him. Hours during which he would face Andrea's unrelenting disapproval.

She glared at him, then with practiced dignity sank into her chair. "To answer your original question, based on the *facts* as I see them, I have reasonable doubt Darvin Ray is guilty."

Struggling for composure, he grabbed the back of his chair and fixed his eyes first on Willard Feldman, then on Charlie. "What about you two? Surely you can see where the facts lead?"

Charlie rose to his feet, tucking his fingers into the back pockets of his Levi's. "Sorry, man. I can't go with you. In my gut and based on holes in the testimony, I don't believe the guy's guilty."

Tony turned to the foreman, who was shaking his head sadly. "Neither do I, folks. Neither do I."

"What the hell do we do now?" Chet exploded. "I gotta tell you, I'm sick of you people. I want outta here!" As he spoke, he poked an index finger in the foreman's face. Others picked up the refrain. "Yeah, outta here." "I can't believe this!'' ''Are they stupid? What's so hard to see?''

Feldman got to his feet and waved his hands for order. ''All right. See what you think of this. We'll take one more written ballot. Then if we still lack agreement—'' he was interrupted by a snort of disbelief from Chet ''—I'll inform the bailiff that we're unable to arrive at a unanimous verdict.''

''You mean a hung jury?'' Arnelle's eyes lighted up.

A dim ray of hope penetrated Tony's gloom and self-disgust. He heard someone, Shayla maybe, say, ''Sounds like a great idea.''

''All right, then.''

Quickly the jurors once again marked their ballots.

ELECTRICITY FILLED THE ROOM as the twelve awaited the judge's response. On the verge of tears, Andrea covered her stomach with one arm. She was both angry and humiliated. How could these people—Tony among them— assume that because she was female, she couldn't be logical? Why hadn't Tony confronted Charlie or Willard as forcefully as he had her?

Or was his attack something personal after all? Maybe their differences—her idealism, his cynicism—were insurmountable.

The animosity on the faces of most of her fellow jurors was very, very real. Except for Shayla. Even though she and Shayla didn't agree about the verdict, Shayla had never succumbed to the rampant emotionalism in the room. Why couldn't the others understand that differences of opinion happen?

She'd been stunned when Tony had cast a guilty vote. Now that she thought about it, maybe she shouldn't have been. She'd assumed, because they'd had so much fun and—she choked back a sob—shared so much more, that they saw eye to eye. And the way he'd been with Nicky—warm, helpful, compassionate—she'd naturally thought he'd have that same outlook on Darvin.

And where had that remark about her "advantages" come from? That was unworthy of the gentle man with whom she'd made love. And it had hurt. Badly. Irreparably?

She reviewed the past week with amazement. How could she have thought she knew Tony? Have entertained the idea that maybe, the two of them... Even without looking up, she felt his eyes on her. But she couldn't face him. Not now. She'd cry. And, damn it, she wouldn't give him or Chet or any of them that satisfaction.

At the sound of a knock, the room quieted. Willard opened the door and received from the bailiff a folded piece of paper.

"Hurry up and read it, damn it," Chet growled.

Andrea raised her eyes to the foreman, who unfolded the note, then scanned it without speaking. The tension in the room was palpable. He adjusted his glasses and began reading aloud. "Please continue your deliberations. If you have not arrived at a unanimous verdict by seven-thirty, I request that you adjourn, then reconvene tomorrow morning at nine o'clock."

A communal groan went up before those who had been standing slowly found their seats again.

Andrea clenched her fists, determined to weather what would surely be another storm of protest directed straight at her.

CHAPTER NINE

ANDREA FLUNG HER PURSE on the kitchen counter, shucked her coat, then put the kettle on to boil. She was drained of the capacity to perform any but the simplest tasks. Right now all she wanted was a cup of tea and a few moments of peace and quiet. It seemed eons since she'd arrived at the courthouse this morning. In retrospect, the hours felt like both a blur and slow-motion torture. It was agonizing to be the target of verbal attack from so many. And especially from someone she'd begun to trust…and care for.

Mechanically she retrieved a mug from the cupboard, dangled the tea bag over the rim and poured in the boiling water. Cupping the drink between her hands, she wandered into the living room and sank down in her favorite chair. The first swallow of tea renewed hope that she'd feel warm again after being chilled all afternoon by the shock of what had happened. How was she going to marshal her resources for tomorrow's inevitable confrontation? She closed her eyes. She'd have to. No way was the evidence strong enough to condemn Darvin Ray to a life in prison. She'd just have to endure the contemptuous looks of some of her fellow jurors and act from the courage of her convictions. She lacked the energy even to ponder which fellow juror had blown the whistle on her and Tony. Did it really matter?

At the sound of the doorbell, she got to her feet. That would be Daisy bringing Nicky home. Dear Daisy! When Nicky had objected to spending another full day with his grandparents, Daisy had taken him under her wing for the afternoon. Walking toward the door, Andrea had one last thought about the trial. She could almost understand where people like Chet and Arnelle were coming from and obviously Shayla had her reasons. But she'd thought Tony had more discernment. Obviously another error of judgment.

Her outlook improved the minute she clapped eyes on Daisy and Nicky. His effusive greeting and Daisy's infectious smile were guaranteed mood elevators.

"We come bearing gifts," Daisy said, holding out a brown bag. "Chinese food."

Andrea, suddenly aware of being ravenous, gratefully took it from her. "Sounds wonderful."

Daisy threw her black satin-lined opera cape over the sofa back and held out her arms. "You look like you could use a hug."

"At the very least."

The hug, combined with the tea and food, made Andrea feel almost human again. As they ate, Nicky chattered about the fun he and Daisy had had going from antique store to antique store hunting for vintage clothing for a theater production Daisy was costuming.

Daisy ruffled his hair. "Nicky made a great hat model."

The boy leaned forward eagerly. "Andie, I got to try on a top hat and a rebel cap and—what was that weird thing, Daisy?"

"Ah, *mon petit ami,* you mean zee artiste's beret?" Daisy struck a pose.

Nicky giggled. "You're funny."

The muscles in Andrea's abdomen eased still more. Their playfulness was welcome after a day of lunacy.

When they'd finished the meal, Daisy threw down three fortune cookies. "Okay, gang. The big moment. Go ahead, Nicky, pick one."

Nicky hesitated, then selected the cookie nearest Andrea, carefully unwrapped it, bit it open and pulled out the tiny scrap of paper. He scowled, then read his fortune aloud. "The wise man invests in health, then wealth." He tossed down the strip of paper. "That's stupid."

Andrea grinned. "Maybe that's why Mimi tries to get you to eat broccoli." The look she received in response required no translation.

"Ha! Listen to this, you two." With a flourish, Daisy read in her best thespian voice, "'A mysterious stranger will bring abundant blessings to your life.'" She waggled her eyebrows. "A tall, dark, handsome one who's not *that* much of a stranger, I hope."

Andrea slowly flattened the curled edges of hers and, scanning her fortune, felt a premonition of dread.

Daisy leaned on her elbows and stared at Andrea. "To-*night,* pal!"

"Yeah, Andie. What's it say?" Nicky asked.

The words swam. "It says," she took a deep breath, "Where truth abides, there justice and love prevail."

Nicky screwed up his face. "What's that mean?"

Daisy cast an appraising look at Andrea, then quickly rose and led Nicky away from the table. "That means it's bedtime, squirt. Why don't you go get ready, then Andie can come up and tuck you in?"

Nicky stood uncertainly, then shrugged. "Whatever. Thanks, Daisy, for the ice cream and the hats and stuff."

"My pleasure."

Andrea watched as he started up the stairs. Before she could begin clearing the table, Daisy sat down, tilted her chair back and folded her arms. "Okay, Andrea, let's have it." For once the pixie mouth was set in a straight line.

"Have what?"

"Oh, so now you're going to play innocent. Won't work." She raised an accusing brow. "Not with your old pal Daisy who's known you since second grade. What's bothering you? The handsome stranger who's entered *your* life?''

She and Daisy did go way back, and through the years, they'd withheld few secrets from each other. ''No, I'm just tired, Daisy. This trial is getting me down, especially since I really need to be at the store.''

''How's the case going?''

Andrea fought the temptation to tell Daisy everything. ''We're in deliberations now. I have to go back tomorrow.''

''What's the deal? Can't you all agree?''

Andrea sighed. ''I'm sorry, but I can't discuss it.''

Her friend zeroed in. ''I'm not so sure that's all.'' She tilted Andrea's chin up. ''What about what's-his-name?''

''Tony,'' Andrea mumbled absently.

''Tony, then.''

''We had some nice times, but nothing that's going to last beyond this trial.''

''And you're disappointed?''

Andrea thought about the question. She was irked with herself. Embarrassed, too. She should have known better than to fall so quickly for Tony. That uncalled-for remark today about her advantages, whatever that meant, and his strange reaction to his father's phone call on Thanksgiving troubled her. There was an underlying bitterness in him. And yet…despite all that, perversely, she *was* disappointed. She shrugged.

''C'mon, girlfriend. 'Where truth abides, justice and love prevail.'''

Andrea smiled sardonically. ''Truth may lead to justice. But not necessarily to love.''

''You talk like the voice of experience.''

Wearily, Andrea rose to her feet, gathering up the utensils. ''You could say that.''

"Do you need me to keep Nicky tomorrow? I'm hitting the flea markets for cheap vintage jewelry."

"Daisy, you've already done so much."

Daisy grabbed the takeout containers and followed Andrea into the kitchen. "You act as if being with the kid is some kind of work. We get along great. Frankly, I'd love the company."

Andrea studied Daisy and could tell that, as always, she meant every word she said. "Thanks, I'd appreciate your help."

"It's settled. Now you run on upstairs and tell Nicky good-night while I clean up."

Nicky was sprawled on his bed reading. "Did you brush your teeth?" Andrea asked as she hung his robe over the back of a chair.

He looked up from his book. "Yes. How come you always ask me that?"

"Hmm. There must be a reason." She grinned at him, then sat beside him on the edge of the bed. "Nicky, I'm sorry, but I have to go back to court tomorrow."

"It's Saturday," he protested.

"I know, honey. But Daisy's promised to take you on another of her adventures. Won't that be fun?"

He scooted back against the headboard and closed his book. "Sure. But I miss you. And I was kinda hoping—" He stopped speaking and ran his fingers nervously over the cover of his book.

"Hoping what?"

His eyes, through the lenses of his glasses, were large and hopeful. "That you and me and Tony could, like, do something?"

"Oh, honey." Andrea's heart sank. Surely Nicky hadn't already gotten his hopes up, not after one short week. "I'm afraid that's not possible."

"But I'll see him tomorrow night, won't I?"

Oh, Lord, the dinner with Claudia and Bert. How could it have slipped her mind? Easily, apparently, under the stress of the jury deliberations. The last thing she needed was a ceremonial social appearance with Tony, but if she canceled, Claudia would have the satisfaction of being able to say, "I told you so." Right now, though, even that sounded preferable to an evening of forced politeness with Tony. Carefully, Andrea removed the book from Nicky's hands and tucked the covers around him. "We'll see, honey." She bent over and hugged him before turning off the light and leaving the room.

At the head of the stairs, she paused, gripping the bannister. It was all too much—Tony, Darvin, the jurors, Nicky, the shop, the Porters. She was dead on her feet. She started down the steps.

In the living room, Daisy was fastening the voluminous cape around her shoulders. "Gotta dash. A mysterious man awaits me at The Jazz Spot." She pecked Andrea on the cheek. "Get some sleep, sweetie. I'll pick Nicky up at eight." Then with a swish, she was out the door.

Daisy was a lifesaver, in more ways than one. Crazy and eccentric, she had a heart of gold. And Andrea had needed her tonight.

A HALF-EATEN PIZZA, the mozzarella cold and congealing, sat on the counter. Tony slumped on the kitchen barstool gazing vacantly at his bizarre Picasso print with the surreal, accusing eye smack-dab in the center. Okay, okay, he'd blown it big time. Maybe Andrea had been right after all. Apparently he couldn't separate the trial and his social life. She had every right to her opinion about Ray's guilt or innocence, and he had to admit she'd brought up some pertinent points in the kid's defense.

So why had he acted that way? How could she have aroused such a spontaneous and unworthy reaction from him? Damned if he knew. But there was no doubt about it. He'd hurt her feelings and he didn't have a clue what to do about it. Normally he was on the outside orchestrating solutions. But, in this case, he was trapped in the middle with nobody manipulating the strings.

He picked up his napkin, balled it in his fist, then threw it directly at the offensive geometric eye. He needed advice and he needed it quickly. Before he could talk himself out of the notion, he reached for the phone and punched in Kelli's number. Patrick answered and after some guy talk, Tony asked for Kelli. While he waited for Patrick to put her on the line, he nearly chickened out. He wasn't accustomed to having any female tie him in knots the way Andrea had.

"Tony, what's up?"

Kelli's warm, breathless voice filled him with hope. "I need your help, and before you get too smug, *yes,* it's about a woman."

"Heck, and I thought you were going to surprise me." Then her tone turned more serious. "What is it?"

"I've screwed up. Royally." He waited for the sarcastic comment that didn't come.

"Hmm. Sounds serious. Tell me about it."

Without going into the trial particulars, he related Andrea's accusation about his cynicism and his subsequent ill-considered retort.

"Do you care about this woman?" Kelli asked.

He swallowed several times. "Yes."

"Then what are you calling me for? You know exactly what you need to do. So get on with it!"

ANDREA HAD JUST COLLAPSED against the soft pillows when the phone rang. She sat up, grabbing the receiver before another ring would awaken Nicky. "Hello?"

"Andrea, it's Tony."

She clutched the receiver, furious at the way her pulse quickened. "Hi." She couldn't think of a thing she wanted or needed to say to him. Not anymore.

"Are you okay?"

"Why wouldn't I be?"

"Well, I can think of one or two reasons."

"None that we need to discuss." She knew she sounded curt. She didn't want to be petty, just very, very careful.

"Andrea, I owe you an apology. I was way out of line today."

"Yes, you were."

"I'm sorry."

"Tony, I'm tired. Can't this wait?"

"I don't think so. You didn't deserve that crack about your advantages, and I'm not proud of where it comes from."

"And where is that?"

"From an overdeveloped case of self-pity and class envy."

For a proud man, that had to be a difficult admission. "I don't understand."

"No," he sighed, "you wouldn't. You're much more tolerant and trusting than I am." He paused before continuing. "Andrea, what I'm about to tell you is not in any way an excuse for my behavior. Only an explanation, and an inadequate one at that. I'd like it if you'd hear me out."

"Go ahead." Andrea listened, struggling to remain objective, dispassionate. Yet the longer he talked and the more he told her about the lonely little boy he'd been—brokenhearted by his mother's death, angry about his father's cold indifference, determined to take on the world—the more she felt her natural compassion coming into play. No wonder he related so well to Nicky.

When he finally finished, the phone line virtually crackled with expectancy. "Well?" he said.

"Thank you. I accept your apology." That was all she could give him at the moment. She was confused and exhausted.

"I think there's one other thing we should discuss." The silence lengthened. "Are you upset about Wednesday night? Especially in light of…today?"

Upset? That wasn't it exactly. He made love like… Damn, her body wasn't supposed to be involved here, yet she couldn't help quivering with remembered passion. No, she wasn't upset. She was furious with herself for having so little control, for not waiting to learn more about the kind of person he really was before… "We're both adults, Tony. I knew what I was doing."

"Good. Uh, I'm glad. Me, too." He hesitated. "Nick doing all right?"

"Fine."

"About dinner with the Porters… If you want to forget about it, I'll understand."

"Let's not make any decisions tonight. We've both had a long day." Besides, she needed time to think, to consider the ramifications of her choices.

"Okay. We'll talk about it after we see how the morning goes."

Canceling the dinner with the Porters would solve some of her problems all right. But Nicky would be disappointed. Somehow he had to be let down gently. She shut her eyes against the projected image of Claudia's smug, superior smile. And never mind that, despite everything that had happened today, just hearing Tony's voice caused her to tremble with desire.

"Andrea?" He sounded tentative.

"Yes?"

"I hope there's a way back for me."

"Tony, I don't know what to say."

"That's all right. I don't expect an answer now. See you in court tomorrow."

"Good night." Carefully she replaced the receiver and rolled over on her side, cradling her pillow in both arms. *In court tomorrow.* He'd see her, all right. He'd watch disbelievingly when, once again, she voted for acquittal. And when she looked at him, what would she see? A talented, if assertive adult or the valiant and needful boy he'd been? Maybe still was.

An hour and a half later she was still staring at the clock by her bed, the digital readout changing with devilish slowness. She was too tired to sleep. The paradox didn't escape her. And the harder she tried to relax, the more clearly she saw Darvin Ray's soulful look fixed on her, as if everything depended upon her vote.

And maybe it did.

TONY'S EYES FELT SCRATCHY from his restless night, and his throat was hoarse with repeated attempts to sway the holdouts to the majority opinion. How long could this ordeal drag on? He didn't want to think about what a delay might mean for his prospects of getting to New York rested and prepared. Surely if something didn't break soon, the judge would be forced to declare a hung jury.

He glanced across the table. Andrea looked exhausted. Dark circles underlined her troubled eyes and her normally rosy complexion was ashen. He leaned back in his chair and permitted his mind to wander while Shayla once more explained her reasoning and the impact the DNA testimony had made on her.

Despite last night's phone conversation with Andrea, it was no surprise their differing opinions and his stupid remark had created distance between them. Not just about this trial, but maybe about their approaches to life. She undoubtedly saw him as a coldhearted cynic. And Andrea? If ever anybody was too trusting, it was her.

How difficult could it be to admit he'd fallen for her? To admit how natural and right they'd felt together Wednesday and Thursday? For the first time, he'd actually begun, on the fringes of his mind, to imagine a future with a woman.

But there were any number of reasons to avoid further entanglement. Their life-styles were very different. He could not afford, especially now, to be sidetracked from his career.

Willard's voice brought him back to the tense scene in front of him. "Is there something further anyone wants to say before we vote again?"

"If we're still deadlocked, are you gonna send a note to the judge?" Dottie asked.

The foreman sighed heavily. "I don't think there's any other choice."

The silence in the room was broken by the sound of the heating unit kicking in. Willard examined each face, his eyebrows raised in question. Then his gaze fell on Andrea.

She grasped the edge of the table with her long, finely shaped fingers, then lifted her eyes. Her voice, soft and tentative, competed with the whir of the fan. "I realize that many of you do not understand my position. I hope, however, you respect my right to differ with you, as I respect yours to differ with me. The judge talked at length about the concept of reasonable doubt. What's at stake here is the difference between possibly sending an innocent man to prison or letting a guilty one go free. I'm well aware that Darvin Ray may be guilty."

Her voice grew stronger. "But I don't know that for a fact." She paused as if marshaling her thoughts. "And until there is something more compelling than circumstantial evidence to convince me otherwise, in my heart I do not believe Darvin shot Angelo Bartelli. I cannot in good conscience, then, vote guilty.''

"Hurry up, Feldman," Chet barked. He slammed a fist down on the table. "Nothin's gonna change here."

"Very well, ladies and gentlemen. Mark your ballots."

As Tony scribbled his "guilty" on the slip of paper, he thought about Andrea. Beneath that gentle, optimistic exterior was a hell of a woman. One not only strong enough to advance her opinions in the face of stiff opposition and withstand hours of censure in this room, but one strong enough to take on the care of her nephew and launch a successful business. He glanced up then, and something volcanic erupted inside him. Andrea's huge, wonderful eyes were fixed on him—with an expression at once both intimate and regretful.

He barely heard the vote result—still nine to three. If she agreed to go through with the dinner this evening, what would the night hold? The last thing he wanted to do was subject himself to the scrutiny of the Porters, but it could be his final shot at redeeming himself with Andrea.

The jurors, many of them numb from too much talk and too little sleep, waited quietly, lost in their own thoughts, until the bailiff reappeared with a note from the judge.

"The judge wants to see us in the courtroom," Willard announced.

Hope brightened the juror's faces, as they hastily assembled and filed into the jury box.

As he walked down the row behind Andrea's on the way to his seat, Tony had the desperate urge to reach out and touch her blond hair, to graze her shoulder with his fingers, but, of course, he didn't.

After what seemed an interminable amount of time, the judge, her lips pursed, uttered the magic words Tony had been waiting for. "Ladies and gentlemen of the jury, this court appreciates your efforts to arrive at a unanimous verdict in this case. However, since there has been no movement since late yesterday afternoon, I must conclude there is no reasonable expectation of a unanimous verdict. Mr. Foreman, is that correct?''

"Yes, Your Honor.''

"Very well, then. I declare this jury deadlocked. The defendant is remanded to custody pending further proceedings in this case.'' She glanced at the court stenographer to be sure she had recorded her words, then turned back to the jury. "Thank you, ladies and gentlemen, for your valuable service in this important privilege of citizenship.''

Hardly were her last words out than the bailiff's "All rise,'' brought the jurors to their feet. Tony felt as if a heavy weight had been removed from his shoulders.

Back in the jury room, there were a few desultory handshakes and goodbyes, but, mostly his fellow jurors fled like kids released from school for summer vacation. As Charlie Franklin passed him, Tony overheard him say to Chet, "No thank-God-it's-over celebration tonight for me. I've got a part-time job over at Le Bistro.'' Well, Tony mused, that clears up one mystery. He loitered, watching Shayla and Andrea exchange phone numbers, then hugs, before sidling alongside Andrea. Shayla sent him an encouraging smile before leaving the room. Only he and Andrea remained.

He hadn't felt so tongue-tied with a female since junior high. He wanted to touch her, to reassure her, yet he had no idea how such a gesture would be received. "Did you ride the Rapid in?'' She nodded. "Could I walk you to the terminal? Buy you a cup of coffee?''

She buttoned up her coat. "No coffee, thanks. I desperately need to get to the store.''

He handed her her purse, then cupped her elbow, propelling her toward the elevator. "I'll settle for the walk then.'' They didn't speak again until they stepped out on the street where a weak sun struggled to send light through a misty cloud cover. ''You've got guts, Andrea,'' he finally said.

She walked along a few paces, head down, before responding. ''I don't think it was a matter of guts. I was scared the entire time. What if I made a mistake?''

''I think each of us had those feelings.''

She looked at him. ''But you seemed so certain.''

He nodded thoughtfully. ''As certain as I could be with the evidence presented.''

''But how could—'' she stopped speaking then and shook her head sadly. ''I think this is a topic we probably shouldn't discuss, even now. Not if we want to remain friends.''

''Friends?'' The word had a neutral connotation that suggested nothing of the wild, wonderful intimacy they'd experienced Wednesday night.

The look on her face signaled that that was exactly how she'd intended the word. ''Yes. Friends.''

He put his hand on the small of her back to steer her around a large puddle in the middle of the street. ''I don't want this to be over, Andrea.'' God, what was he saying? ''I'll settle for friends. But I'd like more than that.''

She didn't say anything until they were at the entrance of the Terminal Building. She turned and faced him. ''I'm not sure, Tony. We don't have to decide anything right now, though.''

''Of course. Except for whether you want me to come with you to the Porters' tonight.'' He hoped she couldn't sense the fear in him.

She searched his eyes for a long moment, then said, ''Nicky would be disappointed if you didn't join us.''

He expelled his held breath. ''I'll be there. What time should I pick you up?''

"Six forty-five?"

"Fine." He stood, his hands hanging impotently at his sides. But just as she turned to leave, he couldn't help himself. "Andrea!"

She hesitated and without pausing to think what he was doing, he hugged her close and kissed her gently, aware of her soft lips on his, aware that he'd acted with complete spontaneity.

When she pulled away, Andrea gazed up at him, a puzzled look on her face. Pedestrians scurried past them and pigeons fluttered overhead. But for the space of an instant, when she joined the crowd headed into the terminal, he felt as lost and uncertain as he could ever remember.

"ANDIE, WHEN WILL Tony be here?" Nicky had followed her from the back door, through the kitchen and dining room and up the stairs. Now he stood in the doorway of her bedroom, his hair awry, his voice pleading.

Andrea felt her patience unraveling, the dark miasma of exhaustion settling over her like a dense fog. "I've already told you, Nicky. Quarter to seven." She glanced at her watch. "That gives us exactly forty-five minutes to transform ourselves." She eyed him up and down. "Starting with you." His baggy jeans and chocolate-stained sweatshirt would never do in Claudia's formal dining room. "March into the shower, young man. Then put on your nice cords, a shirt and tie."

He groaned. "A tie!"

"Yes, a tie. You can wear your green sweater instead of a sports jacket if you like." He stood there scowling, as if it was all her fault that social expectations included a dress code. "Nicky." Her tone sharpened.

"Okay, okay." He shuffled off, muttering just audibly enough so she couldn't fail to hear. "I hate ties."

Andrea crumpled onto her bed, massaging her temples

with her fingertips. Her morning in court had been nerve-racking. Should she have argued more forcefully? What would become of Darvin Ray now? She sighed. This afternoon hadn't been much better—chaos had reigned at the store. And tonight loomed like a dreaded obstacle. So Nicky hated getting dressed up? As if she really wanted to go to the Porters' either. Bert and Claudia would be difficult in their own right, but after the grueling past two days, she wasn't prepared for another evening with Tony. Especially when Nicky had talked about him the entire way home from Daisy's.

Slowly she shed her clothes and when she heard Nicky turn off the water after his shower, she started hers. It would have to be short if she was to be dressed and ready when Tony arrived.

Later as she stood trying to tame her rebellious hair, she realized that the sole object of her thoughts the past few minutes had been Tony. The kiss at the Terminal Building today had undone some of her resolve, that coupled with last night's admissions and the forlorn look in his eyes. The hard man he presented to the public was easy to deny; it was the lost, yearning expression he sometimes got that softened her heart and jump-started powerful and, frankly, sexual feelings. He was mysterious, alluring and, inexplicably, vulnerable. A dangerous combination.

Darn! Halfway through applying her makeup she heard the doorbell ring. She glanced at her watch. He was early. "Nicky, can you answer that?" But already she could hear her nephew clattering down the stairs. Within a few minutes she'd put on her dark-green wool slacks, red silk blouse and plaid blazer. Adjusting her gold hoop earrings as she walked downstairs, she uttered a silent prayer that this evening would go well.

Nicky and Tony were sitting together on the couch, huddled over some magazine. They both looked up when she walked in. Tony slowly rose to his feet, and she inwardly cringed. He looked like every woman's dream—a lazy smile on his face, his navy blue suit perfectly tailored to his broad shoulders, narrow waist and firm legs. "Hi," she managed huskily.

"You look great, Andrea." His eyes locked on hers.

"Look what Tony brought me." With difficulty she turned to Nicky. He was holding out a thick copy of *Sports Illustrated*. "It's all about basketball. Me and Tony—"

"Tony and I," she corrected automatically.

"Yeah, Tony and I, we were lookin' at the NBA teams. 'Specially the Cavs." Andrea couldn't remember when Nicky had displayed this much enthusiasm. "Hey, Tony, do ya think maybe sometime we could go to a game?"

Tony caught Andrea's eye. She shrugged.

"Maybe, sport. We'll have to see." He checked his watch. "Right now, though, we need to leave." He grinned at Andrea. "Unless we want to be fashionably late."

"I'll get my coat," she said, using the few moments to compose herself. She couldn't let her emotions run away with her where Tony was concerned. She wasn't in any position to indulge herself with a fling, and that was the last thing Nicky needed. Friends. That was safe. She felt hands settle on her shoulders as Tony assisted her with the coat. Nicky stood in the entry hall, looking adoringly at his new hero.

During the short drive to the Porters', Nicky kept up a running inquisition about basketball. Even Andrea knew some of his questions were uninformed and naive compared to those of other boys his age. But Tony's answers were unfailingly nonjudgmental and thorough. Andrea hadn't realized how much Nicky had needed the company of a man his father's age. She snuggled deeper into her coat. Poor kid. He was missing so much. And she could do very little about some of it.

The windows of the Porters' imposing Tudor-style home were ablaze with lights. Tony pulled into the circle drive and stopped the car. "Wow," he said. "Some house."

"I think it kinda looks like a castle," Nicky ventured.

Andrea nodded toward the door. "And the lord and lady of the manor are waiting." She looked over at Tony. "Ready?"

"As I'll ever be." He got out and came around to the passenger side to assist Andrea. Nicky had already escaped the back seat and was ringing the doorbell.

Tony pulled her close and whispered in her ear. "Do we look like a scandalous couple?"

His warm breath stirred memories of their night in bed. "To them, we probably will."

He had just enough time to utter, "I'd do it all over again," before the heavy door swung open and Bert stood there, his bald head bathed in reflected light, his gray trousers, camel cardigan, and dress shirt and tie marking him from head to toes as a "club" man. He held out his hand. "Andrea, good evening." He put an arm around his grandson. "Nicholas, my boy." Then he nodded at Tony. "Mr. Urbanski."

"Tony, please."

Bert smiled wanly. "Tony, then. Come in. Let me take your coats."

Andrea smelled the mixed aromas of meat, spices and fresh bread. Her stomach growled. She'd missed lunch. Despite the strained circumstances, maybe for once she could do justice to Claudia's meal.

Bert ushered them into the dark-paneled living room, where a thick Persian rug carpeted the wood floors and a lighted oil painting of a sailing ship dominated the room from above the mantel. "Please sit down and make yourselves comfortable while I tell Claudia you're here.'' Claudia would want to make a grand entrance. Tony sat in a straight-backed armchair by the hearth, his fingers clasped loosely over his stomach. Oddly, he looked as if he belonged. Why ''oddly''? Why shouldn't he be at ease? Just because his roots were vastly different...

''Andrea, my dear, and Nicholas!'' Claudia sailed into the room, her diminutive body clad in a stunning mauve silk dress with a cowl neckline. She held out a thin bejeweled hand to Andrea. ''At last, our Thanksgiving dinner.'' Then, like a robin appraising a worm, she turned and studied Tony. ''Mr. Urbanski.''

That's all she said. As if he didn't merit further notice. Andrea watched as Tony politely rose to his feet and inclined his head. ''Mrs. Porter, how gracious of you to include me in your family dinner.''

Andrea felt the corners of her mouth twitching. It was as if she were watching some British drawing room comedy. It wouldn't have surprised her one bit had Tony picked up Claudia's hand, bowed and brought it to his lips.

Even Claudia seemed momentarily disconcerted. ''Er, Bert, give our guests some sherry while I serve the canapés.'' She departed for the kitchen while Bert stepped to a sideboard and picked up silver tongs. He turned to Nicky. ''Your usual, Nicholas?''

Nicky sat at the end of the sofa, one arm draped along the armrest, obviously on his best behavior. ''Yes, Grandpa.'' Bert opened the ice bucket, clunked several cubes into a cocktail glass, then poured a cola over the ice. ''Here, son.'' Nicky scrambled off the sofa to get his drink.

Claudia reentered, carrying a huge silver tray of tea sandwiches, raw vegetables and hot puff pastries, which she set on the square coffee table flanked by the two sofas.

"Try Mimi's special hot spinach hors d'oeuvres, Nicholas." She held out one of the puff pastries.

"No, thank you."

"'No, thank you'? Is that what you say to Mimi's good food?" Andrea felt her nerves kick in. Claudia wouldn't take no for an answer. Andrea knit her brows and stared at Nicky.

"Okay. I guess I'll try one." He took it in his hand, studying it as if it were a form of exotic animal life. He nibbled at the crust.

"How is it?" Claudia chirped.

"Fine."

Then Claudia wheeled around to the rest of them. "Please. Help yourself."

By now Bert had distributed the wine and had settled on the sofa with Nicky. Claudia perched with Andrea on the other sofa while Tony remained in the chair. "We missed you, Andrea, on Thanksgiving," Claudia said pointedly.

"I'm sorry I couldn't make it." She didn't like where this conversation was going.

"Andrea and I got snowed in down in the Flats. We couldn't get a taxi. In fact, we barely made it to my apartment." Tony's bland expression betrayed nothing, but Andrea could swear he was taking mischievous delight in this exercise.

"Your apartment?" Claudia arched her eyebrows. "How very convenient." The word "convenient" came out with four very distinct syllables.

"You needn't have worried," Tony went on. "We were nice and cozy."

Andrea cringed. Cozy? She gulped, then intervened. "Fortunately by the next afternoon, Tony was able to dig his car out and bring me home."

Bert harrumphed. "Well, the main thing now is that

we're having our little celebration. And you know Claudia." He winked at Andrea. "She never minds putting on a gourmet meal."

"What're we having, Mimi?" Nicky asked.

Her eyes alight with pleasure, Claudia ticked off the menu. "Beef Wellington, cucumber aspic, carrots à l'orange, potato-parsnip casserole and fresh broccoli."

Nicky somehow managed not to grimace, but hurtled on. "What's for dessert?"

Claudia practically quivered. "Bread pudding with chocolate rum sauce."

Nicky looked dubious. "Will I like it?"

"Of course you will, darling."

Bert raised his glass and took a healthy swig, then smacked his lips. "Tell me, er, Tony, what line of work are you in?"

"I'm with Great Lakes Management Group. Mergers and acquisitions."

Bert leaned slightly forward. "Isn't that Wainwright's outfit?"

"Yes, you know him?"

"We went to prep school together."

When Bert supplied the name of the highly regarded, exclusive school, Andrea noticed Tony's jaw tighten. Bert went on. "Tell us about your people." Beside her Claudia nervously fingered her long double strand of pearls.

Tony turned the goblet between his fingers, then looked up, his face creased in a deceptively calm smile. "My people? I don't think you would know them, sir. My mother died when I was five. And as for my father—" he paused for what Andrea could have sworn was dramatic effect "—he lives in Detroit and is a union laborer in the automobile industry."

"I take it you're a...a self-made man, then?" Claudia made the normally complimentary term sound demeaning.

"You could say that," Tony said, before taking a swallow of the wine. "I worked my way through college."

"Were you a fraternity member?" Bert inquired.

Tony smiled, more to himself than for anyone else. "I'm afraid, sir, I didn't have time for that."

"A pity. A chap makes a lot of good contacts that way," Bert went on.

"Bert," Claudia's voice rose in reproof. "I'm sure Mr. Urbanski was too busy with his employment and his studies for much of a social life."

Tony redirected the conversation. "Have you always lived in Cleveland, Bert?"

Nicky sat kicking one foot against the sofa while his grandfather recited the family history. Finally, the boy edged off the sofa, surreptitiously stuffed the remains of the pastry under a napkin and went to stand beside Tony. At the first lull in the conversation, Nicky grabbed Tony's hand. "I wanna show ya something, Tony."

"What's that, kiddo?"

"My dad's trophies. C'mon." He pulled Tony to his feet.

Andrea, sensing Claudia's body stiffen, interjected, "Do they have time before dinner, Claudia?"

Claudia sniffed. "I suppose." She stood up. "I'll attend to some last-minute touches."

"May I help?" Andrea asked.

Nicky was already leading Tony toward the stairs. "No, you stay here and keep Bert company. Surely Nicholas and that man won't be too long." She bustled officiously toward the kitchen.

That man? Andrea had the sinking sensation that the cocktail hour had been merely a warm-up before the main event.

"More sherry, Andrea?" She looked up, startled to find Bert standing at her elbow, extending the carafe.

"Yes, thank you." She took a soothing sip of the wine, wondering how in the world she would survive this evening.

Bert settled back on the sofa across from her. "That Urbanski chap, how long have you been seeing him?"

Already the screws were tightening. "Not long." *And maybe not anymore.* Before Andrea could divert him with a discussion of the trial, he leaned toward her, his tone conveying confidentiality. "Your young man, he's quite a diamond in the rough, isn't he?"

Andrea dug her fingers into the arm of the sofa. She didn't know which was more condescending—the assumption Tony was "her young man" or the assessment of him as a "diamond in the rough."

She fixed her eyes on Bert's and hoped she looked guileless. "Why, Bert, I don't know what you're saying."

"He's not exactly the kind of person, well, that you grew up with here in Shaker Heights."

She picked up her sherry and clutched the stem for dear life. "Your point?" Darned if she was going to let him off the hook.

He gave a slight nod in the direction Tony and Nicky had taken. "My grandson is everything to me. I believe he needs to cultivate the right kind of friends."

Fuming, she decided to play dumb. "Exactly what do you mean?"

"Boys and girls from the established families whose parents knew Rich." He paused to take a sip of wine. "You know, our kind of people."

"As opposed to?"

Bert at least had the grace to look abashed. "Perhaps I've put it clumsily." He leaned closer. "Claudia and I appreciate the job you are doing with Nicholas. Rich and Tami would be pleased. But we don't want anything to endanger that, and so we assume you will exercise great caution in finding a suitable husband, should you consider a marriage of your own.''

There. It was out. The caveat concerning any man who moved beyond the inner circle of Cleveland society. Someone like Tony. The Porters' attitude was downright medieval. Next thing she knew they'd want to arrange a marriage, predicated on the blueness of a prospect's blood. ''I can't imagine why that should be any concern of yours, Bert.''

He cocked an eyebrow at Nicky's photograph sitting on the sofa table. ''That's why.'' He lowered his voice. ''I can't permit you to take chances with him.''

Can't permit? Andrea choked back her instinctive response. If she went too far, what action might the Porters take? ''I love Nicky. Frankly, I resent the implication that I would have anything but his best interests at heart.''

Then Bert sighed, and when Andrea looked at him, he seemed suddenly haggard and spent. ''Thank you. I'll rely on that.''

Andrea looked down at the wineglass she held in her trembling fingers. Not surprisingly, the amber liquid was sloshing against the sides of the goblet.

SHERRY? CANAPÉS? This place had all the charm of a mausoleum, Tony thought, as he followed Nick up the stairs. At the landing he noticed an oil portrait of a handsome young man. ''Who's this?'' he asked Nick.

''My dad,'' he mumbled, dragging Tony up to the second floor where he led him into a bedroom, still furnished for a boy. ''This was his room,'' Nick said in a hushed tone. ''He was a good athlete, you know.''

Tony stepped forward and saw that the shelves were lined with trophies and sports memorabilia. He laid a hand on Nick's shoulder. ''Looks like it.''

''*Really* good.'' The boy started telling him about a tennis trophy from a local country club, then proceeded to the Little League plaques, the stories all sounding like rehearsed pieces. Finally, he picked up a worn baseball glove. "This was his mitt." The boy sat on the bed, his shoulders slumped, the mitt dangling between his knees. Sensing the boy's discomfort, Tony sat down beside him and waited.

From downstairs, he could hear the low mumble of Andrea's and Bert's voices, the distant clatter of serving dishes from the kitchen. Without looking up, Nick finally spoke. "I'm s'posed to use this in the spring. When baseball starts."

Tony knew there was a subtext to the kid's remarks because from the sound of his voice, there definitely was no joy in this Mudville tonight. "Who says?" he asked.

"Grandpa."

"But you're not too keen on the idea, huh?"

Nick just shrugged. "I can't."

"Can't what?"

"Play."

"Why not?"

"I don't…" Tony watched the boy struggle for a deep breath "…know how. I'll never be any good. Least not as good as Dad was."

Tony wrapped an arm around the boy's bony shoulders. "Who says? Everybody has to start somewhere. But you're right." No point trying to fool him. "You won't be as good as your father was, at least not at first. You'll have to give it some time. But, then, you know what?"

Nick looked up, as if afraid to trust Tony's remarks. "What?"

"Someday you might even be better."

"You think?" His hopefulness was painful to see.

"If you're willing to practice and work at it, yes, that's what I think."

Suddenly the boy deflated. "But how am I gonna learn? Who's gonna teach me? Grandpa's too old, and Andie, well, she's a girl."

"Girls can be excellent athletes, too, you know." Nick looked unconvinced. "But maybe one of your teachers or a neighbor would help."

Nick stood up, walked across the room and carefully replaced the mitt on the shelf. "Nah. I don't know anybody." He turned around. "'Cept you. Couldn't you teach me?"

Oh, boy! He'd weighed his words carefully in boardrooms across America, but, in a strange way, he'd never felt so much was at stake as it was right here, right now, with this vulnerable little boy.

"Come here, Nick." He patted the place beside him on the bed. The boy slowly sat back down and Tony wrapped his arm around him again. "It's like this, sport. I know how much you want to learn to play. Not just to play, but to be good. And you're a pretty smart guy to look for somebody who can help. But I can't promise to do that, even if I'd like to." Nick looked at him with watery eyes. Damn, he was botching this. "I don't know how much I'm gonna be around, even how long I'll be living in Cleveland. It wouldn't be fair."

"Even a little while'd be all right," Nick said in a strained voice.

"Nick, look at me." The boy squared around and raised his eyes. "I won't promise you something I might not be able to deliver. But if it works out, I'll help you when I can. We're buddies, right?"

A tear trailed down the boy's cheek. "Right."

"Okay, then." Tony stood up, pretending to ignore the tear, and pulled Nick to his feet. "We've got a deal. Meanwhile, I'm not sure your grandpa's as old as you think. Why don't you ask him to help?"

"Grandpa?" Nick looked dubious.

Tony pulled him close in a half hug. "Why not? Who do you think taught your dad, huh?"

"Yeah," Nick said. "I never thought about that."

"We better head back downstairs. I figure your grandma doesn't like people appearing late for one of her dinners."

"You got that right." Nick flipped off the bedroom light, then paused. "Tony?"

"Yeah?"

"Thanks a lot. I'm glad you're my buddy."

It took Tony nearly the whole flight of stairs to dissolve the lump in his throat so he'd be ready to eat. God, he felt for the kid. Pops hadn't been there for him either. The older kids in the neighborhood had taught him everything he knew about sports—the hard way. He could count on the fingers of one hand the number of times his own father had pitched him a baseball, passed him a football, or shot baskets with him. His old man was far more expert at criticism. "Hey, why didn't ya go fer the bucket!" "Jeez, only two hits? Whatsa matter with ya?"

Tony closed his eyes against the unwelcome memories. Maybe what he'd had that Nick lacked was the anger— the white-hot, go-for-broke fury that served to catapult his one-hundred-sixty-pound frame into monstrous interior linemen or drive his body toward the finish line.

He glanced at the boy scooting into the dining room chair, slowly unfolding the large damask napkin. No, Nick had anger in him. He just hadn't tapped into it yet. And when he did… A fierce ache shot through Tony's chest. Would the kid be prepared for how ugly and uncontrollable it could be?

"Sit here by me, Mr. Urbanski." Tony blinked. Claudia was gesturing to the place to her right. "I want to learn all about you."

Tony took his seat. *I just bet you do. And you want to*

know exactly what Andrea and I did the night of the storm. Lady, in your wildest dreams, you couldn't imagine it!

He felt Claudia's cool hand patting his. "Now, tell me what clubs you belong to and which boards you sit on."

CHAPTER TEN

ANDREA CUT INTO the beef Wellington, cooked to perfection, and tried to savor the bite she put into her mouth. But it was difficult when, from the other end of the table, she heard Claudia's incredulous tone. "No memberships? Surely you understand if you want to make your mark in a town like Cleveland, social contacts are extremely important. Why, Richard belonged to—" And the list rolled.

Andrea concentrated on her food, giving up trying to follow either Claudia's monologue or Bert's hearty questioning of Nicky about his outings with Daisy. She couldn't believe the Porters' insensitivity to Tony, all politely veiled in hypocritical interest. She swirled a fork through her potatoes, steaming and delicately flavored with...maybe nutmeg.

Bert fell quiet when Nicky didn't seem particularly responsive to his inquiries. Claudia, however, prattled on to Tony about Rich's glowing credentials. Andrea masked her discomfort by asking Bert to pass the butter.

Nicky, who apparently had been listening to Tony and Claudia's conversation, interrupted his grandmother. "Mimi, whaddaya mean, a cotillion? Tony, you don't go to those, do you?"

Tony shook his head, the corner of his lip quirking.

"Well, then, Mimi, I don't wanna go either." Claudia drew a napkin to her mouth in dismay. "It's just some dumb dance."

"Andrea will see that you go, Nicholas, won't you, dear?" Claudia's eyes were beadlike.

"I don't think we have to decide that tonight. We're several years away."

"But you can't be too careful, my dear. You wouldn't want to do anything to offend the cotillion committee."

Again the between-the-lines comment was obvious. An unsuitable mate might have a deleterious effect on the committee. It was general knowledge among the Porters' set that only so many escorts were chosen from among the group of socially acceptable young men.

Tony rescued her. "I'm sure Andrea would never knowingly offend anyone."

Andrea mentally completed his thought. "As you have just done." Then she experienced a disturbing realization. It truly was as if she could read Tony's mind, finish his sentences, feel his reactions. Well, enough of that. There were sound reasons to end her relationship with him, but darned if the Porters and their narrow thinking would be among them.

Meanwhile, Tony sat relaxed, eating heartily. She'd have to hand it to him. He'd let the insults slide right on by. He was one cool customer.

She glanced again at Bert, who seemed preoccupied. Despite the Porters' outrageous behavior tonight, she couldn't help feeling pity for them. When Rich and Tami died, their whole world collapsed. Now, their lives revolved around Nicky.

And it wasn't healthy. For anybody.

IT WAS AFTER ELEVEN when they arrived back at Andrea's. As she hung up her coat, she could hear Nicky talking to Tony. "No kidding, I can really go with you tomorrow?" His voice was buoyant.

"I'll pick you up at two. My game's at three. Afterward we'll kick the ball around awhile, okay?"

She came into the room just in time to watch Nicky give Tony a high five. "Cool."

Andrea squared Nicky around by the shoulders. "Enough. It's late. Off to bed, young man." This intense interest in basketball earlier, and now soccer, befuddled her. Obviously it had its roots in Tony. She still couldn't determine if he was simply being polite, or if the two really had bonded. Either way, it was a problem. "I'll be up soon to say good-night."

She turned toward Tony. "Thanks for putting yourself through this evening and for being so nice to Nicky."

"Why does that have the ring of dismissal?"

"It's late, Tony, and—"

"You don't want to talk about it?"

"What?"

"Us." He rested his forearms on her shoulders and linked his fingers behind her neck. His brown eyes were utterly serious.

"Not now, Tony." She tried to squirm away, but he cupped her head in his warm hands.

"It's not going to get any easier, you know."

He was right. Even though she was tired, too much ambiguity stood between them. For Nicky's sake, they needed to talk. "I suppose you're right. I'll put some coffee on before I tuck Nicky in."

"Good. I'll be waiting for you."

I'll be waiting for you. It sounded ominous. She excused herself, fixed the coffee and went upstairs to Nicky. Poor kid, he was already asleep. She looked down at him, suddenly filled with a longing for Tami so fierce her knees nearly buckled. Would her sister approve of how she was rearing Nicky? And what would she advise her to do—

about the Porters, about Tony? She brushed the hair off Nicky's forehead.

Would it be better simply to remove Tony from their lives now, before Nicky got too involved with him, before Tony became so immersed in work that he didn't have time for them? Or should she give them all a chance? She wasn't that sure of her own feelings, either, and it would be unconscionable to put Nicky through another loss. Besides, she had no idea exactly where Tony stood. She drew a deep breath, then tiptoed from Nicky's bedroom. Well, maybe Tony was right. No time like the present.

Back in the living room, she accepted the mug Tony held out to her and settled in the armchair. He'd hung his suit jacket over the newel post and stripped off his tie. Now he sat, ankles crossed on the coffee table, studying her. "Are you avoiding me?" he asked, indicating with his mug the chair she was sitting on.

"Not avoiding you, exactly. I thought it might be easier to talk from here."

"Any particular reason?"

She flushed. "I can be more objective."

"You mean when I'm not touching you?"

A thrilling quiver, like an alarm, raced through her. "Yes."

"Okay. I can live with that. For now."

"Where do you want to start?"

"Why don't we get the trial out of the way before we get on to more personal matters." He took a swallow of coffee. "I gather you weren't too pleased with my position during the deliberations."

Andrea considered her words. "You have every right to your opinion, but…you came on pretty forcefully."

"I felt strongly."

"Obviously." She spoke with thinly veiled irony. "Are you always so sure of yourself?"

He grinned sheepishly. "Are you saying what I consider confidence comes across as arrogance?"

"Something like that, yes." She slipped off her loafers and hooked one by the toe, dangling it from her foot. "You're pretty overwhelming."

"I'm the first to admit I lost control. As I said last night, I'm really sorry, Andrea. That was a crude remark by a kid from the wrong side of the tracks."

"Does your background bother you that much?"

He frowned. "Every day. But, hey, I'm rising above it. Or trying to."

"I know that." She hesitated. "Something else about the trial bothers me. How could you be so indifferent to Darvin's future?"

"I feel as bad as you do about what may happen to him, but if he killed Angelo Bartelli, then he made his own future."

"You're convinced Darvin did it?"

"Absolutely. Believe me, I weighed your arguments. But in the final analysis, so far as I'm concerned, the facts proved his guilt."

She frowned. "I guess what troubles me is that the trial brought out how very differently you and I think."

"I agree with you. At least about the case."

"No, I mean we have different attitudes toward life. You're much...more detached, objective."

"Cold and calculating?"

"I didn't say that." She set down her mug. "You seem willing to believe the worst of people."

"In my business, caution helps," he said dryly. "I don't suppose you'd admit to wearing rose-colored glasses?"

"Sure. Why not? I like people. I tend to trust them until they give me some reason not to. What's wrong with that?"

"Is that why you keep giving the Porters the benefit of the doubt?"

"Partly. But it's more than that. They weren't always like this. Before Rich and Tami... They even knew how to have fun then." The loafer dropped with a thud to the floor. She looked at Tony. His jaw was working. "They were pretty awful tonight, weren't they?"

"Bigoted, snobby, patronizing—all of that," he admitted.

"I'm sorry. I suppose they were punishing me for what they consider the impropriety of the other night."

"Does that bother you?"

"Personally, no. But I can't risk giving them cause to sue for custody of Nicky."

"Do you think that's a possibility?"

"I hope not." She leaned over and put her shoes back on.

He set his mug on the coffee table. "How *do* you feel about the other night?" His eyes never left her face.

"This isn't just about the other night." Maddeningly she felt tears fill her eyes.

He rose to his feet, approached her chair and stood looking down at her. "It was pretty damn terrific if you ask me." He held out his hand.

She grasped it, but remained seated. "You're not trying to confuse me, are you?" She looked up. He was smiling that sexy smile of his.

He pulled her gently to her feet. "I might be. Let's see..." Enclosing her in his arms, he kissed her. Her thoughts whirled, but soon were lost in the welcome pressure of his mouth, the heady sensation of his hands stroking her back, the tremors coursing through her. She didn't even want to struggle against her body's betrayal. All she wanted was to curl up in the strength and security of his embrace.

He slowly withdrew his lips from hers and stood, holding her, searching her eyes. "Did I succeed?"

"Succeed?" She couldn't even think.

"In confusing you?"

She moved toward the sofa, where she sat down, waiting to speak until he joined her. "I've been confused ever since I met you."

He draped an arm along the sofa back. "I know. I'm not your type."

"I didn't say that."

"You didn't have to. The Porters did it for you."

"I'm not a Porter."

"Andrea, the bottom line, as the saying goes, is that I'd like to continue seeing you. But not if it's going to create problems for you or Nick."

She reached for his hand, the connection warming places deep within her. She had to be careful what she said. How she said it. "Try to understand. I have to do everything I can to avoid upsetting Nicky. He's still very fragile."

"And you think I'd upset him?"

"He's quite attached to you. In his mind, I think he already sees us as—" she forced out the words "—as a threesome. I can't let him build up his hopes."

"Especially with someone like me?" He turned and tilted her chin so he could search her face.

"Tony, that's ridiculous! It has nothing to do with your background. None of that makes a bit of difference to me! But Nicky's been hurt as badly as a little guy can be. Not just by the death of his parents. At that time, well, I was engaged, and..." Her voice trailed off.

"What happened?"

"My fiancé wasn't as committed as I thought. After the funeral John must've realized that responsibility for Nicky was part of the deal." She looked into Tony's shocked eyes. "He...he didn't love me *that* much."

Tony beat his fist on his knee. "The worthless son of a bitch!"

"So you see why I won't permit that kind of rejection to happen to Nicky again."

"Yeah, I see. It shouldn't have happened to Nick. And it shouldn't have happened to you." His arm settled around her shoulders. "But what about you? Your feelings? Your future?"

"Nicky comes first. It's that simple." The empty place inside her was growing exponentially. She knew how this had to end. Tony wasn't the settling down type.

"So where does that leave us?"

"Honestly, Tony, I don't know. And I'm not sure I'm prepared to risk finding out."

He shrugged tiredly. "I don't like your answer, but I guess I have to respect it. Would you at least think about it?"

"Tony, I need time. Please."

He got to his feet. "You've got it." He crossed the room, picked up his suit coat and then turned to face her. "Andrea, I may come across as cynical, but I wouldn't hurt you or Nick for the world." He shrugged into the coat. "If it's okay, I'll still take him to the soccer game tomorrow. After that, I'll be in New York on business. I'll let him down carefully."

She took two steps toward him. "Tony—"

"It's all right. I understand." With one hand on the doorknob, he turned and gave her a crooked smile. "For a little while there, we had a great time. So long, Andrea."

The click of the door shutting behind him echoed through the small entry hall. Andrea stood motionless staring at the spot where just seconds before he had stood.

The finality rammed into her stomach. He was gone. Really gone.

Finally she made herself go to the door and turn the dead bolt. When she turned back toward the stairs, she could hardly see for the tears in her eyes.

"FOR HEAVEN'S SAKE, BERT, lie still."

Claudia's hand clamped down on his shoulder, holding him in place. He'd kicked off the blanket, and the sheets were tangled around his hips. "Sorry," he mumbled. "Did I wake you?"

"Wake me? Who could sleep with you tossing and turning?" She turned on the bedside lamp and sat up, arms folded across her chest. "What's the matter? The dream again?"

Bert threw a forearm over his face to shield his eyes. "No." He waited for the next question, knowing full well Claudia wouldn't be satisfied until she'd probed his psyche.

"What then?" Irritation masked any concern she might be feeling.

"It should be pretty obvious."

"Oh." Her voice fell. "You mean that man."

Without thinking, he supplied the name. "Urbanski." His heart pounded. "What do you think he's up to?"

"More to the point, what's Andrea doing bringing a man like that into Nicholas's life?"

"The boy certainly seems taken with him." He let his arm flop down by his side, then turned to look at his wife. "You don't think Andrea would—"

"Marry him?" She frowned. "I hope not, but I suppose we have to consider the possibility that eventually she'll settle down with someone."

Bert shut his eyes against the thought, seeing very clearly in his mind the image of Rich so proudly holding

Nicholas the day he was born. He couldn't stand the thought of a man, any man, supplanting Rich in Nicholas's affections. He groaned.

"Bert?" Claudia poked him. "We've got to do something. I think perhaps Andrea slept with him."

"Who?" For a moment, he couldn't get his bearings.

"Who?" She rolled her eyes. "Who are we talking about?"

Bert felt a pain squeeze his abdomen. He turned over on his stomach and punched his pillow. "No. I don't believe it. Let's get some sleep."

Claudia leaned over to turn off the lamp. "You can believe it or not, but something's going on."

As she arranged herself next to him, he put one hand on her shoulder. She never rolled over into his arms anymore. Ever since Rich had died, she didn't like to be touched. Not that way, at least. He shivered. Where did she go when she pulled away from him? He didn't know her anymore. It was as if when Rich died, Claudia deserted him, too. He didn't understand. And he was lonely, so lonely.

He finally turned away from her and closed his eyes, but sleep continued to elude him. All he could see was Urbanski's smug smile, Urbanski's hand on Nicholas's shoulder, Urbanski's arm around Andrea's waist. They looked like—Bert choked back the phlegm rising in his throat—a family!

"KEEP YOUR EYE on the ball." Lounging against the screen, Tony watched as the kid swung the bat, finally connecting. "Attaboy! That was much better. Heads up, now!" Nick missed the next pitch flung at him by the machine. "You're swinging a little late. Get that shoulder into it."

Tony got a kick out of the way the kid furrowed his

brow in concentration, his tongue poking the side of his cheek. For a beginner, he didn't have a half-bad swing. Nick's eyes had lighted up like fireworks when Tony had suggested coming to the indoor batting cage after the soccer game.

"Didja see that one, Tony?" Nick's voice was elated.

"Yeah, good job." He checked his watch. "One more round, then I need to take you home."

Home. To Andrea. Last night had been weird. First the Porters with their inquisition, barely disguised as a civilized dinner party. Then Andrea's surprising revelation about that idiot John. He couldn't blame her for being cautious where men were concerned. But he wasn't like John, was he? Yet, in honesty, he couldn't say just how permanent he was prepared to make a relationship with Andrea. And she needed him to know.

Maybe cooling it with her was best. Andrea didn't need further pain. Tony looked at Nick, returning the bat and making his way toward him, a big grin splitting his face. Best for the kid, too. He didn't need adults screwing with his well-being. Tony clapped his hands on his knees and stood up. "Want a soda for the road, Nick?"

As they walked to the concessions booth, Tony caught himself before he put an arm around the boy's shoulders. No point building up the kid's hopes. He slapped some bills on the counter. "Two giant orange drinks." He wasn't looking forward to the ride home when he'd have to tell Nick he wouldn't be seeing him for a while. A long while.

Yeah, best to call it quits before anybody got hurt. Besides, he reminded himself, he didn't have time for this stuff. He needed to focus on work. On DataTech, Cyberace and his own ambitions.

Not on the unsettling feeling in the pit of his stomach.

On the drive to Andrea's, Nick asked him lots of questions about famous hitters. Finally, he said tentatively, "Tony, do ya think—" he hesitated "—I could maybe be any good?"

Tony realized that it was a courageous question that required an honest answer. "It depends. You have some natural ability, but you have to want it badly. As I told you before, you have to practice hard and be willing to accept coaching. Do you think you could?"

Nick nodded vigorously. "Yeah. I liked this afternoon." Then his smile dimmed. "But Grandpa..."

"What about him?"

"He wants me to be as good as Dad."

This time Tony didn't draw back; he laid a hand on the boy's shoulder. "It's what you want that counts. Set your own goals, son." He swallowed hard. Damn. He hadn't meant for that to slip out. Son. What he wouldn't give to be the kind of father his old man had never been able to be!

"Thanks, Tony. I'm cool with that." They rode for several blocks in silence, then Nick spoke. "Do ya think we could go again to the batting place next week?"

Time for the truth. "I'd really like to help you, Nick. But that's not going to be possible."

Nick ducked his head and kicked a foot nervously. "I'm sorry. I shouldn'ta asked."

God, why was this so damned difficult! "Of course, you should have. It's just that...I'm going to be out of town. Then when I get back, I'll be real busy at work. I won't be hanging around you and your aunt for a while."

"You don't like us?" He turned an imploring face to Tony.

"It's not that, Nick. It's just, well, Andrea and I have decided we won't be seeing each other." Out of the corner of his eye, he saw Nick bite his lip. "It's kind of a...grown-up thing. Understand?"

Nick shrugged, then stared out the passenger window the rest of the way to Andrea's.

When they arrived, the boy dashed out of the car without saying a word, brushed past Andrea and raced upstairs. Andrea looked anxiously at Tony. "What happened?"

"I told him."

"Told him?"

"About us. That we're cooling it." He stuffed his fists in his pocket. "I tried to be tactful, but it looks as if I blew it."

Andrea stood awkwardly, as if she didn't know quite what to do with her hands. She lowered her eyes. "Better now than later, I suppose."

"Right." He should leave. Why was he still standing here staring at her?

"Tony?"

He searched her eyes, hoping for what? It needed to end. She was right. But… "Yeah?"

"Good luck in New York. And thank you."

"For?"

"Understanding."

"Good luck to you, too." He wasn't any good at this. Should he shake hands, what? He moved toward her, laying his palms on her shoulders, and pecked her on the cheek. "If you change your mind, call me."

Then he was out the door, aware that she stood watching him, a woeful expression on her face.

ANDREA FELT AS IF her heart would break. This was a man she could love, or had thought she could. But he was so different—cynical where she was trusting, worldly where she was naive, sophisticated where she was homey. Besides these very real obstacles, what was the point of going up against the Porters? A clean break. The best possible resolution. She wiped away the tear streaking her cheek and turned to go up to talk with Nicky. But he was standing at the top of the stairs glowering at her. "Nicky?"

He stomped down the steps and stopped directly in front of her. "Why don't you like him?"

She felt flustered. "What are you talking about?"

He stood, feet spread apart, glaring at her. "Tony."

She sighed. "C'mon, Nicky, sounds like we need to talk." She led him into the living room. "What's the matter?"

She sat on the edge of the sofa, but he wouldn't sit down, even when she invited him to join her. "He said he wasn't coming over anymore. Why?" His voice rose.

"He's busy."

"Does he hate us? What did you do to him?" His cheeks were fiery.

"Do to him? Nicky, I—"

"I thought you guys might, you know, get married or something. Then I'd have a father."

Andrea rose to her feet and extended a hand to him. "Nicky, I never intended for you to believe that. Besides, no one can replace your father."

"He's dead!" Nicky yelled, his fists balled at his sides. "I'm sick of hearin' about him. How wonderful he was, how good he was at sports!" He flailed his arms and stepped back. "If he was so wonderful how come he went out in that storm, huh? How come he left me?"

"Nicky, stop it. Calm down."

"Look!" He marched to the shelves and picked up a model of a clipper ship. "He liked sailing better than me. I hate him!" He raised the model above his head and smashed it on the floor.

Horror flooded Andrea. She'd never seen him like this. "Nicky!" She crossed the room and gathered him in her arms. "Nicky, stop it."

He shoved her away and looked at her with murderous

fury. "Don't call me that. My name's Nick. Nicky's for sissies." He walked past her, then started running toward the stairs. "Leave me alone," he shouted over his shoulder. "I hate you."

Andrea crumpled to the floor, the sound of his bedroom door slamming audible over the sobs that threatened to tear out the lining of her chest. Oh, God. What had she done?

THE LAST THING TONY had needed after the afternoon with Nick, after reading the finality in Andrea's eyes, and after receiving a summons to report to Wainwright's office at seven-thirty in the morning was this call from his father.

"Hey, big shot, ya didn't come Thanksgiving, ya didn't come this weekend. So what? I'm just your old man. But the guys from the neighborhood, they want ya back for the basketball team reunion at the high school on the twelfth. I'll bet you'll bust your ass for that, huh?"

"You'd bet on anything, wouldn't you?" He couldn't keep the bitterness out of his voice.

"I'll overlook that. It won't hurt ya to come home once in a while, ya know."

"Pops, all right, all right. I'll come the weekend of the reunion. Are you satisfied?"

"Good. Maybe while you're here you can figger out what to do about my disability insurance."

"Disability? What are you talking about?"

"I'm gettin' laid off at the plant."

Tony ground his molars. "What disability?" He waited, knowing damn well what disability.

"Blacking out. The doc calls it stress."

"That's not what I call it. I call it Kentucky bourbon." Knots coiled in his stomach.

"That's my kid, goddamn it. Always the jokester."

Tony felt rage threatening to boil over. He had to get off the phone. "I'll deal with you the weekend after next."

"Ooh, I'm scared." He heard his father's laugh dissolve into a fit of coughing. "Meanwhile I'll tell Jimmy and the boys you're comin'. Oh, and by the way, bring money, kid. I could use a few C-notes."

Only the exercise of great restraint prevented Tony from rocketing the phone across the apartment. The old man's timing was uncanny! Right now when he needed to focus on New York. He kicked at a stack of newspapers on the floor. Son of a bitch!

Trembling, he plucked a soda out of the refrigerator, popped the top and took a swig. You can't let him get to you like that. It's always the same. No matter what. Face it, your father doesn't love you. Never has. Never will. There. That was the truth.

So why did he keep trying to earn the impossible? And why the hell did rejection still hurt after all these years?

He slumped into the Eames chair. Damned if he knew.

CHAPTER ELEVEN

LATE WEDNESDAY AFTERNOON Tony sat at the conference table in DataTech's New York City hotel suite hammering out last-minute details of the stock transfer, inwardly cursing the inadequate ventilation system. Soda cans, bottles of Perrier and several dishes of nuts littered the surface. A headache beat relentlessly at the base of his skull.

Rodney Steelman and his attorneys were waiting on another floor for him to resolve this latest sticking point. Tony winced recalling the Cyberace CEO's words, barked into the phone in their conversation earlier in the day. "Get it done. I'm due back in Texas for a three o'clock meeting tomorrow. I intend to be there with or without this agreement. If it's without, we're picking up our marbles."

Tony stood up, walked to the window and stared idly down on Central Park. Something was bothering Ed Miller. What? Ordinarily, given the millions of dollars riding on a deal like this and at this stage of negotiations, there wouldn't be nit-picking over dates for stock transfers. Maybe the guy was scared. Once the deal was consummated, he'd have to get DataTech's new technology into production fast, or answer to his stockholders. And Rodney Steelman might have the bluster of a Texas promoter, but Tony had played poker with him. The man didn't bluff. If he said he was going to be out of here tomorrow, he meant it.

Behind Tony the lawyers huddled, making their points with Miller. Maybe they'd talk sense into him. Below, cabs darted in and out of lanes choked with late afternoon traffic and pedestrians moved purposefully toward their destinations. Exciting as New York was, it always reminded him of a human anthill.

"Skee?" One of the attorneys beckoned to him. "Look at this. Think Steelman'll go for it?"

Tony examined the rewording, trying to concentrate on the implications of the change. "Give me a minute." He considered the gist of the proposal and Steelman's possible reactions. "Gentlemen, let me understand you. You need the transfer of sixty-five percent of the cash on or before the end of your fiscal year, is that correct?"

"If we're going to meet our obligations to our subcontractors, yes." Miller drew on his cigarette, then exhaled, filling his immediate area with a blue-gray haze. A flicker in the man's eyes betrayed him. He *was* afraid. Timing of the closing was the significant element for him.

Tony knew he had to move fast. "I suggest we adjourn. I'll go talk with Cyberace. Let's meet back here, say—" Tony consulted his watch "—at eight. That'll give you time for dinner."

He sprinted down the fire-exit stairs to his own room, dashed water on his face and took several deep breaths. If he didn't pin down Steelman now, he had the sick sensation Miller just might pull the plug himself. Massive egos were at stake, not to mention big bucks.

He picked up the phone and dialed Steelman's suite. "Rodney? Looks as if, except for a little tweaking, it's all going your way. I'd like to come up and fill you in on this last fine point.... Great. I'll be right there."

TONY THREW HIS JACKET in the general direction of the chair, unbuttoned his collar, pulled off his tie and collapsed on the bed. Two o'clock in the morning. In the end, he'd pulled it off. Neither Miller nor Steelman had wanted to blink. Ultimately, however, Steelman knew a good investment when he saw one. In a gesture calculated to be perceived as Texas magnanimity, he'd acceded to DataTech's revised payment schedule. At ten the two principals had shaken hands and signed on the dotted lines.

Even before the requisite celebration, Tony had felt as if his brains had been subjected to several hours in a centrifuge. As a result, he was flat-out drained, a condition augmented by generous amounts of champagne.

But he'd done it! Now in the silence of his own room, he could quietly exult, secure in the belief he'd satisfied any remaining questions Wainwright might have about his competence. He'd nailed this deal.

Not bad for the punk from Detroit!

"WHAT'S THE MATTER with you? You look like mud soup!" Daisy leaned over the counter of Never-Never Land and examined Andrea's face. "Littlest Angel? No way. Try Grumpy or Sleepy. Do I need to make you a dwarf costume?"

Andrea adjusted her halo and finished securing a bow to the last of the day's purchases requiring gift wrapping. "Gee, you really know how to make a person feel good."

"Still thirteen shopping days till Christmas. Sure you're gonna make it? You need a girls' night out. How does Reynaldo's sound? They serve great coconut shrimp. Am I tempting you?"

Andrea suppressed a sigh. Daisy meant well. And she was right. She *did* need a girls' night out. Just not now. Not with Nicky the way he was. Sending Daisy a tired smile, Andrea picked up the package and set it on the table with the others. "Not tonight, thanks. I need to get home."

"Something the matter?" Daisy picked up a yo-yo from the basket by the cash register and looped the string over her finger. "I'm waiting," she said without looking at Andrea.

Andrea watched the multicolored yo-yo spin toward the floor, then travel back up into Daisy's hand. A yo-yo. That's how she felt. Her emotions were all over the place. "I'm just tired, that's all."

"Am I gonna have to drag it out of you?"

Before Andrea could answer, Phil approached the counter. "Hi, Daisy. Can you close up, Andrea? My son's got a church-league game tonight. I'll lock the front door on my way out."

"No problem, Phil. Hope his team wins." Andrea began gathering up the cash and receipts from the register.

Daisy "walked the dog" and did a couple of other tricks before replacing the yo-yo in the basket. "Is it Nicky or Tony?"

Andrea stopped, her hands hovering over the counter. The sound of Tony's name was unexpectedly painful. Since that Sunday he'd taken Nicky to the soccer game, she hadn't talked to Tony, but willing herself not to think of him had been far more difficult. She knew her friend wouldn't give up, so she might as well get the true confession over with. "Okay, Daisy. C'mon back while I change, and I'll tell all." She closed the cash drawer.

"Hot diggity." Daisy followed her into the office and perched cross-legged on Andrea's desk while she changed.

"It's like this," Andrea began as she hung up her angel costume. "Tony was fun. Briefly. But we didn't have a lot in common."

"And you found this out in a matter of…what? Ten days? For God's sake, give it a chance. If I'm not mistaken, those were megawatt stars I saw in your eyes."

"The brightest lights burn out quickest," Andrea commented dryly as she stepped into her slacks. "I haven't talked to the man since just after Thanksgiving."

"Hmm. A pity." Daisy sat quietly while Andrea pulled on her sweater and then her shoes. "What about my little buddy?"

"Nicky? Er, excuse me, Nick? That's what he wants to be called now."

"Yeah, what's up with him?"

Andrea sank into a chair. "Oh, Daisy, I wish I knew. He's not happy with me. About Tony. Nicky attached himself to Tony like a fly on flypaper. He blames me because Tony doesn't come around anymore."

Daisy tucked her knees up under her chin. "He liked your Tony, huh?"

"Yes." She tamped down the credit card receipts she'd taken from the cash drawer and filed them. Then she began making out the cash deposit slip.

Daisy waited patiently until Andrea had prepared the deposit. "You could do a lot worse than have Nicky like a guy you like."

"Please, Daisy. Just leave it." She shouldered her bag, turned off all but the night-lights and opened the back door. Once they were outside, Andrea turned to Daisy. "I have other things to worry about with Nick."

Daisy stopped in her tracks. "Oh?"

"His teacher called this afternoon. He's causing problems in class."

"*Our* Nicky?" Daisy's mouth was an *O* of disbelief.

"That's what she said. I have an appointment with her after school tomorrow. I don't know whether to tell Nick or not."

"Why don't you wait until after you hear what the teacher has to say?"

"Maybe I will." Andrea turned and gave her a big hug. "Thanks, for being my friend."

"The feeling's mutual. Let me know how it goes." Daisy turned and strode toward her car. Andrea paused, listening to the canned Christmas music coming from the shopping center speakers. The message of "O Little Town of Bethlehem" seemed to come from another planet. How was it possible at this glorious holiday season to feel so at odds with the world?

Her father might have been able to explain it. But he was gone.

Avoiding puddles of melted snow, she made her way to her car. And what of Darvin Ray? She hadn't been able to stop thinking about him. What kind of holiday would he have behind bars?

"FIGHTING? NAME-CALLING? What do you mean?" Andrea felt diminished enough without having to sit in this student desk that put her about a foot below Mrs. Elliot, Nick's teacher.

"It started about two weeks ago. On the playground. Nick shoved one of the other boys and called him a four-letter word. That was the beginning of what I'm afraid has been a kind of 'acting out' ever since."

Andrea gasped. "I'm shocked. Nicky isn't permitted to use foul language of any kind."

The teacher cocked her head. "Can you think of any reason Nick might be particularly angry?" She paused. "Is everything all right at home?"

"Yes, although I've noticed Nick seems more sullen lately."

The teacher waited. Andrea felt herself growing hot. If she was going to help Nicky, she guessed she needed to come clean herself. "The only change I can think of is that I was briefly seeing a man to whom Nick became quite attached. He wasn't happy when I broke off the relationship."

"I see. That might help explain Nick's behavior. Up to now, he's been quiet, withdrawn. But in the past few days he's become loud, even aggressive." Mrs. Elliot leaned forward. "I'm aware of the tragic loss Nick suffered. His parents and all." Her voice faded. "Sometimes youngsters bottle up their feelings, and then they surface later. I'm wondering if that isn't what's happening in this situation."

Andrea clenched her hands. "It's possible, I suppose. What can we do? It's really unacceptable for him to behave this way in school."

"Let me try setting some boundaries with him here in the classroom. It would be really helpful, too, if you could get him to talk about his parents, about his anger. And to find some kind of outlet for him. Sports, for example. Or something like tae kwon do."

"I'll do my best. Meanwhile, please keep me informed."

"Certainly. If need be, I could recommend him to the school counselor." The teacher smiled and rose to her feet. Andrea stood up, too. "Thank you for coming, Ms. Evans. It can't be easy raising a nephew, but from what I've seen, he's lucky to have you."

It took all of Andrea's self-control to prevent herself from running to the car. Her chest was crushed by the weight of unshed tears—tears of shame, confusion and frustration. Reaching the car, she threw herself down in the seat and leaned her hot forehead against the cool steering wheel. How would the Porters react to this development?

Tami, help me. I don't know what to do. Have I botched everything?

"EAT, TONY, EAT." His father's sister shoved the bowl of potatoes toward him. One thing he'd have to say about Aunt Olga, you never went away hungry from one of her meals. "Stan, you want more ribs? More kraut?"

"Nah, I've had plenty." Tony's father belched in a fashion Tony supposed might be an attempt to flatter the cook.

The three of them sat at the chrome and metal table wedged against the wall of the double-wide. When his aunt had heard about his visit, she'd insisted on coming down from Flint to see him. When he was a kid, she'd show up once or twice a month. He'd always believed she came to try to fatten him up. When she was there, his father acted better. All in all, Olga's was a welcome presence.

"Tony, what time's your get-together with your pals?" Olga asked.

"We're going to the high school game about seven, then out to party afterward."

"Punks," his father said.

Tony let the remark pass. If it hadn't been for his friends, God knew where he might be today.

"Say, Olga, didja know my hotshot son's a big executive now?" Tony mentally shut his eyes. "Yeah, he's a partner, wouldja believe it, in some hoity-toity Cleveland firm. Damned if I know what they do. Management? What the hell kinda job's that?"

"It means I don't get my hands dirty, Pops."

He'd meant it as a joke, but his father angrily shoved his plate to the center of the table. "Somethin' the matter with gettin' your hands dirty? Seems to me it was good enough when I was doin' it to support you."

"Stan," Olga tried to intervene.

"Supporting me? Not since I was old enough to work!" Tony could feel the tension gathering across his back.

"What? Didja forget about the time I worked overtime to get you the money for your senior prom tux?"

"What tux? You got drunk the night before the prom and gambled the money away. I wore my old suit." He felt the same red creep up his face he had experienced when he'd picked up his date that night and watched her face fall when she came down the stairs and saw him.

"Bull!" Stan lunged across the table and grabbed him by the wrist. "You're one ungrateful bastard."

Tony jerked his arm away and stood up so fast, he knocked his chair into the wall. "Don't you ever call me that, you sorry—" He was almost too angry to continue. "You've called me all kinds of names through the years and demeaned me any way you could think of. But you won't defile my mother's memory by calling me a bastard." He moved around the end of the table and stood over his father. "Have you got that?"

His father shook his head sadly and spoke to Olga. "What are you gonna do when you raise a kid that turns out to be as ungrateful as that?"

"Oh, hell. I'm leaving." Seething, Tony grabbed his coat and stepped out onto the tiny redwood porch where he paused to get a good breath. The man would never change! Why did he punish himself coming back here, anyway?

He heard the latch of the door and turned to see Aunt Olga, a shawl pulled around her shoulders. She came and stood beside him, but didn't say anything for a while. From the mobile home lot next door, Tony could hear someone trying to fire up a motorcycle. In the distance a locomotive whistled for a crossing. "He's never been himself, you know, since your ma died."

"I wouldn't know. I can't remember what he was like before that." He didn't look at her.

"I know. You were just a little fella." Then he felt her hand on his arm. "He loved her very, very much. It near to killed him when she died."

Tony's heart felt cold, still. "So that excuses the way he's treated me all these years?"

"No." She moved closer to him. "It doesn't. You

haven't deserved a minute of it. He should be proud of a man like you.''

"That'll never happen."

She laid her forehead against his shoulder. "I'm afraid you're right. And…it breaks my heart."

He gathered her in his arms, his small, roly-poly aunt who was sniffling against his coat.

"I wish…you'd known him then."

"I do, too, Aunt Olga. I do, too." He patted her back. "But I'm afraid it's too late."

She hiccuped. "It's the booze. It's gotten him. He just won't stop."

"I know. We've all tried, but…" he shrugged.

She stood back, wiping her nose on a wrinkled handkerchief. "You're a good boy, Tony. Your mama would be proud. You just remember that." She flapped her arms in a shooing motion. "You go on, now. Have a good time. I'll deal with your papa."

She slipped back in the trailer. He stood looking up at the moon, then at the lights reflecting off the chrome stripping on the nearby mobile homes. A dog howled across the street. Coming home was always like this. And he always arrived at the same conclusion. The best peace he could make with the situation was simply to let his father be. He couldn't change him. He didn't know if he'd ever be able to forgive him. No, there was only one way to make sense of this. When it was his turn, he'd be the best damned father any kid ever had.

When it was his turn…? Andrea's face swam before his eyes.

He stomped toward his car. Hell, maybe he'd never have a turn. Something heavy shifted deep in his gut.

But he desperately wanted one.

IT WAS LATE AFTERNOON before Andrea arrived to pick Nicky up from his grandparents' house. The sky was already dark and the air smelled of imminent snow. Claudia, her mouth set in a rigid line, beckoned her inside. *What now?* Andrea didn't know how much more stress she could take. The store had been a madhouse today, this last Saturday before Christmas. She'd have to go in tomorrow just to set the stock back on the appropriate shelves.

She turned off the motor and reluctantly trudged toward the back door. According to a phone call from Mrs. Elliot, Nicky was behaving better at school although his grades were slipping. But at home? He refused to talk to her about his parents, sulked for hours in his room and, more often than not, sassed her rather than meekly complying as he'd always done before.

Claudia waited for her inside. In a low voice she said, "Andrea, we need to talk." She jerked her head in the direction of the library. "In there. Bert and Nicholas are upstairs playing checkers."

Once in the room, Claudia closed the sliding doors and gestured to a chair. Andrea gingerly perched on the seat. "What is it, Claudia?"

The older woman sat in an adjacent chair and primly folded the pleats of her skirt before looking up. "Nicholas."

"What about him?"

"Now, Andrea, you know very well he's not in the habit of being rude. But, lately—" she shook her head indignantly "—he talks back to us and is highly disrespectful." Andrea forced herself to remain quiet. "What do you intend to do about it?"

"I'm not excusing his behavior, Claudia, but a certain amount of rebellion is normal at his age."

"That doesn't make it acceptable." Claudia gripped the arms of her chair. "We cannot permit him to speak to us in the manner he has adopted lately."

"What does he say?" Andrea dreaded hearing the answer.

Claudia arched her eyebrows. "Among other things, that we're old-fashioned and that he doesn't care to hear any more about Richard's achievements. He even had the impertinence to say that if his father had cared about him, he wouldn't have taken his mother out sailing and left him behind." Claudia's chin trembled. "Richard loved that boy."

Andrea licked her dry lips. What could she say to this woman—so demanding, so set in her ways? "Of course, he did. And I don't think Nicholas means to hurt you. I think perhaps he's going through a rough time right now."

"What on earth do you mean? It's been eighteen months since the accident."

"Psychologists tell us it sometimes takes quite a while for a child to express his emotions. Maybe he's taking out some of his anger on those of us closest to him."

Claudia looked at her as if she'd just advanced an outlandish hypothesis. "Nonsense. We have to move beyond our grief. It's all we can do. No, something else is going on here."

Andrea waited. There was no reasoning with the woman.

"What about that man of yours?" Claudia fixed her eyes on Andrea.

"Tony? What about him?"

"I haven't heard you or Nicholas mention him lately, thank goodness. What kind of ideas do you suppose he planted in the boy's head?" She raised her chin. "Obviously, he wasn't a good influence."

Incredible. Andrea clenched her fists, driving down the anger threatening to erupt. Claudia might not approve of Tony's background, but he'd been nothing but caring with Nick. "If it's any of your business, Tony and I are not seeing each other anymore, but I hardly think he's responsible for any change you've noticed in Nicky."

Andrea could hear Nick and his grandfather coming down the stairs. Claudia rose to her feet and opened the library doors. "I wouldn't be too sure about that, my dear."

"Hi, Andie." Nicky stood slightly behind his grandfather, his attention concentrated on the floor.

"Hello, Andrea." Bert nodded to her. "Nicholas and I finished our Christmas shopping today, didn't we, lad?" Nick nodded uncomfortably. "We'll expect you around eleven Christmas Day, right, Claudia?"

"That will be fine." She eyed her grandson's feet distastefully. "And, Nicholas, do Mimi a favor. Do not wear those awful shoes you have on."

Nicky flushed. "I like them," he muttered.

Andrea sent him a warning glance. "Thanks for keeping Nick today."

"*Nick?*" Claudia turned a disapproving look on Andrea. "That's what that Urbanski man called him."

Nicky stepped around his grandfather and, his voice raw with emotion, confronted Claudia. "Mimi, why are you always like this? I hate it when you talk about Tony that way." The boy's chin trembled in defiance.

Bert stepped forward and laid a hand on Nicky's shoulder. "Now, son—"

But there was no stopping the boy, who went right on speaking, oblivious to his grandmother's shocked expression. "And you better start calling me 'Nick.' I hate my other names! 'Nicholas' sounds geeky and 'Nicky' is for babies!"

Claudia gasped and clutched her chest. "Nicholas, that will be quite enough." She turned to Andrea. "That's exactly what I'm talking about. Bert and I expect you to do something about both this attitude and his insolence."

Andrea, shaken, put her arm around Nick's shoulder and whispered, "Get your coat, honey." When he slipped out of the room, she turned to the Porters. "Rich and Tami entrusted me with Nicky's care, and I'm trying to do the best job I know how. It would help if you'd accept the fact he's a little boy with a great deal on his mind."

Before she turned to leave, Bert caught her eye. She couldn't be sure, but she thought she read approval in his expression. He had his crosses to bear, too, Andrea thought, as she led Nicky from the house toward the car amid the gently falling snow.

Nicky slumped in the passenger seat and folded his arms defiantly over his chest. "They can't tell me what to do."

"Nicky—" he shot her an angry look "—*Nick*, they're your grandparents. They love you."

"Ha!"

She tried again, praying for the right words. "What's the matter, honey? Why are you so angry with them?"

"They don't like anything I do." He spat out the words. "They don't like my name, they don't like my shoes, they don't like my friends."

"Your friends?"

"And neither do you!" His voice cracked.

She was puzzled. He had few friends. "Who are we talking about?"

"Tony." He rested his chin on his chest. "He was cool. And he liked me just the way I am."

Andrea felt close to panic. The snow was coming down harder and she had to keep her attention fixed on the road. "I do, too."

"Mimi doesn't."

She was at a loss for words. "Maybe Mimi's got her own troubles."

"Do we hafta go over there Christmas?"

How she wished she could say no, they'd have their own

holiday. But she couldn't. The Porters didn't have custody, but that didn't mean they wouldn't someday try to get it. "Yes, Nick, we do."

He didn't say another word. When they got home, he clumped past her, up the stairs to his own room and didn't come down until dinner.

After he was asleep, Andrea sat in the living room window seat staring out at the flakes drifting down from the dark sky, blanketing the earth. She hugged her knees to her chest, remembering the last big snowstorm, the breathless hike up the hill to Tony's apartment, the cozy warmth of his robe and the wonder of being in his arms. Nick wasn't the only one who missed Tony.

But she had other considerations beyond her own needs. She laid a cheek on her knees and watched the snow fall. And wondered where Tony was, what he was doing.

And why life seemed so complicated. And unfair.

CHAPTER TWELVE

TONY DIDN'T KNOW what had drawn him here on Christmas Eve. Shaker Square was nearly deserted. A few cars made their way up and down the streets, but most people were at home with their families. He turned up the collar of his coat and stared at the lighted sign. "Never-Never Land." Snow crunched beneath his feet as he moved closer to the shop window with its holiday display of toys and books. No angel with a gilt halo welcomed him this night.

He'd known Andrea wouldn't be there, so why exactly had he come? Some maudlin longing for Christmas past? He might as well be that little boy he once was, his nose pressed against the glass, coveting gifts that would never be his. Like a father who loved him.

He thrust his hands in his pockets and studied the items in the window—a whimsical electric train with a smiley-faced locomotive, a life-sized teddy bear, Victorian-style doll clothes, jigsaw puzzles. He closed his eyes briefly, trying vainly to remember Christmases before his mother died and imagining a home of his own filled with the laughter of children and a Christmas tree that grazed the ceiling. He sighed. Not to be confused with his own childhood reality—a tiny metallic tree sitting on the coffee table of the double-wide and, if he was lucky and his father wasn't drunk, a few bills thrust in an envelope and tossed to him with the standard comment, "Merry Christmas. Buy yourself somethin', kid."

He noticed the pub down the street was still open. Maybe he'd slip in there and get a brew and a bratwurst sandwich. Not exactly turkey and dressing, but what the heck?

Sitting in the booth after he finished his sandwich and nursing a beer, his thoughts turned to Aunt Olga's words as they often had since he'd been in Detroit. So his mother's death had busted up his dad? Made him the distant, addictive person he was? Tony didn't buy it. The busted-up part, yes, but the rest? A man worth his salt didn't turn his back on a little kid. God, it was almost as if his father blamed him for his mother's cancer.

He tossed back the rest of his drink and signaled the waitress for his check. One thing was for sure. He could either go on wishing his childhood had been different—or move on. Face the reality that until his father wanted help, there was nothing he could do for him. And no way he could please him. But there was something he could do for himself. Accept the past, bury it and move on.

The waitress took his money and when he told her to keep the change, smiled and said, "Thanks. You have a merry Christmas!"

Right. He left the warmth of the pub and stepped into the frigid night. Once again he looked at the sign. What would it be like to work in a place called "Never-Never Land"?

A chill shook his body. The previous four days he'd visited three different cities trying to work out a franchise deal for a quick-print business; made urgent phone calls from airports, taxis and restaurants; and listened to Harrison Wainwright exhort him to do more to bring in new business now that he was a partner. If Great Lakes Management had a marquee sign, it would read Rat Race.

Once again he glanced in the window of Andrea's shop. She'd said something once that had stuck with him. About the fun of a work environment where imagination had free rein. His colleagues were driven, stressed-out, acquisitive executives. What would it be like to work with kids who didn't know a stock option from a tax shelter? And who didn't care?

Or to be like Kelli's husband Patrick? As excited about his baby's imminent arrival as he was about upswings in the stock market.

He shook his head and strode briskly toward his car. What the hell was the matter with him? He had the world by the tail, didn't he?

AFTER THE HOLIDAYS, it seemed to Andrea that gray day ran into gray day. The first few weeks in January were productive, but restful. Customers dissatisfied with purchases came for returns or refunds and the Christmas decorations had to be boxed up and stored, yet the reduced traffic left more time for planning.

"What's our next big theme after Valentine's?" Phil asked early in February as they rearranged the window display. He looked slightly ridiculous in his Cat in the Hat outfit. But that was the point, wasn't it? Andrea smoothed down her costume. Who was she, Mother Goose, to talk?

She adjusted her granny glasses. "Daisy and I have been conferring. How does Easter with Raggedy Ann sound?"

Phil grinned. "Great, I've always wanted a red wig and shoe-button eyes." He flapped his arms and blinked rapidly, making her laugh at his Raggedy Andy imitation.

"Settled then. I'll ask Daisy to get the costumes ready for our spring promotion."

He handed her a stack of books, then picked up an armload of stuffed animals. "Nicky seemed awfully quiet the last few times he was in. Everything all right?"

Andrea didn't know which was worse—Nick's outbursts around Christmas or the unnatural brooding of the past several weeks. "I'm not sure, Phil. He seems unhappy, but when I ask him what's wrong, he just shrugs."

Phil shook his head in understanding. "Kids. Go figure."

"I enrolled him in a tae kwon do class, but he's refused to go."

"Why?"

"He's punishing me, I guess. I thought he needed some kind of physical outlet. He doesn't feel comfortable with team sports, so I made the mistake of signing him up and *then* telling him."

"Uh-oh. Bad idea, Andrea."

"Tell me about it."

"He'll probably come around, though."

"Let's hope so." Andrea returned the books from the window to the book display in the back of the store. The holidays had been an ordeal. It had taken all her powers of persuasion to convince Nick to behave himself with the Porters. In honesty, she almost felt sorry for Bert and Claudia. They just couldn't find ways to connect with their grandson. The generation gap was a chasm. As if in silent protest, Nick wore the shoes Tony had given him everywhere except to visit his grandparents.

The only saving grace, when the weather permitted, was that he shot baskets for hours on end, his face screwed up in intense concentration. His Christmas gifts had hardly been touched, except for a book Bert had given him—a history of Major League Baseball. She was at her wit's end. Maybe she'd call the school and talk with Mrs. Elliot again. Perhaps there was good news there. She could certainly use some. If not, maybe it was time to consider the school counselor.

She shelved the last book and leaned against the wall. If only the sun would shine. Maybe she wouldn't feel so helpless and out of sorts.

"Andrea," Phil's voice rang out. "Can you help a customer with baby dolls?"

"I'm coming," Andrea said, adjusting her voluminous skirt. Keep busy, she reminded herself. It helped.

NICK STOOD ON THE STAIRS late that same afternoon glaring at her. "I'm not going and you can't make me!" His pugnacious face revealed nothing of the mild-mannered boy who loved computer games.

"It'll be good for you," Andrea implored. "Jason in your class goes to tae kwon do. His mother says he loves it."

"He's a dork." Nick slumped onto the second step, his eyes cold.

"Listen, here, young man, I've paid the money. The least you can do is try it once." Her patience was wearing thin. "So get your things and come on." She walked toward the back door, praying he would follow.

"Dad and Mom wouldn't make me go!"

She wheeled around and confronted him. "They aren't here, are they? So you'll just have to make do with me!"

"You're not my mother," he spat out.

The wound went deep. She grabbed him by the elbow. "No, I'm not. But I'm all you've got. So get your coat and march yourself to the car. Now."

With a backward glance so full of enmity it ripped her apart, he grabbed his coat out of the closet and stomped through the house.

Was the battle worth it? Should she have forced the issue? But if she wasn't in control, what then? She hated this wild indecisiveness. Parenting was no piece of cake!

THE FOLLOWING FRIDAY Andrea pulled in front of the school to pick up Nick to take him to his second tae kwon do class. The metal swings clanged together ominously and the dirty snow on the playground showed signs of being trampled by children's feet. One or two stragglers exited the building, but no Nicky. Exasperated, Andrea finally shut down the motor and trudged toward the school. He was undoubtedly malingering, trying to avoid the inevitable. She was getting very tired of being tested at every turn.

Inside she looked up and down the hall, empty except for one teacher changing a bulletin board display. Quickly Andrea made her way to Nick's classroom. Dark. She tried the door. Locked. Where could he be? She walked rapidly toward the office. The secretary smiled when she entered. "May I help you?"

"I hope so. I'm Nicholas Porter's aunt. Do you have any idea where he might be? I was supposed to pick him up."

The secretary shook her head. "I'm sorry, most of the youngsters are gone, but just a minute." She stood and walked to the door of the principal's office. Andrea could hear her asking about Nick. "No," she said as she returned to her desk. "Mr. Leider hasn't seen him. Is there any possibility he went on home or is at a classmate's house?"

Andrea quelled the fear rising in her throat. "I don't think so, but possibly his grandfather picked him up. Thanks." She ran to her car and, with trembling fingers, fumbled for her key. There had to be a reasonable explanation. Driving slowly and checking the sidewalks carefully, she searched for Nick's familiar blue coat. Nothing. Surely he was with the Porters.

She pulled into their driveway and hurried to the door, ringing the bell frantically. Abruptly the door opened. Claudia stared at her. "Andrea, what on earth?"

Andrea found her voice. "Is Nicky here?"

"Nicholas, here? Why, of course not. Should he be?"

"Who is it, Claudia?" Bert came and stood behind his wife. "Andrea, what a surprise!"

Claudia twisted to face him. "She wants to know if Nicholas is here."

"Here? Why, no. Isn't he at home?" Bert looked at Andrea strangely.

"I...I don't know."

Claudia's voice rose. "What do you mean, you don't know?"

Andrea was already headed back to her car. "Never mind, I'll go check."

"Andrea," Bert called, "we'll be right behind you. Claudia, get your coat."

Cold fingers of dread squeezed Andrea's chest so tightly she could hardly breathe. Please God! She was driving too fast, but she had to get there. Had to see that Nicky was all right.

She careened into her driveway, grabbed her house key from her purse and ran across the lawn. She managed to get the door open on the third try. "Nicky!" she called, racing from one room to the next. "Nicky, where are you?" The silence was overwhelming. She took the stairs two at a time and threw open the door to his bedroom. His bedside clock ticked, the computer sat where it always did, the usual pile of dirty clothes lay on the floor. "Nick!" she screamed. There was no answer.

She crumpled to the floor, dazed. Oh God, oh God, oh God.

"Andrea? Did you find him?" She could hear Bert wheezing up the steps. Then he stood in the doorway, red-faced and breathing deeply. "Nicholas?"

"He's not here." She stood up, looking around frantically. "We've got to do something."

Claudia materialized in the doorway beside Bert. "What's going on here?"

Andrea shoved past her. "Let me get to the phone. There's one more place I can try. Then we have to call the police."

Her hands were shaking so badly she could hardly grip the directory. Finally she located the number for the tae kwon do studio. She gripped the receiver like a lifeline.

"Nicholas Porter? Just a minute." The receptionist put the phone down. In the background, Andrea heard children's excited voices. The woman was taking an eternity. Finally she returned. "I'm sorry, Ms. Evans. There's no Nicholas Porter here."

"Oh, God!" Andrea dropped the receiver. She felt Bert's arms around her, helping her into a chair.

"We'd better call the police," Bert said grimly. "Do you want me to—"

"No, no." Andrea wiped the back of her hand across her face. "I can do it. They may need to know—" she swallowed a sob "—what he was wearing, things like that."

As she dialed the police, in some corner of her brain she registered Claudia's comment. "Bert, what has she done to our grandson?"

She couldn't think about it now. Not now.

Later.

HARTFORD HAD BEEN THE PITS. More wrangling and posturing among supposed adults than Tony could stomach. He'd have an ulcer sooner rather than later if he didn't watch it. It was not an easy matter moving people off long-held positions or getting them to cede their spheres of influence. And, of course, the late Friday afternoon Cleveland-bound plane was overbooked. Hot, stuffy and full of coughers.

He squirmed uncomfortably, wedged beside a corpulent gentleman, who had appropriated their common armrest.

He rubbed his face, feeling the stubble. Closing his eyes, he tried to stop the thoughts racing around in his head. Two proposals to finalize, a heavy-duty meeting in St. Louis with some real estate brokers, three contracts to review. There was never enough time.

But somehow he'd do it. That was his job.

And all he wanted to do was sleep all weekend. Fat chance. Not and live up to his billing.

The plane landed smoothly, only twenty minutes late. He grabbed his briefcase and topcoat, sprinted down the jet way and hurried to the curb, where he hailed a taxi.

Clouds were riding in low off the lake, hiding the moon, and a fierce north wind shook the cab periodically. Tony was relieved the cabbie wasn't talkative. He had quite enough of that in his work, ninety percent of it hot air.

He leaned back against the seat. What was eating at him? Some form of dissatisfaction he couldn't put a name to. Vague. Disturbing. And, more and more frequently, rising to his consciousness.

The cabbie slammed on his brakes in front of Tony's apartment. He paid the driver, got a receipt and walked toward the building. The hell with all this soul-searching. It wasn't getting him anywhere; it just made him tired.

He started up the stairs. He'd have a couple of beers, order in a pizza, maybe catch a little TV and call it a night. He reached his floor and started down the hallway.

Halfway to his flat, he stopped, blinking his eyes. What the hell?

He ran the rest of the way. Lying on his side in front of his door, his knees pulled up to his chest, was…Nick?

Tony knelt and gently nudged him. ''Nick, buddy. Hey, you all right?''

Slowly the boy rolled over and opened one eye. The other, Tony saw, was black-and-blue, swollen shut. ''Hey, kid, it's me. Boy, that's some shiner you've got!''

Shaking off sleep, Nick squinted up at him, then, recognition dawning, threw himself into Tony's arms. "Tony, Tony. I thought you weren't coming!"

Tony found himself cradling the boy, whose fingers dug tenaciously into his shoulders. "It's okay," he said softly. "You're fine. I'm home." Nick gave a convulsive shudder. Tony pushed him far enough away to study his face.

"What are you doing here, buddy? How'd you find me?"

"I—I needed to talk to you. I looked up your address and came downtown on the Rapid."

"Since you're here, whaddaya say we go inside, and I'll fix us a sandwich while you tell me what's going on?"

Nick ran a fist under his nose, sniffled loudly, then nodded his head. Tony stood, opened the door and, putting an arm around Nick's shoulders, led him into the apartment. "Sit down, sport. You like grape pop?" Nick nodded, staring at Tony as if his life depended on him.

Tony hung up his coat, took off his jacket and rolled up his sleeves. This was one situation that had to be handled delicately. He knew a hurting kid when he saw one.

Tony poured the grape soda over ice and handed the glass to Nick. "Here you go." The boy gulped thirstily. "I'm going to change my clothes. Then I'll make us some double-deck peanut-butter-and-jelly sandwiches. After dinner, whaddaya say we talk?"

Again the boy nodded.

"Does your aunt know where you are?" Tony asked gently.

Nick looked up with frightened eyes, then managed to speak again. "No." He studied his hands. "Do you hafta tell her?"

"Yeah, kid, I do."

"Please, Tony, could you tell her I'm okay, but I wanna stay with you tonight?"

Andrea wasn't going to like that idea. But Nick seemed to be hanging on by a thread. "I'll see what I can work out. No promises, though."

The boy smiled weakly. "You can do anything, I betcha."

If Tony hadn't had the weight of the world on his shoulders before, he sure did now. He went into the bedroom, took a deep breath and picked up the phone.

BERT COULDN'T SIT STILL. He paced between the fireplace and the entry hall, then back again. For Claudia's and Andrea's sakes, he was trying to remain calm, but panic lurked just beneath the surface. The detective had finished taking down all the information Andrea could provide. In the kitchen Claudia prepared coffee. Andrea sat shriveled into the corner of the sofa, her face pale, her fingers gripping the phone directory. They'd already called everyone they could think of, including Urbanski, who wasn't home.

"I just don't understand it," he heard Andrea saying. "Nick's never done anything like this before."

Claudia entered the room, the tray in her hands wobbling. She set it down with a clatter. "Sorry. I can't seem to stop shaking." She stood there clutching her pearl necklace as if it were a rosary. "Officer, do you...do you think he's been abducted?"

"Oh, God," Andrea's eyes widened and she drew her knees tight against her chest. "Please, no!"

"It's a possibility we have to consider, ma'am." The detective stood up. "Meanwhile, we have an all points bulletin out for him and we'll be questioning people from the school." He nodded toward the front door. "For tonight, I'm going to post a uniformed officer here. If you need anything or think of any other helpful information, you let him know."

Claudia snagged the detective's sleeve. "You can't just

leave us like this. I mean, what's your plan? What are you going to do?''

Bert took hold of her and pulled her back. "Let the man do his job, Claudia."

Andrea stared straight ahead, never acknowledging the detective as he left.

Bert led Claudia to a chair, helped her sit, then handed her a cup of coffee. Then he poured one for Andrea, who waved it away with her hand. He kept it for himself and sat on the sofa beside Andrea. "It'll be all right," he said. "It has to be."

"I'm so frightened," Andrea whispered. "Nicky, baby, where are you?"

Suddenly Bert became aware of the sound of china rattling against china. He watched with alarm as the cup and saucer slipped from Claudia's hands. Coffee spilled all over the floor. He leaped across the room and gathered her into his arms. "Claudia, what is it?"

Her gaze was fixed on the shelves next to the fireplace. "I c-can't believe it. It's happening all over again."

"What is?"

She stepped around him, all the time staring at the shelves. "Our boy. He's gone."

Bert laid a hand on her shoulder. "He's only missing, Claudia. The police will find him. I'm sure of it."

"No, no they won't. It's just like last time." She reached out and touched one of the ship models, studying it with a kind of fascinated horror. "Like Richard." She shook her head. "Richard didn't come back."

Bert turned her in his arms and braced his hands on her shoulders. "Stop it, Claudia. This kind of talk isn't helping anyone."

"He just sailed away and never came back!" Her voice rose shrilly and tears trickled down her powdered cheeks.

"And now it's Nicholas. He's never coming back! It's all my fault."

"Andrea," Bert barked. "Get a blanket and some brandy." Andrea jumped up and ran from the room. "Claudia!" Bert took her face in his hands. "Claudia, listen to me. The boy will be all right. He's got to be. Nothing is your fault."

Her eyes cleared and she turned and looked at him curiously for a moment, as if she'd never seen him before. Then unexpectedly she crumpled against him. "Richard?" There was a moment of anguished silence before it broke in a crescendo of sobs. "My baby! I didn't mean to."

Bert held her upright by sheer force of will. She was crying uncontrollably and not making much sense. He'd never seen her like this. Not even...when they'd first learned about Rich. He led her to the sofa and laid her down just as Andrea arrived with a blanket, which she tucked around Claudia. "Bert?" Andrea looked at him questioningly.

Claudia clutched at the blanket and pulled it up to her chin, her unrelenting keening cracking his heart. Bert felt his own eyes fill. "It's coming out, all of it," he said softly.

"What?" Andrea asked.

"The grief." He shook his head, then pulled out a handkerchief and blew his nose. "I thought...I thought she didn't care."

Andrea put a hand on his shoulder and gently pushed him down on the edge of the sofa. "She's had it bottled up for a very long time."

Bert sat there for what seemed many minutes, holding his wife's hand and brushing the tears from her cheeks. "Rich is gone, Claudia. He's gone." He leaned over and kissed her. She looked up at him with the soulful blue eyes he remembered from their courting days. "But Nick will be fine, Claudia. We'll find him. You'll see."

Claudia struggled to sit up. "Nicholas?"

Somewhere in the house the phone rang. Dimly, he heard Andrea speaking to someone. "*Nick.* That's what he wants to be called, Claudia. Nick."

"Nick?" She sighed and fell back against the pillow.

Bert squeezed his eyes shut. He prayed he was right. The lad had to be fine. Otherwise, he didn't think he could bear to go on living.

"Bert? Claudia?" Andrea stood in the doorway cradling the phone to her chest, tears streaming down her cheeks. "He's okay. Nicky's okay."

"Where? Who found—"

"Tony. He's at Tony's."

Bert let his forehead drop gently against Claudia's. "Thank God. Did you hear that, sweetheart? Our Nick's been found."

CHAPTER THIRTEEN

HEARING ANDREA'S VOICE, reedy with relief, Tony realized what a welcome sound it was, how much he'd missed her. After he assured her Nick was okay, she asked to speak to him. Tony carried the phone to the living room and handed it to Nick.

"I'm okay, Andie.... I'm sorry. I guess I didn't think you'd be so worried...."

Be so worried? Didn't the kid know how much Andrea loved him? Tony put eight slices of bread on the counter, opened the peanut butter and began making the sandwiches, one ear cocked to Nick's conversation. Andrea wasn't going to be happy about his request to spend the night here. Tony wasn't sure what he had to offer the boy, but if Nick wanted to stay, he'd do his best to help.

"I don't know 'zactly why. Lotsa things. Stupid tae kwon do, Ben, you and Mimi raggin' on me, school.... Can't you understand? I just needed to talk to Tony."

Tony made a mental note of Nick's concerns, but he'd bet his last dime there was a lot more to it than school or his grandmother's criticism. The kid needed a man to talk with. And, for whatever reason, he'd been elected.

"Please don't make me come home yet. Not tonight... Tony said it was okay with him. *Please,* Andie." Nick signaled a plea with his eyes and handed back the receiver. "She wants to talk with you."

"Tony, thank God you found him. Is he all right? I need to see him."

In her voice Tony heard fear mixed with relief. "He's fine, Andrea, just a little tired. I know you want to see him, but spending the night seems very important to him." He tried to stress the word "important" without alerting Nick. He had to make her understand. Distractedly, he ran a hand through his hair.

"I don't know, Tony. It's quite an imposition."

"Lemme put it this way. We're doing a guy thing here. And it's kind of…heavy."

"If you're sure—"

"I'm sure. I'll bring him home after breakfast." He paused, picturing her worried face. "Would you like to talk to him again?"

"Please."

While Nick concluded the conversation, Tony smeared grape jelly on top of the peanut butter, unearthed a package of potato chips and set two places at the table.

Nick got out of his chair and set down the phone. "Thanks, Tony, for fixing it so I can stay."

Tony studied him, then opened a drawer and pulled out a couple of paper napkins. "You look like you had hand-to-hand combat with a meat grinder." He gestured to Nick's place. "Sit down and dig in, and while you're eating you can tell me how you came by that shiner."

Nick attacked the food. Poor guy had had a rough day and it had probably been a long time since lunch. After wolfing down half a sandwich, he took a swig of milk and tentatively began. "Me and Ben got into a fight."

Tony arched his eyebrows. "Oh? And what does Ben look like?"

"He scraped his knee when I pushed him down. That's all."

"Who started it?"

"I did." He still hadn't looked up.

"Wanna tell me about it?"

The boy swallowed hard, then fiddled with a crust, peeling it away from the bread. Tony waited. "He's been on my case all year. I hate him!"

"So what was different about today?"

Nick fixed his good eye on Tony, as if gauging his potential reaction. "He called me a name."

"What name?"

"Bastard. He said everybody has a mom and a dad, but since I don't have any parents, I must be a bastard!" Tony watched the boy's throat work. "So I pushed him down and kicked him as hard as I could, but he got up and ran at me and punched me in the face." He paused, then hung his head again. "He's lots bigger than me."

"That was a pretty awful thing to say. Sounds like you did the only thing a man could do." Tony leaned back in his chair and watched the boy's chin come up, his shoulders straighten.

"You think so?" His voice quavered with hope.

"Absolutely. A guy can only let a bully push him around so long, and then he has to take action."

Nick shoved a piece of crust around the edge of his plate. "Can I ask you somethin'?"

"Shoot."

"What's a bastard?"

Tony was tempted to laugh, but the kid looked so forlorn and uncertain. It was a hell of a question, especially since Tony didn't know how much Nick knew about the birds and the bees. "It's a name insensitive bullies use when they want to get at somebody by saying he has no parents." He hoped he wouldn't have to get more specific. Or tell Nick how much being called that by his own father had wounded him.

"So it's really bad, huh?"

"Yeah, it is." So bad Tony realized, with blinding perception, that although Stan Urbanski might be his biological father, he had never succeeded in earning Tony's respect. "How'd it make you feel when he said that?"

"Mad. Really, really mad."

"Why?"

"'Cause I had a mom and a dad and they loved me a lot and I can't help it that they—" he swiped the back of a fist across his good eye in a futile attempt to forestall the tears "—drowned in that dumb old lake!"

Tony knew a defining moment had arrived. "Tell me about it, Nick."

"I shoulda been there. I shoulda gone with them. But I had a dumb ol' birthday party to go to. Mimi said she'd take me and pick me up. She told my parents to go on sailing."

God, no wonder the woman was so bitter. She probably couldn't live with herself.

"If I'd been there, I coulda seen it. Seen that ol' boom coming around. I coulda hollered. I coulda thrown a life jacket." The sobs were coming faster now, and his little shoulders were shaking violently.

Tony shoved his chair back and went to the boy, kneeling in front of him, looking directly at his tearstained face. "Nick, listen to me. There is nothing, *nothing* you or anyone else could have done. It was an accident. Accidents happen. We don't like them and we don't understand them, but they're nobody's fault. Not yours, not Mimi's." Suddenly Nick lunged toward him, wrapping him in a huge hug. The boy's body moved convulsively and his tears dampened Tony's shirt.

Tony held him for several minutes, then when the sobs abated, picked him up and carried him to the sofa, where they sat side by side, Tony's arms around Nick. Tears pooled in his own eyes, and he understood that at the same time Nick was mourning the mother and father he'd lost, he was finally letting go of the father he'd never had.

Tony cleared his throat and finally managed to speak. "You know about the storms on Lake Erie, don't you?"

Nick shook his head. "Whaddaya mean?"

Hadn't anybody thought to tell the boy this at the time? "They're sudden and vicious. It's a shallow lake and storms gather without warning and move so quickly that it can be very dangerous."

"But Daddy was a good sailor. Grandpa keeps telling me that. Why did he let it happen?"

"Your dad was surprised, son. And he did a very brave thing. He tried to save your mom. Never forget that. He must have loved her a great deal."

The boy seemed to be considering what he said. Tony realized he hadn't completed a necessary part of the thought. "And he loved you a great deal, too. Neither your mom nor your dad would want you to feel responsible." He tilted Nick's chin up. "Look at me. I'll bet they told you to go to the birthday party and have a good time, right?"

"Uh-huh."

"So you were doing exactly what they wanted you to do and you were exactly where you were supposed to be. Don't ever forget that, okay?"

"Okay." He laid his head against Tony's shoulder.

"Tired, sport?"

"A little."

"One other thing. Andrea and your grandpa and Mimi love you very much, too. I know sometimes that love can feel stifling, but think about it. You're pretty lucky to have them!" As he was lucky to have Aunt Olga. You took love where it was offered.

Nick sat up with more energy than he'd had all evening. "Tony, do you think I could sit in that funny-looking thing?" He pointed to the Eames chair.

"Sure. Go on." As the boy scrambled into the chair,

Tony smiled and shook his head. Kids had a way of saying "end of discussion" that more than a few of his clients needed to emulate.

"Tony?"

"Yeah?" Even the boy's good eye was scrunched up and his gaze was fixed on the Picasso print.

"You have weird stuff here!"

"Not like your house, huh?"

Nick grinned at him. "I don't wanna hurt your feelings or nothin', and I guess this is cool for an old guy, but I like my house better."

Tony laughed. "You know what, kid? So do I!"

AFTER CALLING PHIL to ask him to open the store, Andrea bathed, dressed, ate breakfast and now waited impatiently for Tony and Nick. The flawless blue sky and bright sunshine seemed providential this special Saturday morning. She couldn't keep herself from running to the window every time a car slowed outside.

The overwhelming relief of learning her nephew was safe at Tony's had been only slightly marred by Nick's insistence on spending the night there. Much as she'd wanted to get him home and hug the daylights out of him, she knew he had problems she hadn't been able to address. Maybe Tony was right. It could be a "guy thing." And she trusted him to deal with Nick.

But it complicated her life. Nick's actions made ending her relationship with Tony more problematic. Her nephew was attached to the man, pure and simple. What if Nick wanted to continue to be friends with Tony? Well, she'd just deal with that when and if it happened.

Then there was Claudia's breakdown. She who was never fazed had completely fallen to pieces. Andrea didn't quite know what to make of it. Bert had bundled the tearful Claudia off as soon as she was steady enough to walk to the car. Andrea shook her head. That was a side of Nick's grandmother she'd never seen before—a vulnerability that made her infinitely more human.

Another car! She peered out the window. There they were. She hurried to the door and flung it open. "Nicky!"

The boy ran toward her. She gasped as she took in the black-and-blue bruises all around his swollen eye. But even that was forgotten when he threw himself into her arms. "I'm so sorry, Andie."

"Me, too." She pulled back and examined his eye. "Are you all right?" He nodded. "You can tell me all about it later, okay?" Then she hugged him again, burying her face in his hair, which smelled strongly of Tony's woodsy shampoo. Her stomach flip-flopped at the incongruous memory of standing in his shower all those weeks ago.

"Hello, Andrea." Tony stood over them, blocking the sun, holding Nick's backpack. His voice was hesitant.

As she rose to her feet, she became lost in the intoxicating warmth of his gaze. Nick stood with an arm around her waist. "Tony...thank you so much," she managed.

"Tony's got this cool apartment and he cooks great flapjacks and me and him are gonna go to the park and practice fielding today, right, Tony?"

Flapjacks? They'd always called them pancakes.

"Only if Andrea gives you permission." He gave Nick a knowing look. "You could be in a little trouble, kid."

Nick's face fell. "Oh. Yeah."

Andrea realized she'd been staring at Tony. She found her voice. "Why don't we go inside and discuss it over a cup of coffee?"

"I hate coffee," Nick said.

The tension in Andrea dissolved in genuine laughter. "Then maybe you'd like cocoa instead."

"Cool!"

Tony followed them into the house. Nick took his backpack from Tony, started to go to his room, but then paused and looked at Andrea. "I thought you'd be mad."

"There are issues we need to discuss, young man. But mainly I'm relieved that you're safe and sound—except, of course, for that shiner."

Nick grinned a face-splitting grin. "It's pretty neat, huh?" Then he ran up the stairs.

Andrea looked wonderingly at Tony. "He sounds proud of it."

Tony smiled. "As you'll find out, he has every right to be."

Later, sitting around the kitchen table with their coffee and cocoa, Nick told her about the fight. Although she disapproved of fighting, she decided she might've decked Ben herself had she heard him call Nick a bastard. She'd need to phone Mrs. Elliot and alert her to the situation.

"So is it okay, Andie?"

Her attention had wandered. "Is what okay?"

"If Tony takes me to the park today. We only got a few months before baseball starts, and I gotta get good."

How could she deny him when he looked so animated, so happy? She looked at Tony questioningly.

He nodded. "It's fine." He turned to Nick. "Why don't you go upstairs and change your clothes, sport?" After the boy left, he moved his chair closer and lowered his voice. "Frankly, I think it would be a good idea for him to run off some steam. Don't you have to work, anyway?"

Andrea nodded. "He usually goes to his grandparents' on Saturdays, but—" Claudia's tortured face rose in front of her "—I don't think they'll mind if he comes later. Could you run him over there when you finish?"

"No problem." His fingers toyed with the coffee mug. She couldn't keep her eyes off his hands. Strong, veined hands that had touched her in intimate places and drawn quivers of response from her.

She forced herself to concentrate. Where were they? Oh, yes. "I'll call them."

"Fine, but before you do, I think there's more you need to know about what he told me last night." She gripped the handle of her mug, totally unprepared for Tony's next words. "He feels responsible for his parents' deaths."

It must be the sun shining through the window, she thought wildly. *All I can see are spots.* Dimly she heard a voice. "Andrea, are you all right?"

She pressed fingers against her eyes, then opened them. Tony was leaning toward her, his hand on hers. "What did you say?"

"He thinks he should have been on the boat with them," Tony said quietly.

"Oh, God."

"There's more." He hesitated. "He thinks his grandmother encouraged them to go."

It was all coming too fast. "You mean he blames Claudia, too?"

Tony nodded solemnly. "Looks that way."

"What should I do?"

"I think he'll be better now that he's talked about it. But encourage him to let it out if he brings it up with you."

Maybe she should consider the school counselor, after all. She felt suddenly exhausted. "Oh, Tony. I don't know how to thank you."

He looked at her intently, and she had the sense that with any encouragement at all he would kiss her. And that she might have let him, but the moment passed. When he spoke, his voice was husky. "I do. At least let me be a friend to Nick. It doesn't have to be about you and me."

An instinctive protest rose in her, but her rational side prevailed. He was right. They weren't the issue; Nicky was. She only had time to murmur, "Okay, just you and Nick," before the boy clattered into the room, dragging a bat and holding a ball.

"I'm ready," he said, looking expectantly at Tony.

Tony pushed his mug away, then rose to his feet, pausing to send Andrea another one of those melt-your-heart looks. "Thanks, Andrea. I'll take good care of him."

After they were gone, the house was too quiet. Andrea turned on the local easy-listening station before she put the mugs in the dishwasher. Last night was catching up with her. So many things to think about. Mainly about Tony and the welcome yet disturbing way his presence lingered.

Just before she left for work, she called the Porters. Claudia answered the phone. She sounded weak, very unlike herself. Andrea carefully explained Nicky's plans for the day, fully expecting Claudia to respond with comments about "that man Urbanski." But she did no such thing. Instead, she simply said, "Andrea, when you come to pick up Nick this afternoon, I'd like to talk with you. Privately."

After Andrea hung up, she stood a moment, puzzled. Although she'd definitely been summoned to an audience, she hadn't heard the customary edge in Claudia's voice. She'd sounded almost…agreeable. But it wasn't until she started for the car, that the lightbulb went off in Andrea's head. Surely she was mistaken.

Claudia had referred to her grandson as "Nick"!

TONY THREW THE sporting equipment in the back seat and made sure Nick was buckled up before he pulled away from the curb and headed for the Porters' house. "You did pretty well for the first time. You might make a good second or third baseman."

"You think?"

"You're agile, you've got a good eye and you're quick."

"But I don't catch very well."

"Not yet. Give it some time. And remember what I told you. You gotta be ready."

"You mean get my mitt positioned."

Tony tousled his hair. "Exactly."

"That was really fun today. Can we go again?"

"We'll see. I want to talk to your grandfather about it."

"Grandpa? Why?" The kid didn't sound too happy.

"It'd be a lot easier if there were three of us. One to pitch, one to catch, one to bat. Also for infield practice."

"But Grandpa?"

"He taught your dad, didn't he?"

Nick shrugged, then seemed to consider the idea.

Tony, whistling a few choruses of "Take Me Out to the Ball Game," said no more until they arrived at the Porters'. "One last thing, Nick. Remember, at the same time you lost your father and mother, your grandparents lost their only child. Sometimes us guys have to put aside our own needs and kinda, you know, take care of older people. It's the nice thing to do." To the extent they'll let you, he added silently, thinking regretfully of his own father's stubborn resistance. He held out his hand and shook with the boy. "Understand?"

Nick grinned and nodded his head. "I got it!"

"Okay, then, let's do it!"

Hand in hand they strolled up the walk to the Porters' front door.

BERT KNELT AND CLASPED his grandson against his chest, his voice unsteady. "Oh, son, I thought we might not see you again. We were so frightened."

Nick's voice was muffled. "I'm sorry, Grandpa. I didn't mean to scare you. I'll never run away again."

Bert didn't want to let go. Holding Nick, smelling the faint odor of little-boy sweat, he was flooded with relief. Slowly, his knees creaking, he got to his feet, gripping Nick's hand in his. "Mimi will want to see you. Then you can tell me how you got that black eye, Nick."

"Nick?" The boy beamed up at him. "You called me Nick."

Bert chuckled. "Well, that's your name, isn't it?"

Nick giggled. "It sure is."

"All right, then. That's what Mimi and I will call you from now on."

So preoccupied had he been with his grandson, that only now did he realize he'd left Urbanski standing in the entry hall. "Er, Urbanski, could I offer you something to drink? A glass of wine, perhaps."

He'd thought surely the man would refuse after that awkward dinner, but Urbanski surprised him by saying, "Thank you, Bert. I'd like that."

"Tony's my friend, Grandpa. My best friend."

Bert considered Nick's words. If Urbanski was good enough for Nick, he was good enough for him. After all, according to Andrea, the man had done them all a service by helping Nick. "Why don't you go along upstairs, lad, and visit with Mimi. She's resting in her bedroom, but she'll be delighted to see you and hear about all your adventures. But—" he held up his hand in caution "—go easy on the details about that eye of yours."

"Okay." Nick literally skipped up the steps. It had been a long time, Bert noted, since the boy had seemed so happy, at least in this house.

He gestured toward the library. "In here, Tony. Port or sherry?"

"Port will be fine. Thank you. This will give me the opportunity to discuss something with you."

Bert poured their drinks, handed a glass to Tony and

settled across from him in a leather armchair. "Before you begin, let me say this—my wife and I are grateful for everything you've done for Nick." He raised his glass, then took a sip. "All right. I'm listening."

Tony set down his port and leaned forward, elbows on his knees, hands clasped. "Let me level with you. I'm aware you may not think much of me. I lack the polish and advantages of a man of your class. But I care about your grandson. And I think it would be in his best interests if we tried to get along. He very much needs both of us in his life right now."

Bert felt the wine warming his stomach, easing the tension knotted there. "Go on."

"Nick needs some toughening up. And he needs men who love him to help him do that."

"Does the black eye have anything to do with this?" Bert had been shocked by the ugly bruises, but he hadn't wanted to spoil Nick's welcome.

"In part." As Tony told him about the bully at school, Bert felt himself growing hot under the collar. Damn schoolyard bullies! "Now I don't know exactly why, but Nick seems to have selected me as a kind of mentor and coach." Tony went on to explain about Nick's interest in sports. "But you're his grandfather. I think it's important for you to be involved."

"I had no idea he needed help. I just naturally assumed—" What had he "naturally assumed"? Fathers helped sons learn to play games. But Nick...didn't have a father. Where would the boy have learned? He knew what he'd assumed—that his grandson would just naturally pick up the skills.

"I'd like you to come with us."

"What?" Bert shook his head. "Excuse me, I lost the train of thought there."

"Nick wants to get ready for the baseball season. We'll

be going to the park on nice days to practice. We'd like you to come along and help.''

"To the park?'' He hadn't been to the park since…he tried to remember. Since Rich played city league ball for his company. He treated his rumbling stomach to another swig of port.

"Could I pick the two of you up next Saturday?''

"Why, I—'' he felt an idiotic grin spread across his face "—I'd be delighted.''

"That's settled, then.'' Tony finished his drink, then rose to his feet. "I'll be running along now. Enjoy the rest of the day with your grandson.''

Bert stood and clasped Urbanski's shoulder. "I will, believe me.'' He walked him to the door, where he paused and extended his hand. "Thank you, Tony. For everything.''

"You're welcome.''

After he was gone, Bert hesitated before climbing the stairs to see how Claudia and Nick were doing. He scratched his head. Darned if he could remember why he wasn't supposed to like that fellow.

AT WORK, ANDREA TRIED—unsuccessfully—to forestall thinking about her unsettling reactions to Tony. On one level she interacted courteously with customers; on another, she couldn't help remembering the way her spirit had soared when she'd seen him, how his voice had sent shivers down her spine and, above all, how gently and appropriately he had handled Nick. The boy worshiped him.

Closing time came none too soon. The emotional events of the past twenty-four hours had taken their toll. All she wanted was supper, a hot bath and a warm bed. On her way to pick up Nick, she turned her attention to Claudia. If she hadn't been there to see it for herself, she would have had trouble believing that the impeccably groomed, tightly controlled woman had gone so completely to pieces. Could Claudia really have held such powerful emotions in check for so long? That was heavy-duty denial.

Andrea shook her head. She guessed she'd find out soon enough, although it was anybody's guess whether Claudia would talk about yesterday or not. In truth, Andrea didn't have any notion why Nick's grandmother wanted to see her this afternoon.

When she arrived, Bert gave her an uncharacteristic, somewhat clumsy hug before ushering her upstairs to the master bedroom. Claudia, sitting up in the king-sized bed, looked tiny, frail against the massed pillows. Her satin bed jacket did little to conceal the crepelike skin of her neck or her protruding collarbone. She wore only lipstick and Andrea couldn't help being startled. The woman looked ten years older. But the harsh lines in her face were softened by a tentative smile. "Come in, dear." She beckoned toward a small damask-covered chair pulled up to the bedside. "Nick's just putting our game back in Richard's, er, *his* room."

"Game?" Andrea was aware her mouth was gaping.

"Yes, we've been playing Battleship."

Battleship? In her wildest dreams, Andrea couldn't imagine it. It was usually Bert who entertained Nick.

As she sat down on the edge of the chair, Claudia shooed Bert away. "Go find your grandson and get him a snack, Bert. The boy's been holed up with me for too long. He must be starving."

Andrea bit back the objection. It was nearly dinnertime, but in a situation as delicate as this, the regular rules didn't apply.

When they were alone, Andrea felt a compulsion to fill the silence. "How are you, Claudia?"

"Tired. Ashamed. And, believe it or not, better than I have felt in many months."

Andrea didn't know which of those conversational threads she should pick up. "I hope you're not ashamed about last night. You had every reason to be overwrought. We all were."

Claudia smiled sadly, her thin fingers worrying the satin edge of the blanket. "I regret very much that my actions made a difficult situation even worse for you and Bert."

When Andrea demurred, Claudia held up a hand. "Let me go on, my dear. Bert and I had a long talk this morning. I'm not only ashamed of my overreaction last night but of how I've let my narrow-mindedness stand between us. Of how I've denied Nicho—*Nick* the freedom to be a little boy. Over the past few months, I suppose I've made life quite difficult for you, Andrea."

Andrea didn't know what to say, but settled for honesty. "It hasn't been easy."

Claudia shook her head regretfully. "I don't know how to make it up to you and Nick." She hesitated as if organizing her thoughts. "No, 'ashamed' isn't strong enough. The correct word is 'guilty.'"

"Claudia, you don't have to—"

"Oh, but I do. For too long you and Nick have had to put up with an old lady's pride and bitterness. Frankly, I scared myself last night but, with Bert's help, I've done a lot of soul-searching since then. I've come to several conclusions." She reached for Andrea's hand, pulling it onto the blanket, then covering it with her own cool, dry one. "That's what I want to talk to you about."

Scooting her chair closer, Andrea shifted to a more comfortable position. In the depths of Claudia's pale blue eyes there was a flicker of indecision. She closed them briefly, then opened them and looked straight at Andrea. "I lost my only child in Lake Erie. And much as I regret it now, without ever speaking of it, I took responsibility for the accident and for what happened afterward. The only way I could deal with my grief was to close myself off from other people. I see now that I was also indulging my selfish need for the dramatic."

"But how could you have been responsible?"

"I convinced myself that Richard and Tami would still be alive if I hadn't encouraged them to go sailing so that I could take Nick to the birthday party. I loved showing him off. Tami didn't want to go sailing that day. She was a good mother, and she had promised Nick she would take him to the party. But I insisted she go with Richard."

Tami's dear face swam before Andrea's eyes. She felt sick. "But the storm wasn't your fault."

Claudia sagged against the pillows. "I realize that, but I needed someone to blame. Me. Then when Bert couldn't handle Richard's death, I made a conscious decision. Somebody had to take control, be the strong one." She smiled ruefully. "A role I was born to play. But…it wasn't until last night, when I thought—" she covered her eyes with her free hand briefly "—we might have lost Nicholas, too, that I let myself face the full impact of Richard's death." She leaned forward urgently and grasped Andrea's hand in both of hers. "I loved my son. You've got to believe that."

"Of course I do. I never doubted it."

"But grief, especially denied grief, turned me into a critical, bitter, unpleasant person. Andrea, I've wronged Nick and I've wronged you."

Tears welled in Andrea's eyes. Such self-revelation required courage, especially for someone as proud as Claudia. "Please, I—"

"Not yet, Andrea. Let me finish. I want, somehow, to try to make it up to you both. I don't know if that's even possible. It won't happen overnight and I'll make mistakes.

I can't undo the past, but if you'll let me, maybe I can learn to be a better grandmother…and a better friend.''

The enormity of Claudia's turnaround was almost too much to take in. But welcome. Oh, so welcome. ''I'd like that, Claudia,'' Andrea said quietly.

''I've thought a lot about how to begin.'' She released Andrea's hand and scooted upright in the bed. ''First, I will stop second-guessing your decisions about Nick. Grandparents often have old-fashioned ideas, and you're right—the boy needs to feel he fits into the crowd. Frankly, you're doing a great job, a better one than stuffy old grandparents could, and it can't be easy all by yourself.'' She ticked off number two on her middle finger. ''And second, would you be willing to give me some suggestions? I think Nick's afraid of me.''

Andrea was at a loss for words. This was a new Claudia. One she wanted to get to know. Finally she spoke the words rising straight from her heart. ''Thank you for your honesty.''

''Can you forgive me, my dear?'' Her plaintive expression eliminated any last reservations Andrea harbored.

''Of course.'' She leaned over and patted Claudia's slender blue-veined hand. ''As a token of good faith, maybe I could give you your first grandmother tip?''

''Please!''

''Try peanut butter and jelly instead of broccoli.''

Andrea didn't think she'd ever heard a more appealing sound than the tinkling of Claudia's laughter.

CHAPTER FOURTEEN

WHO WAS HE SUPPOSED to be, anyway—Captain Marvel? Stewing over his hectic schedule and one particularly troublesome client, Tony stood in his office, loading his briefcase with the revised proposals for the latest deal and dreading this, his fifth trip to San Diego since the end of February. He was turning into a jet jockey!

Okay, okay, so this was what he'd thought he wanted—all the pressure of super deals, recognition for his finessing abilities, not to mention the money and status partnership had won him. But the eleventh-hour posturing of self-important suits, the incessant quid pro quo of bargaining and the same-old-same-old nature of the game were growing old.

Why? He snapped shut the case and leaned on his desk. What was so damned bad about what he did? It was legal, necessary and profitable. Was he one of those guys who achieved his goal only to grow bored? Or to crave keener, more high-stakes competition?

"Why the long face, Tony? I thought you were off today to the glorious fields of battle." Kelli stood in the doorway, an amused grin on her face. "You got that memo I sent you about the liability clause, didn't you?"

"Yes, I have the memo and, yes, I'm off to San Diego. But the 'glorious fields of battle' part? Try descent into an active volcano."

"Just the kind of challenge you like." She stepped into his office and perched on the arm of a chair.

"Is it?"

"What's with you? You sound downright bleak."

He leaned on the edge of the desk and folded his arms across his chest. "I don't know. I've worked hard, I'm exactly where I'd hoped to be professionally."

"But?"

"There's no end product. Just the next deal. After a while, they all start to seem alike. And the clients? It's like a revolving door. As one set sweeps out, another comes in. Only the names and faces change. There's no ongoing connection, no real relationship."

"This sounds serious. Sure you're not merely having a down day?"

He shrugged. "Maybe. But...I don't think so."

"You know what I think?"

He watched, fascinated, as in an unconscious protective gesture she wrapped her arm over her rounded abdomen, as if cradling the unborn infant. Now *there* was an "end product," an "ongoing relationship." She and Patrick were lucky.

"Tony?"

Her voice startled him. She'd asked him a question. What was it? Oh, yeah. "You're going to tell me what you think, like it or not, right?"

"Absolutely." She smiled fondly. "So professionally you're frustrated. How about personally?"

He felt his shoulders tense. "Personally?"

"It's simple. Are you happy?"

Happy? What did that have to do with anything? "I guess."

"Well, guess again. You don't look happy, you don't sound happy, so how could you *be* happy?" She eyed him shrewdly. "What's going on with Andrea?"

"Not much." Nothing really, except for the brief moments he saw her when he picked up Nick for baseball practice. Even those glimpses were infrequent, since more often than not he had to disappoint the kid because work interfered.

"Umm." She made that vague sound doctors do when they're probing a body for symptoms. She checked her watch. "I'm due in a meeting." She stood and put her hands on his shoulders. "But, Skee, if you'll take some motherly advice, you need to slow down long enough to figure out what you really want. Frankly, I think you know very well. You just haven't admitted it to yourself." Then she started out the door, pausing just long enough to say, "Have a good trip."

"Thanks, Kell." He stood there a minute, staring into space, before turning back to his desk to be sure he wasn't leaving anything important behind. *You just haven't admitted it to yourself.* The hell of it was, he was afraid she was right. Disgusted with this counterproductive train of thought, he grabbed his topcoat and briefcase, then took the elevator to street level where he hailed a cab.

"Airport, please," he said as he sprawled in the back seat of the taxi, then added the name of the airline. The pavement was wet with melted snow and ugly splotches of slush splattered the windshield. He hoped to God the cabbie could see better than he could drive. He was in mortal combat with every other vehicle on the road. The grim thought came to Tony that this ride was a metaphor for what was wrong with his career—lots of slush, too much testosterone and questionable goals—all made palatable by the civilized label of "service."

"Can you turn down the heater? It's hot in here."

"Gotcha, boss," the cabbie replied, looking at the heater control, taking one hand off the wheel at seventy miles per hour and scaring the wits out of Tony.

His life flashed proverbially before his eyes. If it wasn't Great Lakes Management, what *did* he want? And what was so unfulfilling about what he was doing? He forced himself to consider the questions. Was it only the job that was eating at him? Or was it something more? Was it…Andrea?

Despite the jouncing of the taxi, he managed to focus on the issue Kelli had raised. Was he happy? He wasn't used to such painful soul-searching, and the answers he was coming up with scared him, because they pointed to an entirely new and uncharted direction for his life. And because, no matter how skillfully he negotiated, how persuasively he presented his case, or how desperately he wanted it, this goal might not be attainable.

Nevertheless, the conclusion was unavoidable. He wanted time for a personal life, for a family. He wanted to be somebody's loving husband, some child's caring father. He wanted what he had never had—a real home. Bottom line, he wanted Andrea, and he wanted Nick.

The squeal of brakes and a jolt that nearly threw him into the back of the driver's seat caused him to curse under his breath. But the abrupt stop was nothing like the jolt of his own sudden and inescapable revelation.

"Here we are, sir," the cabbie announced, turning to give Tony a toothless grin of triumph.

"There is a God," Tony mumbled as he paid the man, then gratefully escaped the deathmobile, prepared to move on with his life.

ANDREA GLANCED AT the kitchen clock, worry lines pinching her forehead. Usually Bert had Nick back before six. Something must've delayed them. She'd been astounded, and touched, when Bert had announced he was joining the tae kwon do class, and instead of being embarrassed by his grandfather's presence, Nick had been enthusiastic. Now, the whole class called Bert "Grandpa."

Andrea turned down the burner under the potato soup.

It wasn't like Bert not to call if he was going to be late. Surely nothing had happened to them.

She began paring apples for apple crisp, one of Nick's favorite desserts. She enjoyed pleasing him. He seemed happier lately. He especially looked forward to his Saturday outings with Tony and Bert, although last week, Tony hadn't been able to get back to town in time. Nick's acute disappointment served once again to remind Andrea how much the boy depended upon Tony. Unfortunately, five or six other times the two of them had had something planned, Tony'd had to cancel, thereby corroborating her reservations about the relationship. The man was obviously committed to his high-pressure job. It was unrealistic to expect him to continue making time for one small boy. Thank goodness Bert was now taking such an active role in his grandson's life.

Besides, if Tony were out of the picture, then she wouldn't have to see him herself or experience the spontaneous tug of longing that both excited and appalled her. It would be foolhardy to fall for someone whose goals so opposed hers. After John's rejection of Nick, why would she even consider making herself vulnerable to further heartbreak?

It was best all the way around for Tony to fade from their lives.

She was mixing the butter, flour, sugar and cinnamon when she heard the car in the driveway. Seconds later, Nick burst into the room. "Andie, wait'll you see! You'll never guess where we've been. Grandpa—"

Just then, Bert materialized behind his grandson. "Sorry, Andrea, we should've called, but—"

Nick couldn't contain himself. He stepped aside and pointed at Bert's feet. "We went past this shoe store that was having a big sale."

Bert grinned sheepishly. "Nick was pretty persuasive. I

couldn't resist.'' Pulling up his pant leg, he extended one foot.

Andrea couldn't help herself. She started to giggle. ''Bert, those are the most obnoxious athletic shoes I've ever seen in my entire life.''

Nick was practically jumping up and down. ''Yeah, aren't they cool?''

Bert shrugged, beaming at Andrea. ''I don't know what took me so long. These are the most comfortable darned shoes I've ever had!''

A shadow crossed Nick's face. ''Whaddaya think Mimi'll say?''

''Mimi? Heck, if she's lucky, I just may buy her a pair.''

Andrea, a grin still playing over her features, turned back to the counter, then sprinkled the crumb mixture over the apples while silently uttering a prayer of thanksgiving for the wonderful change in Bert and Claudia.

ON THE RETURN FLIGHT from San Diego, Tony eyed the phone on the back of the seat in front of him. He'd always thought it looked pretentious to make a call from 38,000 feet above the ground, but... He checked his watch again. It would be too late by the time they landed in Cleveland. And, for reasons he didn't want to examine too closely, it seemed urgent that he reach Andrea. Now.

Saving himself further second-guessing, he went through the maneuvers necessary to dial her number. When she answered, it was almost surreal—as if her voice came from the cloudless night beyond the fuselage. ''Andrea, it's Tony.''

''Tony?''

He couldn't read the inflection. ''Listen, about tomorrow—''

''It's okay. I'll tell Nick you can't make it.''

This time he could tell she was ticked. "Whoa! Let me finish. I'm on the flight back."

"On your way back?"

"From San Diego."

"You're calling me from a plane?" She sounded faintly disapproving.

"I couldn't wait."

"I beg your pardon?"

"I couldn't wait to hear your voice." Silence. "Andrea, are you still there?"

"Yes."

"I'll pick up Nick as usual tomorrow. But that's not the main reason I called."

"It isn't?"

"Could you have dinner with me tomorrow night? I thought it would be a good idea if we talked."

She hesitated a beat. "Yes. I think we *do* need to talk."

Somehow he'd expected at least a hint of enthusiasm, not this prissy schoolteacher voice. "I'll pick you up at seven."

"Fine. I'll be ready. And thanks for calling. I'll be sure to give Nick your message. Goodbye, Tony."

Tony stared at the receiver in his hand, then returned it to the console in front of him. Damn. He was going to have his work cut out for him.

Maybe he was the only one who couldn't shake the memory of one snowy night.

IT WAS A CRISP, frigid early March evening—one of those nights when it's too cold to snow and your breath comes out half-frozen. When Tony tucked an arm under Andrea's elbow to escort her from the parking lot to the restaurant in the picturesque town of Chagrin Falls, she held herself erect, avoiding contact with him. She had important things to say to him, and she couldn't afford to be unnerved by his masculinity.

During the drive to Chagrin Falls, they'd made small talk, mainly about Nick and the Porters and his recent San Diego trip. The conversation had felt stilted, as if both of them were rehearsing the lines of some dull play.

Inside the restaurant, Andrea pretended to study the menu by the intimate light of the single candle. She couldn't concentrate on food. She was too nervous. As he'd implied on the phone, he clearly had an agenda. So did she. Which of them would go first?

"White or red, Andrea?"

She looked up. A smile quirked Tony's lips, lips she found herself thinking of all too often. "What?"

"Wine."

"Oh." The waiter stood silently, his hands folded behind his back. "Whatever you're having will be fine."

Tony nodded to the waiter. "A bottle of your best merlot, please."

They discussed the relative merits of tournedos of beef and pecan-encrusted chicken breasts until the wine arrived. Then, seeking her eyes with that mesmerizing look of his, Tony picked up his glass. Before clinking it to hers, he offered a toast. "To old friends and new beginnings."

Much as she wanted to, she couldn't break his gaze. Instead, she raised her glass and almost imperceptibly touched it to his. *New beginnings?* Yes, she guessed that was what this was about—going their separate ways, getting on with their individual lives. That was what she'd decided, wasn't it?

Except she'd miss the burnt umber of those simmering eyes.

"What are you thinking? You're pretty quiet tonight."

Andrea fumbled with the evening purse in her lap. She needed something to hold on to. He'd given her an opening, and she might as well get this over with. "You're right. I haven't been very good company."

"I didn't say that."

"That's because you're a gentleman." She smiled wistfully. "We need to talk about Nick."

"Is something wrong?" The concern on his face was genuine.

"Not really. In fact, he's been more animated and happier lately than he's been since his parents died. And, in part, I have you to thank."

Tony shrugged off the compliment. "I haven't done that much."

"I'd call sharing your free time quite a bit." She summoned her courage. "And that's what I want to talk about. I can't expect you to continue spending your valuable time with Nick. I know how busy you are."

"Is this a brush-off?"

"What do you mean?"

"A polite way of saying, 'Butt out of our lives'?"

She was speechless.

"Let's get one thing straight. I don't spend time with Nick because I have to. I do it because I like the kid. But if I'm making you or him uncomfortable, just say the word." He leaned back in his chair, the fingers of one hand idly caressing the base of his wineglass.

She'd known this would be difficult, but she hadn't expected this pain lancing through her. She tried again to make him understand. "I know you like Nick. But you're a busy man. I mean, look how often you have to break dates with him."

"Irresponsible, huh?"

"I didn't mean that. What I'm trying to say is—" She heard the edge in her voice.

"That I get the kid's hopes up, and then don't follow through?"

"Something like that." She picked up the merlot and took a sip.

"And you don't want him disappointed. I can understand that. For years I lived that scene big-time."

Haltingly she set down her glass. "What do you mean?"

"You already know something about my charmed childhood." His tone took on bitterness. "The difference between Nick and me is that I never expected anything of my old man. It was easier that way. Then I was never disappointed." He leaned forward. "You think I don't know it hurts Nick when I let him down? Hell, it hurts me!"

"Then don't you think it might be easier on everybody if you just forgot about Nick and went on with your life? That way you wouldn't be bothered and he wouldn't become overly attached to you."

"No."

"No?"

"No, I don't think that would be better. Besides, there's more to it."

"What?"

"You."

The word struck her heart. "Me? I don't understand?"

"We're not finished with each other. At least, I'm not finished with you, Andrea."

A shudder went through her. "Tony, don't. I'm fond of you, but we're two very different people."

"No kidding?" Inexplicably, he grinned. "Isn't it great? Think how boring sameness would be."

"Tony, there's really no point in this—"

He reached across the table and grasped her hand. "Give it a chance, Andrea. *Please.*" Need, raw and exposed, sat in his eyes.

It required every shred of willpower to resist the compelling argument of her desire-filled body. "It's too risky, Tony. I can't have Nick hurt again."

His hand tightened on hers. "Nick or yourself?"

Her eyes filled. He'd come too close to the truth. But, she reminded herself, he wasn't John. He let go of her hand and raised his fingers to her cheek where he gently wiped a tear she hadn't been able to blink away. "Don't fight us, love. Let me prove to you how much I care."

"Tony, I won't lie to you. This is all very tempting. But you're a skeptic, I'm an optimist. You're ambitious, sophisticated. I'm a family person. You're all business—"

"Whoa!" He held up his palms. "Rebuttal time." He took both her hands in his, fixing liquid eyes on her. "First, I don't know if you've noticed or not, but some of your optimism is rubbing off on me. Second, ask Nick. I like your homey house a hell of a lot better than my sterile bachelor pad. And as for being a workaholic wed to Great Lakes Management—" he paused for emphasis "—what if that changed?"

"Tony, be serious. You've sacrificed so much to get where you are."

"I am serious. What if I also told you that the brass ring isn't all it's cracked up to be?"

"Meaning?"

"I don't exactly know just yet. There's only one thing I'm sure of." He turned one of her palms up and lowered his lips to it, gently, seductively.

"What?" she managed to whisper.

"That I want you to give me a chance. A trial courtship, no pun intended. That's all I ask. Will you?"

Even an iron maiden would melt, Andrea rationalized. "A chance?" Darn, she was going to cry again. "You're a very persuasive man, Tony Urbanski."

He grinned. "That's what I hear in all those boardrooms." Then he sobered. "But it's never sounded more welcome and it's never been more important."

She drew her fingers away and slowly extracted a tissue from her evening bag. "I'm scared, Tony."

"Don't be. I promise not to hurt you. Or Nick."

She smiled tremulously, then excused herself to go to the powder room to repair her face. And, if she was honest, to calm her trembling nerves. Could she risk it—a trial courtship? Did she dare trust the love sitting there in his eyes? She dabbed her cheeks with powder and reapplied her mascara. If it came to it, was she willing to compromise between her traditional view of family and his fast-paced, driven life-style? And how would Bert and Claudia react if she and Tony got serious? She leaned on the counter, staring at her pale reflection. Did she love him enough to explore these questions?

When she returned, he stood and held her chair. "Well?"

Before sitting down, she hesitated. Then, her decision made, she looked at him thoughtfully. "No guarantees, Tony. But I've always been an optimist. Why change now? We're worth a chance."

He hugged her, then whispered. "You won't be sorry."

After he'd seated her and resumed his place, he reached into his pocket. "Did you read the paper this morning?"

The comment was a non sequitur coming on the heels of their previous discussion. "No, why?"

He withdrew a clipping. "Here's an item you might be interested in. I think perhaps you'll enjoy watching a grown man eat crow for dinner." The twinkle in his eye charmed her. He gave her an article from the *Plain Dealer*.

She scanned a few lines, then paused and looked up at him, aware that she couldn't stop smiling. "Tony, that's wonderful! I'm so pleased." She read aloud. "...the confession resulted in the release of wrongly accused Darvin

Ray, who was being held in the county jail awaiting retrial for Angelo Bartelli's murder.''

"See? Sometimes you cockeyed optimists are right!"

"Tony Urbanski, is this your way of giving me permission to say 'I told you so'?"

"No, *this* is my way." And he leaned across the table and brought his lips down on hers, drawing her last shaky breaths right out of her.

When, after several glorious moments, he pulled back, she tried to recapture some semblance of reason. What, exactly, had she agreed to? Clutching her napkin under the table, she asserted herself. "Tony, remember. This is an experiment."

"Ma'am," he touched the brim of an imaginary Stetson, "that's all I ask."

TWO WEEKS LATER, Andrea sat across the table from Daisy, who jabbed a large coconut-encrusted shrimp in her direction. "See, I told you we needed a girls' night out! I just don't know why it took you so long."

"You were obviously right. I haven't laughed so much since we TP'd Dudley Taylor's house in ninth grade."

"Remember after we got finished, how that awful rainstorm hit?"

Andrea chuckled. "Oh, Lord, I'd forgotten that part. It took him days to clean up the mess."

"Do you think Nicky'll do stuff like that?"

"I suppose. He's no less mischievous than we were. He's a good kid, all things considered, and lately he's been much easier to get along with."

"That's no surprise." Daisy dipped the shrimp into the honey sauce, then continued. "Tony seems to have made a big difference in his life."

"He has."

"Yours, too, from the looks of it."

Andrea toyed with her sesame bread stick. "'Difference,' yes. 'Big,' I'm not sure about."

"A dozen long-stemmed roses looks 'big' to me!"

"Yes, that was nice. But the best part is, I'm enjoying simply having fun with him. Going to ball games, dancing, taking in a concert. Frankly, I wasn't sure he knew how to have fun."

"Give the guy a break. He can't be *all* business." Chewing thoughtfully, Daisy eyed her. "Are you getting serious about him?"

Andrea felt a twinge of exasperation. She still wasn't sure the "new Tony" was a permanent condition. "Why does it always have to be about commitment? Why can't I just relax, enjoy going out with him and see where it goes?"

Daisy shrugged elaborately. "Okay by me. It's your life."

"Yes," Andrea said, "it is." She was reluctant to admit the degree to which she was enjoying life right now. Or how much she hoped, somehow, it could always be like this.

"Chuck it in here, Nick." Tony crouched at first base, awaiting the boy's throw from second. "Aim for my mitt." The ball was a foot wide. "Close. But you can do better. Don't make the first baseman step off the bag."

Bert stood on the pitcher's mound, bundled in a heavy windbreaker. "Now, son, what happens if there's a runner on first when the batter hits the ball to you?"

"I look to second to see if the shortstop's covering."

"Then what?"

"If he is, I try for the double play. If not, I throw to first to be sure to get one out."

Bert beamed. "Good boy!"

Tony strolled toward the mound, where Nick joined him. "Had enough for today, fellas?"

"It's a little cool out here for this ol' grandpa. What do you say I treat the two of you to a burger and shake?"

They walked to the diner across the street, perched on stools at the counter and dug into their food. Tony ruffled Nick's hair. "When are the Little League tryouts?"

"A couple of weeks. April 17."

"You know what? I think you'll be ready. What's your opinion, Bert?"

Bert licked a greasy finger. "Gee, these hamburgers are great." He looked up. "Ready? No doubt about it."

"Grandpa, won't this snack spoil your dinner?"

"Not if you don't tell Mimi on me. That woman monitors my eating like a hawk."

"Do you have another date with Andie tonight?" Nick asked.

"Sure do. Guess it's about time I asked you two if you approve."

"You and Andrea have been spending a lot of time together. Is this getting serious?" Bert held a French fry halfway between his plate and his mouth.

"I'd like it to be." Tony held his breath. Bert's reaction was very important to him.

Bert set down the French fry, wiped his fingers on his napkin, then reached across Nick, to shake his hand. "I couldn't be more pleased."

"Me, either," Nick whooped. "Are you gonna marry her?"

"I'd like to. There's just one problem," Tony said. "Andrea."

"Huh?" Nick looked incredulous. "Whaddaya mean? She talks about you all the time. She's always askin' me about what we do and stuff."

"Really?" Tony grinned. "That's good news." He

chewed thoughtfully on his burger. When he finished, he wiped his mouth, then turned to the other two. "But I'm not sure how she feels. I'd like to do something really special to…to show her how much I care. I'm wondering if you two could help me think of something."

"What do you have in mind?" Bert asked.

"I'm not sure. Something unexpected. You know, romantic."

Nick frowned. "That might be kinda hard. She says you're all business. That you don't know how to play, whatever that means. I don't get it, do you?"

Tony smiled begrudgingly. "Yeah, I think I do. That's why I'm open to suggestions."

"You prob'ly wanna do somethin' mushy, right?"

"Mushy is very good," Bert said. "Trust me, I'm the voice of experience."

"Okay, so you're telling me it has to be playful and mushy." Tony was beginning to wonder if involving Nick and Bert had been such a good idea. "That's a tall order."

All three sipped on their shakes. Finally Nick slurped noisily. "Know what that sound means in Cleveland?" he asked, looking hopefully from Tony to his grandfather.

"I'll bite," Bert said. "What?"

"It's all gone!" Nick laughed uproariously. Not for anything would Tony tell him that joke had been around forever.

Bert was peculiarly unresponsive. "Grandpa?"

Bert waved his hand as if calling for time. Finally, he dug in his pocket, placed some bills on the counter, then announced triumphantly, "I think I've got an idea." He chortled. "But I'm not sure you're gonna like it, Tony."

"Is it playful and mushy?"

Bert laughed so hard, he had to wipe tears from his eyes. "Oh, yes!"

Tony bit. "Well, then, let's hear it."

As Bert unfolded his plan, Nick could hardly contain himself. He was literally bouncing on the stool. Tony wasn't so sure. It sounded like overkill to him. Uncomfortable, embarrassing overkill. "So Nick, my lad," Bert continued, "do you think you can enlist that woman—what's her name? Maisie?—to help?"

"Daisy, Grandpa. I'll call her tonight." Nick turned a glowing look on Tony. "This is about the neatest thing we've ever done, right, Tony?"

Tony silently groaned. Neat? It was crazy! But the smile on Nick's face was powerful persuasion.

Bert fixed a look on Tony. "You won't back out, will you?"

"Do I have a choice?"

"No!" the two conspirators trumpeted.

Nick ran ahead of Bert and him toward the car. Cold feet didn't begin to describe Tony's reaction to Bert's brainstorm. But he was in love, and love sometimes called for extreme measures. But this was pretty damn extreme!

"Bert, I've gotta ask you something."

"Go ahead."

"Would you approve if I asked Andrea to marry me?" He cleared his throat. "I know there was a time you and Claudia didn't approve of me. And it's true that I come from a working class background and I have some rough edges, but there isn't anything I wouldn't do for Andrea and Nick."

Bert clamped a hand on his shoulder. "Son, in my book they don't come any better. And as for Claudia, you'll have plenty of opportunity to win her over. Something tells me she'll vastly enjoy being charmed."

Tony hardly heard the rest of Bert's remarks, so overwhelmed was he by the natural, affectionate way Bert had called him "son."

CHAPTER FIFTEEN

TONY AWKWARDLY JUGGLED the mewling infant. "I'm gonna drop him, Kell."

"I don't think so." Serene and relaxed in the new rocker Tony had provided for the O'Shea nursery, Kelli seemed to get a kick out of watching him hold the baby. "You're a natural."

"Don't press your luck. Here." He extended the baby to his mother. "I haven't had any practice at this." He breathed a sigh of relief when tiny Paddy settled contentedly in the safety of his mother's arms. "Sure you're feeling all right?"

Kelli laughed. "Tony, I feel fine. After all, having a baby is a natural phenomenon."

"So in a couple of weeks you might be able to help me with something?" Even to himself he sounded tentative.

She rubbed her forefinger over the baby's head, as if exploring a miracle. "Like what?"

"A plan I have to convince Andrea I'm an okay guy." She glanced up, her eyes sparkling. "Er, actually, a plan Nick and Bert and I have."

"Bert?"

"Nick's grandfather." He rushed on. "The trouble is, I don't know if I can pull it off. It's pretty insane. I'll feel ridiculous." He proceeded to fill her in, wishing like hell she'd quit giggling. "It's…it's…not something I'd ordinarily do," he finished lamely.

"No, it's not," she managed between chortles. Finally,

regaining control, she looked straight at him. "So why *are* you doing it?"

He stood up and paced to the window, then turned around to face her. "I just can't disappoint Nick."

"Oh, right. Nick." She chucked Paddy under the chin and spoke as if to the baby alone. "Tony's a good boy. He wouldn't disappoint Nick. No, no, no."

Why did her voice have that faintly sarcastic ring? "I like the kid. He's had it rough." He ran a hand through his hair and strode to the other side of the room.

"Tony? This isn't a cage, you know."

He stopped. "Huh?"

"The room. You're like a restless tiger."

"I am?"

"Yes. You know why?" She didn't wait for a response. "Because you haven't given me the real reason you've agreed to this interesting little scenario of Nick's and Bert's."

"I haven't?"

"No." She lifted the baby onto her shoulder and got to her feet. As she walked toward him, he could feel a thick lump forming in his throat. She stopped in front of him and gazed directly into his eyes. "Tony Urbanski, why exactly have you agreed to do this?"

"Because…" Her face wavered in his vision. "Because…oh, God, Kell, I love her." Like a cork exploding from a bottle, the lump disappeared.

"Right." She laid a hand against his chest. "So shut up and get on with it." She shifted the baby to her other shoulder. "Will I help?" She giggled again. "Skee, I wouldn't miss it for anything."

"WASN'T THAT an exquisite performance of the Brahms?" Claudia inquired, taking Andrea's arm as they negotiated the stairs from the mezzanine to the theater lobby.

"Yes, it was. Thank you so much for inviting me, Claudia. It's been ages since I've been to the symphony. I'd nearly forgotten how much I enjoy classical music."

"Just between you and me, Bert puts up a brave front, but I don't think he cares for it much, so it's a treat to have you along."

"My pleasure." And it was, Andrea reflected. Over the past few weeks, in her own way, Claudia had been trying to reach out to Nick and her. The main thing was that they were all making progress, and any easing of their relationship was welcome after so many months of mutual distrust.

"Do you have time to stop by the coffee shop on our way home? I'd really enjoy an espresso. Besides, there's something I want to share with you."

"I'd like that."

The tiny coffee bar near the Porters' home was nearly deserted, and the waiter led the two women to a cozy booth in the corner window. Over their drinks, Claudia made a surprising admission. "Bert and I are in the process of discovering some things about ourselves and how we coped with Richard's death. Bringing all of our emotions into the open has been painful."

Andrea nodded encouragingly, wondering where this was going.

"We decided we could benefit from professional assistance, so we've been consulting a counselor at our church." She paused to sip from her cup.

"It's hard for any of us to admit we need help. I hope you're finding the experience worthwhile."

"Oh, we are." She pulled a tapestry-covered book out of her handbag. "He recommended keeping a journal. I'm discovering it's extremely therapeutic. I'm amazed at what comes out." She moved her cup aside and made a place on the table for the journal. "This is what I wanted to share with you."

"Oh, Claudia, that's personal. You really don't—"

"Nonsense. I'm convinced it's important that you and I come to a new understanding." Claudia opened the cover, smoothed down a page, then smiled. "As a preliminary step, I want to tell you some things I've learned about myself, thanks to this little book."

Andrea was bewildered. She didn't know anything about journal writing or what Claudia was expecting by way of reaction. But this seemed important to her. The least she could do was listen. She picked up her coffee and held it, warming her cold hands. "Please go on."

Claudia placed her finger at the top of the page, as if deciding where to begin. "A long time ago, I thought I led a charmed life. That nothing could ever happen to disturb my perfect little world."

Andrea's fingers tightened on the mug. Good Lord.

"I had a beautiful home, a successful, devoted husband and a handsome, loving son. Not to mention many friends who moved in the right circles and appeared to accept me. I paid little heed to unpleasantries. Such things only happened to other people. Until, of course, that awful, awful day when—" her voice wavered "—Lake Erie swallowed up my beloved son and his wife."

Andrea couldn't take her eyes off Claudia. Slowly she set her mug down, realizing how difficult this must be for the older woman.

Claudia turned the page and ran her finger over the words written there, as if taking a cue from what she found. "I...I didn't know what to do then. Life was out of my control. Quite simply, my world vanished that bright June afternoon. Bert was no help. His own grief was overwhelming. And the passage of time was little comfort for either of us. Nightmares still occasionally disturb his sleep.

"Consciously or unconsciously, I made a decision. At the time maybe it was the only one I could make." Claudia took a shuddering breath. "Loving seemed too risky, because just when I'd thought my world was ideal, life saw fit to humble me, taking away my pride and joy—Richard. What the counselor and these scribblings have helped me see is that I refused to let other people get close to me because nobody could do the one thing that would restore my faith—that is, bring back my son. So I…buried my heart."

Andrea sat, her hands folded in her lap, her attention never straying from Claudia's soft, determined voice.

"I isolated myself, became cold, unfeeling and bitter. But at least no one could hurt me ever again." She smiled crookedly. "I held love at bay. Except for Nicholas. But even to him, I must have seemed distant, unapproachable." Claudia carefully closed the journal and sat quietly for a few seconds before resuming.

"It was bad enough having to share Nick with you, but then Tony came along. He presented a huge threat. Nick seemed devoted to him, and to add insult to injury, he wasn't one of 'our' people." She shook her head sadly. "Lord, what an arrogant judgment. All the man did was put a smile back on our grandson's face and care for him as if he were his own. And, heaven knows, Nick needed a father figure. But I didn't want to admit any of that."

Andrea fought the sob welling in her throat.

"Nor did I want to admit that you and Tony were falling in love." Claudia raised an eyebrow and Andrea felt a flush creep up her neck. "But facts are facts. It's as obvious as the nose on your face or—" the older woman smiled knowingly "—the blush on your cheek. However, something distressingly familiar seems to be happening."

"Oh?"

"I'm afraid you're becoming too much like me. The 'before' me."

Andrea clutched the napkin in her lap. "I don't understand."

"I'm talking about taking risks. There are no certainties in this world. For too long I was barricaded behind my fears, afraid to love because I'd been so devastatingly—and unfairly—hurt. All I succeeded in doing was failing others and wallowing in my own unhappiness." Claudia captured her hand, and, slowly, Andrea raised her tear-stained face. "Are you going to hide from life, too?"

"I...I'm afraid." The words burned her tongue.

"Then perhaps I can help." Claudia's grip tightened. "The next step is up to you." There was a challenge of the most affectionate kind in Claudia's clear blue eyes. "You love your Tony, don't you?"

"Yes, but—"

"Oh, Andrea, Never-Never Land is a fantasy. We have only what's before us with all its wonderful imperfection." Claudia withdrew her hand, reached inside her purse and pulled out a pen. "Now, dear, I want you to help me with what comes next." She opened the journal and turned to the last entry. "Listen. 'I don't know how Andrea will react, even if I find the courage to tell her all these things. But I'm hopeful. Very hopeful.'"

Andrea lifted the napkin to her face and wiped her eyes, a tremulous smile spreading over her features. "To begin with you could say that I like the 'after' Claudia a great deal. And—" she struggled to find the words "—I confess I used to find you intimidating. I was so afraid that you and Bert would take Nick away." Claudia started to interrupt, but Andrea stilled her with a touch of the hand. "I understand now that isn't going to happen. Because you know what? We've all changed. For the better." Andrea could feel the tension leaving her body, a magical lightness in its place. "You said there's no such thing as perfection. In this world I think only one thing comes close. Love."

Claudia had never begun writing. She'd put down the pen and now sat, elbows on the table, her chin propped on her hands, watching Andrea with what could only be described as delight. Andrea beamed at her before finishing her thought. "You've taught me a valuable lesson, Claudia, for which I'll be eternally grateful. Here's something else you can add to your journal." She paused for dramatic effect. "I'm going to tell Tony I'm not afraid anymore, not so long as he and Nick and I can be together for as long as happily ever after takes."

ON A SUNNY SATURDAY morning, the first in April, Andrea subjected herself to one of Daisy's artistic moments. "Hold still, damn it!" Daisy put a hand on Andrea's shoulder. "Don't move. I've got to get the mouth just right."

"But my wig itches." Andrea reached a hand up and scratched at the red yarn hanging over her forehead.

"Do you or do you not want to look like Raggedy Ann?"

"Yes, but I didn't know you'd have to put those black dots under my eyes, too."

"Tough. It's gonna be great. How do you like the costume?"

Andrea looked down at her black shoes, red and white horizontally striped tights, starched white pinafore and blue and red calico dress. "It's authentic. I'll give you that."

"Okay, so don't rave. I myself consider it one of my finest creations." She began applying the eye makeup. Her voice softened as she changed the subject. "What's eating at you, honey?"

"Lord, is it that obvious?"

"You slay me. You wear your emotions right out there for the world to see." She added one final dollop of black paint and stood back to survey the result. "Historically, only one thing has ever gotten you down. Men. So what's up?"

"I'm not sure I've done the right thing."

"What right thing?"

"I called Tony this morning and left a message on his answering machine."

Daisy moistened the tip of the eyeliner pencil. "That doesn't sound too ominous."

"I've made a decision." Andrea blinked as Daisy came too close to her lid. "I'm going to tell Tony how I feel."

"Oh?" Andrea could tell Daisy was being intentionally nonchalant. "And how's that?"

Andrea stepped back. "Surely that's enough makeup for Raggedy Ann."

Daisy pulled at Andrea's pinafore, straightening the bib. "Answer the question."

Andrea cocked her head, giggling when the floppy fringe tickled her ears. "I don't know what he's going to say or how he'll react, but I'm going to say, 'Tony, you know what? The verdict is in. I love you!'"

Daisy threw both hands in the air. "Thank God." She hugged Andrea, then stood back and smiled approvingly. "You don't have to worry about his reaction."

Andrea straightened the wig. "Now look what you've done. I'm all distracted. Is Phil ready yet? It's time to open the store."

"All but the makeup. You go on. He won't be long."

Andrea paused with her hand on the door. "Daisy, thanks. I appreciate all the trouble you've gone to with these costumes."

Daisy raised one eyebrow. "I certainly hope so."

Andrea paused. Those words had an ominous ring. She shook off her unsettled feeling. She was just jumpy today.

Because, despite what Daisy said, she *was* worried about Tony's reaction.

"PHIL, DO WE HAVE any Monopoly Junior games in the back?"

Phil scratched his red Raggedy Andy wig. "No, I don't think so." He came over to where Andrea and her customer stood eyeballing the stacked games. "But maybe I could suggest something else. How old is the child?"

Phil was the games expert, so Andrea gladly handed the problem over to him and hurried to assist a distracted-looking man in the doll section.

By two o'clock, she, Phil and the two part-time employees had racked up numerous sales. The store was a beehive of activity, so Andrea really hadn't had time to second-guess her decision about Tony, and maybe that was just as well.

Around three, Nick popped in with Bert. "What are you two doing here? I thought you'd be in the park with Tony."

"He couldn't come today," Nick said.

Andrea's heart sank. Not now. Not while things were going so smoothly. No doubt there was a problem at work. She pursed her lips. "I'm sorry."

"Yeah, he said somethin' about tending to business." Nick trailed over to the computer games, leaving Andrea with Bert.

"I'm afraid that man is going to break Nicky's heart."

Bert unzipped his jacket and stuck his hands in his pants pockets. "Oh, I wouldn't be too sure about that."

"Why not?"

"Er…uh, Nick's a pretty resilient youngster."

"Do you think so?"

Before Bert could reassure her, the front door opened and two mothers herding toddlers entered. On their heels came a grandmotherly type and two middle-schoolers. "Excuse me, Bert." Andrea bustled toward the two mothers, checking to see if the other employees were responding to the influx of customers. Phil corralled the toddlers and took them over to the play corner while her other clerks assisted the remaining customers.

The mothers spent quite a while making their selections. Andrea accommodated them patiently and rang up the sale, sighing gratefully when they gathered their entourage and departed.

Hardly had she had time to catch her breath, when a merry-faced, dark-haired young woman with a baby in an infant carrier came into the store. She looked around distractedly, then spotting Andrea marched toward her. "Ma'am, can you help me?"

Darn. She really needed a break, but out of the corner of her eye she noticed Phil straightening the toys in the play area and the other employees were still busy. She pasted on a smile and said, "Certainly. What can I do for you?"

The woman set the carrier on the counter. The baby peered at Andrea with wide blue eyes. "I'm clueless." Grappling in the depths of her purse, she pulled out a wrinkled gift certificate. "One of my neighbors gave little Patrick this. I haven't a notion where to start. I mean, I know I'm supposed to get 'developmentally appropriate' toys. But what does that mean? Could you give me some suggestions?"

Andrea couldn't believe it. The woman looked intelligent. Had she never read *Parents' Magazine?* And apparently she hadn't been out of the house much lately, either, since she kept right on talking a mile a minute as they walked toward the infant-toddler section. "Well," the woman concluded, "at least I know you're not supposed to get things with small parts or pointy edges."

Andrea picked up a mirrored crib attachment with a black, red and white color scheme. "You could start with something like this. These colors are supposed to be the first an infant can distinguish. Then as he gets a bit older, you might want one of these kiddie gyms." Andrea pointed to the model set up on the table.

"Here, would you mind?" The woman thrust the carrier at Andrea. "I want to get a closer look."

Andrea was mentally counting to ten. After inspecting the gym, the anxious mother spread out one of the interactive floor mats so she could examine it, too. While she was on her hands and knees, Andrea surveyed the store. Nick was sprawled in the bean bag with a Goosebumps book and Bert held a kaleidoscope to his eye. The part-time employees were helping more customers, and Phil was nowhere to be seen.

"Oh, here." The woman gestured to the floor beside her. "You can set Paddy down. If you don't mind, could you hand me that fuzzy ball there…yes, that one. I want to see if he likes it." She held the sphere inches from the baby's eyes. "Do you like it, boy-o? See? Isn't it pretty?"

Andrea stared at the ceiling and rolled her eyes. Talk about a doting mother. She cleared her throat. "You've made some nice choices there. Would you like me to carry them to the cash register?"

The woman laughed self-deprecatingly and picked up the baby. "How silly of me! I just got carried away. Yes, by all means. Please."

As they approached the counter, the young mother gave a sudden whoop that nearly caused Andrea to drop the kiddie gym. "Look! Patrick, it's Raggedy Andy, too!" She held up the carrier, as if by doing so, the infant could see better. "Oh, isn't that precious?"

Precious? Andrea made a mental note. She'd have to remember to tell Phil. He'd get a kick out of that remark.

He was making his way across the store. If Raggedy Andy did this much for the woman, Andrea could only imagine what a hit Santa Claus would be. She set down the items the mother had selected and started behind the counter when she paused, observing Phil, a puzzled frown on her face. Something wasn't quite right.

She stared as Raggedy Andy came toward them. Yes, the blue pants with the two white buttons, the little white collar and the red wig were exactly as she remembered. But Phil seemed taller and there was something odd about his walk... Oh, God. She backed into the counter, dimly aware the young mother beside her had covered her mouth with her hand and seemed to be stifling a giggle. Andrea watched, dumbfounded, as Raggedy Andy continued moving directly toward her, smiling broadly. But his eyes weren't gray, they were...dark brown. Under the hot wig, Andrea thought she might faint. It couldn't be. But it was.

"Tony?" she squeaked. "What in the world are you doing?"

He kept walking until he stopped directly in front of her. "I decided I haven't had a whole lot of fun in my life, so it was time I started."

Somewhere in her brain Andrea registered the smiles of people in the periphery of her vision, two of whom were Phil and Daisy. But mainly she studied the totally improbable, ludicrous sight before her. Tony Urbanski—serious, sophisticated deal-maker—in a Raggedy Andy costume!

"Are you out of your mind?" She couldn't believe her eyes, but amid the improbability of it all, she knew instinctively that Tony was giving her a rare and valuable gift.

"Just tell me one thing, Raggedy Ann. Am I playful or what?" Flapping his arms, he pirouetted, then stopped and picked up both her hands. He looked at her lovingly with his own shoe-black eyes. She didn't know whether to laugh or cry, but it didn't matter because she couldn't catch her breath. After a long moment, he turned and nodded briefly to the young mother. "Thanks, Kell. If I had a sister, I'd want her to be just like you."

Kell. Andrea didn't understand. Did he know this woman?

"But now, I need to get to the business at hand." Taking Andrea by the shoulders, he pulled her closer. She was both unwilling and unable to avoid the mute entreaty in his eyes. Then, thinking her rag-doll knees would surely fail her, she watched as Tony did something very peculiar. His gaze never left her face as he stepped back, untucked the red-and-white checkered shirt and slowly raised it, baring a white T-shirt.

There on the left side was a big red heart. And in the center, in true Raggedy Ann and Andy fashion, were words she couldn't ignore. I LOVE YOU.

Tears streaked her makeup, but she didn't care. In fact, she didn't care about anything but flinging herself into his waiting arms. Which she did.

"I love you, Andrea," he whispered against her scratchy wig. "You'll always come first."

She sniffled against his shoulder, then gazed at him. "Oh, Tony. You big ole…" she searched for the words "…optimist! I love you, too!"

Then the applause of the onlookers drowned out everything except for Tony's enthusiastic embrace and Nick's ecstatic voice. "I told you it'd work, Tony. It's *really* mushy. Right?"

Above her head, she heard Tony respond. "Right, son."

EPILOGUE

IT WAS ONE OF THOSE roses-and-honeysuckle summer days, when the breeze off Lake Erie murmurs a gentle benediction. Lush rhododendrons bordering the park were in full bloom. Families strolled or biked along the winding paths, and overhead, fleecy clouds ballooned across the brilliant blue sky.

Andrea pulled into the parking lot adjacent to the baseball diamonds. She'd dashed over from work, but Tony and Nick had come straight from home. Today's game was big! Nick could hardly eat this morning, he was so excited. Both teams were undefeated. Andrea smiled to herself as she walked toward the action. It was hard to believe the difference in Nick. Gone were the sullenness, the aggressiveness, replaced by a confidence that she could only attribute to Tony's influence.

Dear, gentle Tony. A far cry from the single-minded, no-nonsense businessman whom she'd met those many months ago. In an accustomed gesture, she ran the thumb of her left hand over the back of her wedding ring, as if to assure herself it was still there, that the dream really had come true. When he'd asked her to marry him, he'd nearly broken her heart with the poignancy of his words. "All my life I've been searching, trying to prove that I amounted to something. I was looking in all the wrong places. I know that now. Andrea, what I most need is family. And, for me, that's you and Nick."

Other parents fell in around her, some carrying lawn chairs, others coolers. The closer they moved to the appointed diamond, the louder grew the animated chatter of the Little Leaguers. Beyond the first-base dugout, where the Porter Blue Devils were practicing, Tony raised a hand and waved. The crisp sounds of bats hitting balls and balls hitting leather filled the air.

Once settled in the bleacher behind home plate, Andrea located Nick, crouched at second base taking infield practice, the bill of his cap pulled low on his forehead. His expression indicated that he was every bit as competitive about baseball as he was about computer games. Now if only he could get a hit. Batting was his weakness.

Andrea shaded her eyes with one hand, and located Bert kneeling in right field, instructing an outfielder. All the exercise he was getting as Tony's assistant coach made him look ten years younger.

"Andrea, yoo hoo!" Carrying a padded seat cushion, Claudia, dressed in a denim skirt topped by a jewel-studded denim shirt depicting a baseball player, threaded her way through the onlookers and, after arranging her cushion, sat down beside her. It was all Andrea could do not to laugh, because evidently Bert had made good on his promise. Over her hose-clad feet, Claudia wore a pair of cross-trainer athletic shoes in vivid magenta and white.

"I declare. Isn't it a beautiful day?" Claudia stretched out her legs and leaned against the seat behind her. She, too, seemed almost youthful. "Are you glad to be home?"

"The honeymoon was wonderful, but, yes. Both of us missed Nick a lot."

Claudia nodded toward Tony. "He's a good father." Andrea nearly choked. Once, Claudia would never have linked Tony's name with that label. Claudia continued. "How does Tony think he'll like his new job?"

"It's not exactly a new job, just a different emphasis. Great Lakes Management has given him carte blanche to try to franchise Never-Never Land. If the effort is successful, he'll relinquish his duties in the mergers and acquisitions area and take over management of the Never-Never Land subsidiary." Her eyes strayed to the field, and she nudged Claudia. "It looks as if he still needs all his negotiating finesse."

On the field a beefy man, wearing tennis whites, was gesticulating wildly and every now and then punctuating his remarks with jabs in the direction of Tony's chest. Claudia pulled her sunglasses down on her nose. "Who is that obnoxious individual?"

"I'll give you one guess."

"You don't mean it? Ben's father?"

"It figures, doesn't it?" Claudia's laughter warmed Andrea's heart.

"Well, my dear, the world is full of difficult people."

Andrea concealed a grin. *Tell me about it.*

Claudia continued. "Have I told you about Nettie Creighton and Alice Morgan? At your reception, I went into the powder room, but neither of them saw me. They were gossiping, as usual, this time about why in the world anyone would put Raggedy Ann and Andy on top of a bridal cake." Claudia chuckled, then leaned closer. "But that isn't the funniest part. Then Alice asked in this horrified voice what the odd-tasting little tea sandwiches were." Claudia, convulsed, wiped her eyes and finally managed to go on. "That's when I spoke up. I said, 'Ladies, it's the latest rage. Peanut butter and jelly!'"

They were laughing so hard they almost missed the start of the game. And, wonder of wonders, during his first at bat, Nick sent a ball skittering through the infield just inside third base. When he landed on first, Bert moved from his coaching position to give him a hug. More important, his teammates were on their feet cheering.

Andrea sighed contentedly. Family. There was nothing like it.

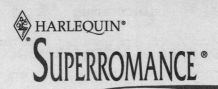

HARLEQUIN®
SUPERROMANCE®

From July to September 1999—three special
Superromance® novels about people whose
New Millennium resolution is

By the Year 2000: CELEBRATE!

JULY 1999—*A Cop's Good Name* by Linda Markowiak
Joe Latham's only hope of saving his badge and his reputation is
to persuade lawyer Maggie Hannan to take his case. Only Maggie—
his ex-wife—knows him well enough to believe him.

AUGUST 1999—*Mr. Miracle* by Carolyn McSparren
Scotsman Jamey McLachlan's come to Tennessee to keep the
promise he made to his stepfather. But Victoria Jamerson stands
between him and his goal, and hurting Vic is the last thing he wants
to do.

SEPTEMBER 1999—*Talk to Me* by Jan Freed
To save her grandmother's business, Kara Taylor has to co-host a
TV show with her ex about the differing points of view between men
and women. A topic Kara and Travis know plenty about.

By the end of the year,
everyone will have something to celebrate!

HARLEQUIN®
Makes any time special ™

HARLEQUIN®
SUPERROMANCE

IN UNIFORM

THERE'S SOMETHING SPECIAL ABOUT A *WOMAN* IN UNIFORM!

WINTER SOLDIER #841
by Marisa Carroll

When Lieutenant Leah Gentry—soldier and nurse—went overseas as part of a team that provided medical care for those in need, she expected long days and hard work. What she *didn't* expect was to fall for Dr. Adam Sauder— *or* to become pregnant with his child.

Watch for *Winter Soldier* in June 1999 wherever Harlequin books are sold.

HARLEQUIN®
Makes any time special ™

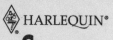

SUPERROMANCE

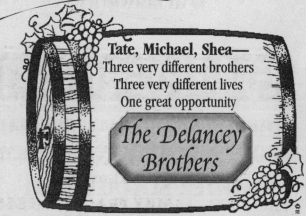

Tate, Michael, Shea—
Three very different brothers
Three very different lives
One great opportunity

The Delancey Brothers

June 1999—Second to None (#842)
by Muriel Jensen

What's a tough cop like Michael Delancey doing in a place like this? Mike was a hostage negotiator in Texas; now he's working at the Oregon winery he and his brothers have inherited.

Michael was ready for a change—but nothing could have prepared him for Veronica Callahan! Because Veronica and her day-care center represent the two things he swore he'd never have anything to do with again—women and children....

And watch for the third story in The Delancey Brothers series, Shea's story, *The Third Wise Man* in December 1999!

Available at your favorite retail outlet.

HARLEQUIN®
Makes any time special ™

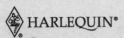

HARLEQUIN®

SUPERROMANCE

Welcome to Hope Springs, Virginia, a town where you can leave your doors and your hearts open, where people are friendly and children play safely. The kind of place you'd be proud to call home.

June 1999—ALL-AMERICAN BABY (#845)
by Peg Sutherland

Heiress Melina Somerset is pregnant and on the run. Hope Springs, Virginia, looks like an ideal place to make a life for herself and her unborn child. The townspeople are friendly and don't ask too many questions. So her secret's safe—unless Ash Thorndyke stays around long enough to find out she's going to have his child.

The newest title in the **Hope Springs** series by popular author Peg Sutherland.

Look for the next installment in the **Hope Springs** series in early 2000.

HARLEQUIN®
Makes any time special ™